THE COMPACT

A story of a destination

PATRICIA SPICER

The Compact
Copyright © 2025 by Patricia Spicer

ISBN: xxxxxxxxx (hc)
ISBN: 979-8894791913 (sc)
ISBN: 979-8894791920 (e)

The Reading Glass Books
1-888-420-3050
www.readingglassbooks.com
fulfillment@readingglassbooks.com

To the reflections on Lake Suttonfield
and the shaded pathways through the park
and to all those who know it when they are happy.

CONTENTS

ASTRID WILLIAMSON BECOMES MRS. W

In the doorway of the darkened kitchen, Astrid Williamson stopped and groped for an explanation. There was a small circlet of blue light floating on nothing at the other side of the room. As it was six o'clock on a foggy morning and barely beginning to get light, the strange circlet was clear, but unidentifiable. She felt for the switch on the right side of the door and pushed it up. In the rush of light the blue halo disappeared. She scanned the room, unnerved. *Did I imagine it?* She pushed the switch down again, and the halo reappeared, hovering over the stove top. No, it was on the stove, not *over* it. A gas burner, set low. With an unsteady finger, she lifted the light switch on again.

"Joyce!" she said aloud, urgent. But of course Joyce wasn't there. Too early. So it must have been burning all night. Very low, luckily, but what a waste! And a possible hazard. Maybe it was burning more than all night. Maybe since yesterday's lunch? Joyce must have left it on. What had they had to eat for lunch? Astrid struggled to remember, but couldn't. Probably some sort of soup with crackers or French bread. The usual thing. How could Joyce have been so careless?

But no. There was also supper. And Joyce had gone by then. *I must have… but what did I eat?* Astrid went to the refrigerator and looked inside. There wasn't much there. Some vegetables in a lower bin. Milk and mayo and that sort of thing on the door. A couple of covered plastic bowls. She took the larger one out and prised off the lid. Yes, that was it! The unappetizing remains of macaroni and cheese, which she had prepared on the stove top and must have left the burner going when she lifted off the pan.

It was me. And suddenly she was afraid again. Not a physical fear, but the other one. The real one.

Seeing the flame still burning, she went to the stove and turned the knob. *Stupid woman! Never, never do that again! So glad Lydia isn't here to see how stupid I've gotten.*

And I won't tell Joyce. When nobody knows, it isn't quite so bad. Though Joyce would be nice about it. She has such a good…what do you call it?… disposition.

Not going out today. Am I? No. Good. I won't have to rush to a public restroom.

I'll make some coffee. I can do that. She picked up the electric teakettle and ran in some water. *No more gas burner. Well, unless I really need to.* Astrid pushed the switch to set the water heating. Then she heard a plaintive noise and looked down to see her cat, Creamy, sitting on the floor next to her empty food dish. Lightly, the cat stood up and meowed again.

"Oh, Creamy, I did feed you last night, didn't I?" But Creamy's reply was the simplicity of a yellow-eyed stare.

Astrid opened the cupboard to get the cat food. Only it wasn't there. Just a couple of boxes of cold cereal. Not something she cared for, but her doctor said it was good for her, so she took down one of the boxes with something about being fortified with vitamin C and riboflavin. But why did it matter? Didn't she take vitamins anyway? And a pill to improve circulation. It was supposed to help the brain somehow, but… it seemed to keep getting worse. Was it time for her pills now?

Maybe she was forgetting to take them, even with that little plastic box. But Joyce usually reminded her. She'd ask Joyce when she came. If she remembered. But she wouldn't tell Joyce about the gas burner.

Cold cereal is cold cereal, with or without vitamins, even if they call it… What do they call it? Something that sounds organic. Wasn't there at least some fruit to go with it? She looked in the refrigerator but didn't find any. The pantry then. That little alcove just inside the back door of the kitchen. She noticed a can with peaches on the label. All right. She was happy to find the can opener in its properly labeled drawer, and properly she opened the can. Good. One thing at a time. A spoon. Cereal in the dish, sliced peaches spooned onto the cereal. A small click. What? Oh yes. The teakettle. She took down her favorite mug from the cup tree, then the instant coffee and the sugar bowl. Joyce really had arranged things logically, even putting labels on most of the drawers. Thank you, Joyce. *I must remember to thank her when she comes.*

Astrid poured boiling water into the mug, which she always warmed beforehand. Habit, not memory. Then she poured the water out of the mug and put in a spoonful of coffee. Not so good, powdered coffee, but easy and this brand was better quality. Who told her that? She could afford the better kind. Fresh, aromatic steam came up. The room lightened with daybreak. Morning improved. She got the milk from the refrigerator and set it on the kitchen table next to the cereal bowl. Then she sat down, stirred her coffee, sipped, but tasted no sugar. She added sugar, stirred again.

Creamy meowed piteously, came and rubbed her whole fluffy body on the leg of the chair.

"Oh Creamy! Didn't I feed you?"

Astrid got up and opened a cupboard door, but the cat food wasn't there.

Only a cereal box. Joyce must have put it somewhere else. Maybe… she began to open cupboards at random. Yes, in a cupboard just above

Creamy's dish, there was the box of dry kibbles. Quite logical, after all. Did she need water too? No, there was plenty in the bowl. Good. Astrid didn't pick up the food bowl, but merely stooped and poured a small stream of brownish kibbles into it and set the box back on the shelf, trying to be methodical. Then she sat down again to her breakfast, while Creamy crunched her food in the background. She sipped her coffee, which was still hot, and tasted the cereal, which was disagreeably cold. A few sliced peaches, even a spoon of sugar, could not save it.

I really must find something better for breakfast. Pastry would be nice, but the silly doctor. Of course Joyce would bring me doughnuts, but not a good idea. And just look at Joyce. Poor Joyce! But she saved my life. Saves it every day.

I can't give up. If I do what will happen? they'll take me and put me in one of those places like where Maman had to go. So I have to be very careful. No breaking my hip or setting the house on fire. Lydia would be furious. I wouldn't blame her. The house is her…what's the word? what you inherit. And if I, if they take me away, she'd have to rent the house, and the renters would wreck it, maybe not on purpose, but, that's how they are. I have to be careful. Very careful.

What's happening to me? I try. I used to be a teacher. I knew lots of poetry by heart. I knew Latin. But I can't remember… Yes, I do! Amo, amas, amat. *And then? The words are all fuzzy, like they're under water. And I drove a car. I could go anywhere, into the city, to galleries. All those places. Berkeley, too. A long time ago. It seems. Until I gave up. Had to give up. The day I met Joyce.*

⚬

It hadn't been so long really. Though Astrid couldn't quite remember, it was a little over a year ago. The middle of July. On her way to the supermarket shortly after lunch, she had come to an intersection and couldn't remember if she was supposed to turn or go straight. And because she didn't know, she wasn't signaling.

The light went green, and someone behind her honked. And they honked again and then someone behind them honked and someone else, and there was a cascade of honking pushing up behind her, and since it seemed easier to turn right, she turned, though she still wasn't sure.

Everything along the street looked different than she expected, so she should have turned left, or gone ahead. But instead of worrying about how to get to the store, she was suddenly more worried about being lost, worried about driving endlessly in a maze of traffic where all the other people knew exactly where they were going.

Astrid was so careful. She had long since given up driving to places where the traffic was difficult or where she had never been before. Only to the market, the bank, the hairdresser. And to visit her old friend, Molly Peterson, until Molly passed away. She had been cautious, and still she had forgotten the way. It wasn't fair. She scolded herself and fate at the same time and cried out inwardly, "Where am I?"

She drove on for a couple of blocks until she saw a little shopping center, not the big one where the market was, but just a few businesses laid out in a row, in a one-story building like an elongated shoebox. At least there was a clear entry and some empty parking spaces. She turned in and parked, clutching the steering wheel in both hands to stop the shaking.

Finally, she picked up her purse from the seat beside her, got out, and began to walk along the front of the businesses, still unsure what to do. The area looked slightly familiar, but not in the context of her house. On a whim she went into the laundromat, thinking of asking someone for directions to the market, thinking that when she got there, everything would fall into place. But no one was inside, only the whir of clothes in a dryer, which someone had temporarily abandoned. Going out, looking up and down the walkway, seeing no one to question, she noticed a coffee shop next door just beyond the laundromat. Maybe that's where the person with the laundry was, or anyway someone who would give her directions.

In the window of the cafe Astrid saw someone moving towards the door, an older woman, somewhat stooped, with short hair the color of gray sand. Wait.

Is that the way I look? Not old like that, surely. More than her years. She had gotten such a sweet, elegant birthday card for her sixtieth birthday from Lydia only last June.

But this woman looked far older. Dismissing the unwelcome image, she straightened up as best she could, opened the door, and went in.

That was how Astrid met Joyce, back of the cash register that filled the space between two tall display cases of pastries, all enticing, and surrounded by the comforting smell of hot coffee. The girl at the register was making change for a customer, who took her coffee and a bear claw to a small table by a window. The girl closed the register drawer with a quick shove and smiled at Astrid, revealing remarkably crooked front teeth that bent together as though leaning on each other, noticeable in an age when everyone had had them straightened. Her blondish hair was held behind her ears with barrettes, and she was probably thirty pounds overweight. It was hard to say which feature dominated her pudgy face, the oddity of her teeth or her clear, pretty blue eyes. As there was no one else waiting to be served at the moment, Astrid went up to her, thinking that, yes, maybe she had been in this coffee shop before, but not in a long time.

"Can I help you?" The girl's chipper voice stopped her pondering the question.

"Well, yes… but no, I don't want anything…" She struggled to frame her problem so that it didn't sound too stupid. "The thing is that I was on my way to the market, and I must have taken a wrong turn, and I was wondering if you…"

"Sure, but what market? You mean the big one? The Safeway?"

"Yes, yes, that's it. The Safeway. I don't think it can be very far. I've shopped there for years, you know. I can't think how I…"

"Sure. No problem. It's sort of near. You go on down E Street to 2nd and turn right. It's about three blocks down, on the corner of B Street."

"Yes, I know, but…"

The girl looked at Astrid expectantly.

"I don't know… what street I'm on now," she admitted.

"Oh, this is E Street right here. You just got a little turned around for a minute. You gotta take a left outta the parking lot. Only the traffic is kind of heavy, so I'd say to take a right out of the lot and go around the block. That'll get you back…"

Astrid sighed. Her internal map was stubbornly blank. "I don't know if I can… remember what you said…"

"Hey, listen," the girl said, inspired. "Can I get you a cup of coffee? I mean, even if that's not why you came in. Maybe you just need to relax a little. And if you can wait about twenty minutes, I'll be off work and I can ride down there with you. I could stand to do a little shopping myself, and I don't have a car. It's either I gotta walk everywhere or take the bus. Maybe we could help each other out, I mean if you want…"

Astrid thought it over, whether to accept the offer or not. In the old days you trusted almost everybody. Now you trusted hardly anyone. But that wasn't right. And besides, beggars can't be choosers and all that.

"Yes," she said after a moment. "Yes, that would be very kind of you. I'm… my name is Astrid Williamson, by the way." Proper. Like a handshake.

"Hi. I'm Joyce. Some people call me Jolly, but either one's okay. So regular or decaf?"

"What?"

"Your coffee. You like regular or decaf? Or cappuccino? Latte?"

"No, no. Regular's fine. Can I have sugar?"

"Sure. There's cream and sugar down at the end of the counter there." She pointed the direction and then turned to pour into a stout mug.

The warm, unhurried atmosphere of the shop, the sweetened coffee with one of those little tubs of half-and-half added did have a calming effect. Astrid felt so much better by the time Joyce emerged from the back without her apron and carrying a bulky shoulder bag that she almost had second thoughts about needing someone to help her, but now that she'd made a commitment, of course she would fulfill it. That was the way she'd always been. And yes, it was a comfort, after all, to have someone along to remind her of the turns and to suggest where to park in the huge lot, because somehow just making simple decisions had become a matter of inexplicable effort. Perhaps because thought itself was an effort.

Inside the door of the cavernous market, Astrid took out her shopping list and reviewed, while Joyce waited to push the cart. The usual things mostly. Multi-grain sandwich bread, various canned soups, some fresh fruit, cheese. When you live alone, you don't vary your diet much, as she remarked to Joyce. Mostly soup and sandwiches and salads. That sort of thing.

"I used to cook a lot, before I lost my husband. But now, you know..."

"Sure. I live alone too. I get it."

Then she told Joyce about Creamy, so not alone altogether. Did Joyce have a cat? No, Joyce did not. It was because she lived in a studio apartment where they didn't let you have pets, but she liked animals. Maybe someday. Astrid looked at her list again and saw that cat food was on it, but couldn't remember where it was located in the store.

"I know what," Joyce suggested, as she moved the cart away from the main entrance. "I mean I don't know either, not having a cat an' all. So let's just go up and down the aisles and get what you need. Then you can check each thing off your list.

Accordingly, they explored the aisles in as leisurely a fashion as one can in the cluttered and crowded bazaar of a major market, and eventually, after adding several items to the cart, they found an aisle crammed with pet food. Since Astrid could not remember the brand, Joyce helped her to recognize a bag of kibbles that looked familiar. A medium sized one.

As they were going around, Joyce pushed the cart and put a few items of her own on the lower shelf. In one aisle she added a package of chocolate chip cookies, but then returned it to the shelf.

"I guess I don't need cookies, do I?" she asked with a rueful smile.

Astrid said she used to bake cookies when her grandchildren came to visit, but not lately. Lydia said that cookies weren't good for them. Anyway, they hadn't been to visit for a while. Too busy.

Joyce gently moved her along. Did Astrid need cereal? No. Anyway, she hated cold cereal. Oatmeal was all right, with warm milk. "I used to cook it a lot. We ate healthier then," she added. "When my husband was alive."

Finally they came to the produce section at the far edge of the store.

She picked up a golden delicious apple and looked at it, as if waiting for it to answer a question. Yes, it was all right. "We'll put two in a bag. And over there, some string beans, but not too many. I live alone, you know. If I buy too much it only goes bad. I could use some potatoes, but not a whole sack. I like baked potatoes and they're easy."

Joyce agreed. "I cook them in my microwave pretty often," she said. "With margarine and sour cream. Maybe I shouldn't," she added, "but heck…"

After many stops and starts and discussions about brands, by the time they neared the check stand, the cart, both top and bottom, was fairly full.

"I'll unload the stuff," Joyce offered.

"No, wait!" Astrid Williamson stopped her.

"Did you forget something?"

"No, no, it's not that." She lowered her voice and bent across the handle of the cart. "I have to… isn't there a restroom in this store? I seem to remember…"

Joyce pondered the question. "Well, I've never used it, but think there's one at the back. Let's go see. Or maybe I can just ask…"

"No, please. Let's look. I should never have had that coffee, you know. I know better…but now I really need to…"

Joyce was right about the restroom at the back of the store and dutifully guarded the cart while Astrid Williamson went in.

"You okay?" Joyce asked when she came out. "Hey, Mrs. Williamson, have you got your purse?"

"Oh…no…it's…" and she rushed back through the door to retrieve it, came out again, clutching it under her arm, like a football receiver guarding the ball.

"Thank you so much. I set it down to wash my hands. I would have… Let's get out of this silly place."

"Suits me." Joyce again took charge of pushing the cart.

"You can call me Astrid," Astrid Williamson offered suddenly. "I know some people are too, well, personal, but I don't mind, really."

"How about Mrs. W?" but the letter sounded rather like "Doublia."

"What?"

"You know, for your initial. Kind of formal and friendly, at the same time. I mean, maybe it's silly, but when I was a little kid, my gramma used to call Mr. Rogers 'Mr. R.' Like she'd say, 'Hey, Jolly, you wanna look at Mr. R?' It sounded friendly… You know?"

"Mr. Rogers?"

"Yeah, you know. The kiddies' show. On TV."

"Oh, oh yes, of course. Yes, my daughter used to watch it. Yes, Mrs. W is fine." She smiled sideways at Joyce. "Or Astrid. Either."

When they got back to the check stand, Joyce unloaded her own purchases on the conveyor, put down the bar, and then unloaded the rest. Very methodical. Joyce paid for her groceries with food stamps and Astrid—Mrs. W—with a credit card, which Joyce ran through the slot for her and then pointed where to sign on the window. As they were crossing the parking lot, Joyce, who was still pushing the cart, now replete with paper bags, asked a question.

"Could you… I mean, if it's not too much trouble, could you give me a lift home?"

Judging from their conversation on the way from the coffee shop, she had concluded that they couldn't be living very far apart, a few blocks at most. Joyce had told Astrid that she was lucky to have found one of those old houses that were converted into small apartments for low-income people. She had her own bath and kitchenette. It wasn't bad for a single person, but it would be nice to have a little yard of her own and a pet. Maybe someday.

Astrid was willing to drive Joyce home, what with the groceries and all, but from the moment she fastened her seat belt, she felt as though the map of her mind had again faded to a blur, like a paper left too long in the sun.

"You'll have to tell me every turn," she said, her hand on the key, "but first help me get out of this silly parking lot."

When she got to the neighborhood she recognized, Astrid automatically turned down her own street and into her own driveway, where she stopped, clutching the steering wheel tightly with both hands, Joyce still beside her and the engine idling.

"Maybe you better turn off the engine," Joyce suggested. "I can help you in with your stuff. Okay?"

Astrid turned off the key and set the brake. When she turned to answer Joyce, her eyes were full of tears.

"I can't do this anymore," she said simply.

"What's that, Mrs. W?"

"Drive this car. I can't do it. I'm too scared."

"That's okay, Mrs. W. I understand. Anyway, my place is only three blocks from here. Two blocks down and one over."

"Oh, I'm so sorry! You needed a lift home. I told you I would, but I didn't think…" Suddenly Astrid sniffed like a child silently weeping.

"No, that's okay. Really. I don't need a ride at all. It's so close. Usually I ride the bus home, which still isn't even this close. Which is good 'cause I can use the exercise. I know that. Anyway, maybe I can help you with your stuff. I'd be glad to. I'm not in any special hurry. Do you need a hanky?" she added.

"Thank you, but no," Astrid sniffed. "I'll be all right."

"Well, at least let me help. Honest."

They both got out then and took all the bags from the back seat to the porch, then said their goodbyes. Joyce picked up her own well-filled bags and set off down the street. Astrid looked back at her car from the porch. She was telling the truth. She couldn't do it anymore.

I'll sell it. I'll call Lydia tomorrow and ask her to help me. Maybe not. She's so busy with the children and everything. I'll call Tom. No…what's his name? Ed, I think. I don't remember. It'll come to me. I'll call him and ask his advice. He knows about things like that. But will he think I'm… senile? Will they put me in one of those places?

⎯⎯◆⎯⎯

For the next few days Astrid contemplated her car, the Toyota sedan she once loved, sitting useless and monstrous in the driveway. Without it, how would she get her groceries? Get her hair done? See her doctor? Go to the post office? All she was sure of was that she couldn't get in it again. So abruptly one afternoon, when she happened by chance to remember the name of their family attorney, she looked up his number in her pop-up directory and called his office. Remarkably he was in and available and suggested donating the car to a non-profit, so she could get a tax credit. Maybe the Council on Aging, if she was sure. They'd be happy with the donation and could arrange for someone to drive her to appointments, take her shopping, all that. He didn't argue with her about giving up the car. Not at all. He even offered to make the call for her and fill out the papers. Nice of him.

The very day they took the car away, Astrid was sitting in a rocker on her front porch in the early afternoon, contemplating the empty carport with mixed feelings of failure and success, when someone hailed her from the sidewalk.

"Hey, Mrs. W. How're you doin'?" It was Joyce.

Although Astrid didn't recognize her immediately, in a minute it all came back. The coffee shop and the supermarket. That nice girl. She invited Joyce up onto the porch and they talked about this and that, and Astrid suddenly complained that her vacuum cleaner wasn't working. It didn't seem to pick up anything at all. Joyce offered to go in and look at it. Astrid told her she thought it was in the hall.

"Back in a jiffy." And she was.

She said that the bag needed changing, that was all. Probably Mrs. W had forgotten to change it for awhile. Accordingly, she put in a new bag and took the old one out to the garbage bin behind the house. It too was overloaded, but she managed to press in this one last item. Suddenly she had an inspiration.

"Y'know...I could stop by here sometimes after work," she said when she went back to the porch. "I mean it's pretty much on my way. I'd just get off the bus a couple blocks sooner and walk over. Like I could help you out with your housework an' stuff."

"Well, I... don't want to..."

"I mean I could just come by once a week, like... Isn't Tuesday when they pick up the garbage? So I mean I could stop by on Mondays and roll it out for you, and the recycling. Whatever. Or maybe something else you don't feel up to doing. So how about it?"

"I, well, if you really don't mind... I'll pay you, of course."

"You wouldn't have to." But on this point Joyce didn't sound firm.

"Of course I would. I'm not rich, but I'm not poor either. My husband, Charles, he left me pretty well off, and I have a pension. I was teacher, a long time ago," she added, wanting Joyce to know that she'd been somebody once. Somebody capable.

"Well, actually, my rent, even though it's like subsidized, …so if you could see your way clear, like minimum wage for an hour or so, well, I could sure use it."

"I'm sure we can arrange something," said Astrid.

Joyce's visits started with Monday, but evolved into twice a week and then almost daily, because it seemed there was always laundry or cleaning or cooking to be done. Lauren Hamilton, a volunteer from the Council on Aging, generally came on Fridays, but she was more of a driver, who took Astrid shopping or to some particular appointment. That sort of thing. It was Lauren who saw to it that Astrid got some cash from the bank once a month, so she could pay Joyce the weekly fifty dollars they had agreed on. Joyce herself made a note on the calendar about the garbage bins and her payment, but other than that, they kept no records, and Astrid paid no Social Security. The arrangement was simple and unofficial.

THORNY AND RICHARD AGREE

John "Thorny" Thornton was washing the remnant of mortar out of the tipped-up wheelbarrow with a high velocity nozzle, stirring up a fine cloud of white mist, while the remaining slightly milky liquid trickled into the sprawling juniper bush at the east side of the driveway. Up and down and around he cleaned out the barrow, intent on his work, even though it was altogether routine. In some ways, he found it better to work without a helper. Do your thing in your own time and your own way. Both more and less responsibility. On the other hand, it was getting too hard to work alone.

Although he was still lean and well muscled, his hands pained him inside his work gloves. His thinning, gray hair spoke to the timing for Social Security—as if there were security. His mouth expressed his effort with a small grimace. A naturally wide mouth made him seem content, almost smiling, but a slight downward bending revealed his weariness.

He had just turned off the faucet when a pale silver Volvo sedan pulled into the drive behind him, paused while the garage door smoothly opened, then disappeared inside. There was no gesture of recognition from the driver, although Thorny knew him from a previous job. A little odd maybe, but then Thorny, his hands full of hose, could hardly have returned a greeting. Stooping, he methodically coiled the hose around the hanger next to the house, conscious of the aching, knobby joints of his fingers. Everything about this yard, except for the disturbances of his recent work, was clean and tidy, reminding him of his own garden, when Clare was alive and kept all the beds in order. A little scrappy now. Unweeded. Untrimmed. Like a gentleman visibly in need of grooming.

Thorny went down the broad flagstone steps he had set in place three years before and examined the nearly finished wall of ledgestone that now bordered those steps. Karen Young, the woman of the house, had a good eye and good plans for the new plantings, mostly azaleas, she said, with a blue potato plant down at the sunnier end. Being on the east side of the house, the steps caught the morning sun, but they were shaded in the afternoon by the house itself and the broad deck behind it.

Thorny reviewed his work. The cinder blocks were well set and mostly finished with ledgestone, up to about ten feet from the top next to the drive entrance. It looked good. The way the new wall tied in with the flagstones. He saw that it was good, just as God kept saying at every stage of creation. If God had existed, he would have been a master mason. Certainly, he would have started with rock. Everything comes from that.

The sliding door on the back of the house opened then. Hearing the swish of it, Thorny glanced up to see Richard Young come out onto the upper deck, just above where Thorny was standing. Young was a sandy-haired man of middle height, causally dressed, not muscular, but visibly fit. He went to the railing and leaned on it with both elbows, either not seeing Thorny or deliberately taking no notice.

It was a moment of social perplexity. Although they'd known each other since the last project, wasn't it Young's place, as the employer, to make some greeting? Unless he hadn't noticed that Thorny was there.

Then maybe it would have been rude of Thorny to simply turn and go back up the steps without saying anything, when, by his movement, Young was bound to notice him.

Thorny cleared his throat. "Hello there," he said, noncommittally. "Nice day," he added, which it was. A typical August late afternoon sky, set like a pale dome over the city and San Francisco Bay. Hardly a drift of cloud. No sign of fog yet, though it could come in at any time, folding like a slow, white wave over the Marin hills.

Young startled visibly, jerked his head to his left, staring.

"Sorry," Thorny apologized. "I was just taking a look at the job. What d'you think?" he fumbled. "Is the missus gonna approve?"

Richard Young didn't answer for a moment, but seemed to stare past Thorny at the rock work, as if seriously considering how to answer the question, but when he did answer, his voice was a swollen croak. Not like the man at all. Someone else.

An impostor.

"It's fine. Of course. Good."

Clearly, Young didn't really want to talk or couldn't. Thorny guessed at laryngitis. But he didn't know Richard Young quite well enough to press for an explanation. He pulled off his gloves and dropped them on the rim of the wheelbarrow.

"Well," he said, turning back, "tell the missus I'll probably be finished tomorrow. Monday at the latest. She said it was okay for me to work on Sunday, if I wanted."

Young nodded. "You working alone?" he asked, in a voice slightly more his own.

"Yeah. Fact is I'm about retired. I think this'll be my last job. That's what I'm thinkin'. Everybody's gotta quit sometime, y'know?"

"Yeah, I know."

Thorny couldn't tell from his flat tone whether this comment was an invitation to more conversation or a dismissal. Probably the latter. But Richard Young kept looking at Thorny in an odd way, expectant, like putting a finger in a book you're reading while you mentally attend to something else.

Thorny went up two steps, putting himself at eye level with the man on the deck, just where the railing opened onto the flagstone. He rested his left hand on the railing's end.

"Well, you know, I don't hafta work anymore. I've got social security now and a little retirement in my IRA. It's not that I don't wanna work. I love it, always have. But it's the arthritis." Thorny held up his right hand to show the knobby joints, as if he needed justification. It was always a matter of pride with Thorny that he wasn't lazy. "Some people don't realize that a mason needs his hands as much as a violinist. Sure, you can take painkillers, but there's no cure. So I figured it was time. I don't wanna stop. My work is all I got. But I gotta be realistic. A person's gotta know when to call it quits," he repeated. "Just a fact."

"You're so right." Young looked away from Thorny then and out across the bay at the crinkled water, dotted with the sails of small boats, like birds with one wing lifted. "Karen told me that your wife passed away," he observed unexpectedly. "A year ago, was it?"

"Two years next month. September thirteenth. Not too long after I laid these flagstones. "Course I had a crew then. I wasn't workin' all by myself, like now." He paused and looked down at his work approvingly. "Anyhow, it turned out okay, don't ya think?"

"Nice job," Young concurred without removing his gaze from the bay. "Karen was sorry. About your wife. She knew her from the garden club."

"Yeah. She wrote me a nice note when Clare died. I still got it."

"It was cancer, is that right?" Young turned his head to look at him directly.

"Yeah." Thorny stepped from the flagstone onto the redwood decking and again rested his hand on the railing. If he was going to explain about Clare, he didn't want to have to talk at a distance. Too personal. "She was the sort who didn't like going to doctors. And why should she? She was hardly ever sick. And so she kind of put off getting a checkup when she started to not feel good, y'know, but he, the doctor, said it probably wouldn't have made any difference. It maybe started in the gall bladder, but it was in her liver by the time they diagnosed it. There wasn't much to do, but make her comfortable, like they say, and get ready to say goodbye. "

Richard Young nodded.

"Y'know, I thought the first anniversary of her death was gonna be the worst, but now the second one's coming up, and I dread it even more. I mean my work kind of helped me out at first. Jus' to stay busy all the time. And in the evenings, read or watch some dumb show on TV. Y'know? In the wintertime there was football, which was about the biggest deal of the week. But it isn't all that big a deal, is it?"

Richard looked at Thorny.

"Sorry. Maybe it's different for you," Thorny apologized. "I didn't mean to carry on."

"No, no. I agree." By now Richard Young sounded like Richard Young, but it still wasn't clear to Thorny whether he wanted to talk or not. He didn't say anything to indicate an end of the conversation, nor a continuation, but stood very still, staring at Thorny, then drew a breath and looked back over the bay.

"I have cancer," he said all of a sudden, flatly.

"You do?" Thorny was perplexed about what else to say. "Well, that's rotten."

"Yeah, it is."

"There's gotta be treatment," he ventured with conventional logic. "If you catch it in time anyway."

"Yeah, sure, but not this time. I just came from the clinic in Ross. Got the latest blood results. Sure, they'll wanna hit it with all the usual treatments, the chemo and everything, but the prognosis; it isn't good. They say there's a new drug for lung cancer, but only to slow it down, not a cure. And it's expensive…"

"You've got insurance, haven't you? With the airline or something?"

"Sure, but the drug treatment they want to use is 'experimental,' which means that insurance wouldn't cover it anyway." For a moment he sounded angry at Thorny for being naive. "Okay, I've looked into all the angles, from the day I got the original diagnosis. Besides, my grandfather died of lung cancer, like twenty-five years ago, but I remember. It was long and painful, and treatments have only gotten more costly. Sure, there's things to do if you catch it early. But I didn't realize I was sick, till the day I coughed some blood. I mean that's when I went to check it out, right away, but even then… Dammit. It's not fair. Granddad smoked. A lot. I never did! What kind of sense does that make?"

"None. But it happens. I know."

"Yeah, it does," but Richard Young no longer sounded angry, just disillusioned, disgusted with the whole thing. "So all I really want is to get it over with. That's about it."

Thorny was stumped for a comment, all the more because he knew how pointless it was to say anything, but the situation demanded something. He walked over and stood next to Young and also leaned his arms on the railing, a kind of companionable gesture that evaded touching.

"Hospice is good," he said at last, lamely. "They really helped us at the last. Anyway, your wife's a nurse, isn't she? She'd know how to take care of you."

Young shook his head. "No way! She doesn't know." The thickness was coming back into his voice. "She's worked with terminal cases from time to time and hates it. I don't blame her. Home nursing is what she does, but mostly with people who are just out of the hospital, recuperating. I mean she could've worked with hospice but didn't want to. So I figure—"

"But she's gotta know…"

Richard looked at Thorny. "Maybe not."

"What do you mean?"

"I've been thinking. Maybe she doesn't have to know, not if I die in an accident." He squinted at Thorny. "Does that shock you?"

Thorny was quiet for a while but not from shock. "Me? 'Course not. I think about having an accident a lot." He'd never said that to anyone.

"If it was a genuine accident, I mean. Then Karen would get the insurance and there wouldn't be all that drawn-out process of dying. For either of us. It'd hurt her, of course, but it'd be clean, in a way. See what I mean?"

Thorny nodded. "Sure. If there's no cure. But hell, you gotta be sure."

"Today was the day, goddam it! I went in hoping. Bronchogenic carcinoma. I knew that already. Elevated LDH. Probably metastasized. So I am sure." He stopped, looked at the bay again. "I love this place," he said unexpectedly, gently. "We were lucky to buy into Tiburon when it was still a little affordable, and the house is practically paid off now. My life insurance would do that easily. And Karen loves it too, as you know. She'd never have to move, and the girls… they'd have their old home to come back to, to visit. Susan and Roy were married on this deck. That was one of the reasons we had the flagstones put in."

"Yeah, I remember the missus telling me." He paused. "It's none of my business, o'course, but how the hell would you plan… I mean what sort of an accident? You mean like a car wreck? Wouldn't that look suspicious? Deliberate? A single car, I mean. And you wouldn't want to—"

"All right. It'd look like suicide. I know that. And I don't drink, except on very special occasions. Like Susan's wedding. No, not a car. Not at all."

"Okay, not a car. So?" It was a necessary question.

"I'm a retired pilot. Commercial. But you knew that"

Thorny nodded. "When did you retire?"

"Nine months ago. The usual story. All the things you were going to do with your family when you stopped working. Right. Well, we did a few during the past year, going to Baja last winter and British Columbia in June. I belong to a flight club. We own a light twin, a Cessna 310. I still love planes, like I guess the way you love rocks. So I'd hate to ever crash a plane on purpose, but at least it's insured. The other guys in the club wouldn't lose anything. Financially, I mean. And I think I'd know how. The mountains can be tricky in the autumn. But I'd have to be alone, and I can't come up with any reason for flying over the Sierras, or anywhere, by myself.

"It's not like I haven't been giving it a lot of thought, even before I was sure about the prognosis. You always have to have to a contingency plan, but I'm not seeing the way." He paused, not as though asking for a response, but just having run out of any way forward.

"I get your point. As for me, well, I thought about it, too. Some sort of accident, I mean, but different."

"Such as?" Richard Young sounded genuinely interested.

"Well, like I was saying…" Thorny cleared his throat, did not look at the man next to him, but out to the deep blue-green of the water. "When I think about it, I think about a place we liked to go once in awhile on weekends, Clare an' me, up on the Mendocino Coast, especially after we lost our son Greg. Mostly we'd garden on weekends, but if there wasn't too much to do, like the end of summer, then we might take a picnic lunch and a bottle of wine and drive up the coast and just stroll along the beach or sit back up against a cliff and watch the surf curling in. You know how you can watch the breakers turning just about forever."

Richard nodded. "Yeah," he assented. One who had been there.

"Well, there's this walk along a bluff a little below Fort Bragg, and it could be dangerous if you slipped. And I got to thinking that if I went up there with a picnic and a bottle and got a little tipsy, then I wouldn't feel scared, and I'd just kind of wander over to the edge and let go, head first, like I was looking over the edge and lost my footing. Like that. It's rocky there, like I said. You couldn't not break your neck. If you see what I mean. If they figured I'd been drinking, well, what of it? You know?"

"Sure, I can see that."

"I haven't got any medical reason to check out. Not the way you do. But I haven't got any reason to hang around either. I cashed in my life insurance after Clare died. No family, to speak of, on my side or hers. Only a couple of cousins on my dad's side. Lost track of 'em. To tell the truth, after Clare died, I didn't even make a new will. Still got the same one we both made years ago. So I guess that's about the same as…what do they call it…?"

"Intestate…"

"Yeah, right. I mean, the way it is, anybody could get my property."

"You should change that."

"Well, sure. I know that. And I've been thinkin' about it off an' on, that there's gotta be some charity…but I'm not a joiner."

"You live in San Rafael, don't you?"

"Since I was born."

"Your place must be worth a lot," Young observed neutrally.

"You bet. It's eighty years old at least, but really sound construction, and I kept it in good shape, if I do say so. And a huge lot. The house was never mortgaged, believe it or not. We inherited it from my dad, y'see. We thought about mortgaging it to send Greg to college, but he never… Well, anyway, the house is like my only real asset. I mean big asset. Sure, developers would love to get their hands just on the property. Forget the house. I swear t'god, I'm not letting it go to somebody who'll come in with a crane and bulldozers and knock it all down. No way. Look, even if I donated the place to a charity, they'd sell it off and put the cash to something else. That's no good."

"I can see that." Richard assured him.

"Did you know my wife was a master gardener? I did the landscaping, but she designed the plantings. It doesn't look so good anymore, but our garden—I mean her garden—was written up twice in the local paper. Anyway, I don't have a clue what it's worth right now, but plenty, I'm sure."

Thorny became aware of how much space his own voice had taken up. "I'm sorry. I talk too much sometimes. You're the one with the… anyway." There was a trailing element in his tone that wound into a new pathway. "If you crashed a plane, it'd look like a car wreck. If you were alone. But if you had a passenger, nobody'd think two bits about suicide."

"You're not serious." A flat statement without inflection.

"Why not? If I could just figure out what to do about my house… I'd hook up with you. Absolutely." Thorny looked at Richard unblinkingly, and Richard looked back. There was a deep silence, filled with speculation.

"Do you gamble?" Young asked unexpectedly.

Thorny shook his head. "I bought a lottery ticket a couple of times. Why?"

"Just an idea. I was thinking I could arrange a little excursion to Reno, just for the two of us, but that wouldn't make sense. I don't gamble either. Maybe fishing…Do you…?"

"I used to go with my dad once in a while, when I was a kid, up around Redding. Always thought Greg and I would, but he never seemed to care about fishing. Anyway, Clare an' me, we sort of honeymooned on a lake up there. I mean in the Sierras." He pondered his recollection for a minute. "She had a friend whose dad had a cabin up there, near Blairsden, an' she said we could use it. It wasn't like any other vacation we ever took. The air was so quiet and crisp in the morning, and the sound of the lake water lapping over the pebbles. God! I'd like to see that place again, a kind of pilgrimage, I guess you'd say. Maybe more like a memorial. Is that crazy? I've got Clare's ashes. Maybe I could scatter them up there, somewhere near where we camped. Is that crazy? I've heard that people do that sometimes…"

"No, it's not crazy. I guess it's sort of common. Maybe we wouldn't quite get there, or maybe on the way back, depending on the weather," Young added as if considering the weather advisories in his mind's eye. "Maybe you could show me where it is—Blairsden, you said?—when you come around tomorrow."

"Yeah, sure," Thorny said with a quick eagerness. "Happy to."

"You probably wouldn't make much out of a flight map. I mean they don't look like road maps. But if we put the two together…" Young straightened up from the railing. "In fact, we can have a look now, if you want to," he added. "After all, Karen isn't here. That is, if you've got the time."

"Sure. I got nothin' but time."

LAUREN AND HARRISON HAMILTON AT HOME

If furniture were sentient, the living room furniture at the Hamilton house would have faded with boredom. Even the furniture in David's bedroom would have little to report, except for his occasional vacations, since he had left for college. The household furniture was used, yes, but so routinely that, if there were any wear, it would show only on a couple of the living room chairs and on Harris's home office desk chair.

Of course the room is tastefully decorated in the upper-middle-class style of the time. It has a fabric-covered sofa of muted floral design and two swivel chairs with molded wooden bases and matching ottomans, covered in pale beige leather, quality purchases from Scandinavian Designs. In front of the sofa is a large, dust-free, glass-topped coffee table, also from Scandinavian Designs, with a scatter of current magazines. Against the wall on the right of the mostly-unused fireplace, is an entertainment center with television, tuner, combination VCR and DVD player. A wide, chest-high bookcase with an orderly set of encyclopedia and other hardbound books stands against the wall on the other side of the room. On top of the bookcase is a low flower arrangement and a modest set of framed family photographs.

There are original paintings on the walls, all landscapes, except for one non-objective canvas above the bookcase. Behind the sofa is a large watercolor depicting a vineyard in the fall, waves of mixed warm colors spreading over low hills with higher unplanted hills in the background. This painting was purchased at a gallery in St. Helena one afternoon twelve years ago when the Hamiltons took some guests from Chicago on a wine-tasting tour in the Napa Valley. The wine they bought that day is long gone, and they haven't seen their guests since then, but the picture is still enjoyed when they think to look at it. On the section of the room that faces the street is an open-plan dining area with a modern, expandable, walnut dining room set and a broad doorway that opens into the kitchen.

Lauren Hamilton, slender and middle-aged with short, dark hair, is sitting at one end of the sofa, next to an end table with the reading lamp turned on. Although it isn't dark, the lower light of late afternoon makes the lamp useful. Lauren is wearing jeans and a casual print shirt. She is reading the latest copy of *The Atlantic*, seemingly absorbed.

Behind her, coming from the kitchen, there is the sound of a closing door, the one that connects to the garage, and footsteps. Harris is home.

"Laurie?" he says before reaching the living room.

"In here." Where else? She closes the magazine, but keeps a finger in it to mark her place.

Harris, a trim man in his 50's, wearing casual trousers, a light blue polo shirt, and a beige sport coat, is carrying a briefcase. Professional in every detail. He pauses just inside of the dining area and addresses his wife.

"I had to tell Bennett that I can't make the forum on gang violence because of the conference at Asilomar. He'll have to ask Peterson to fill in as moderator, which is fine with him. Even if Peterson's more an early childhood development person, but that's okay. He didn't mind. Bennett, I mean."

With the last words, he crosses to the tuner and touches a switch, which immediately produces a Mozart horn concerto. Rather loud. He turns it down, then turns around to Lauren.

"You don't mind not going to Asilomar, do you?"

"Of course not. I told you. I've got plenty to do here, and I'm supposed to take Astrid Williamson for some shopping on Friday. Our regular day, you know. I could change it, but I don't like to. She needs a predictable routine."

"Of course." He doesn't sound very interested one way or another, but notes that Lauren spends a lot of time with the Council on Aging.

"I'm only visiting two women nowadays," she makes an automatic semi-apology. "Astrid on Fridays and Millie Snyder on Tuesdays. And I have a hunch that Astrid won't be living alone much longer. She has help with housework, but she's getting more confused. You know how it goes…"

"Alzheimer's?"

"Maybe. I'm not the doctor, but she definitely has some of the signs. She used to teach at the Marin Academy, but you wouldn't know it now. When I first started seeing her, I used to take her back issues of *The Atlantic*, but she can't focus anymore, just turns pages. As for Millie, she has macular degeneration, so she listens to talking books. Her mind is fine. It's ironic. Astrid sees very well. Maybe I can give our back issues to Larry Peters." She is alluding to their son's high school English teacher.

"That's a thought." Harris pauses at the door into the hall. "Any mail?"

"On your desk. The rest was junk."

"What's for supper?"

"I guess you'd call it pasta primavera. I sort of culled out the garden this morning and got some nice squash and tomatoes. End of the season, but still good. And French bread," she adds and awaits approval.

"Sure. Fine. I was just thinking… we haven't had salmon in quite a while."

"No, I guess not."

"Isn't it in season?"

"Yeah. I'll check at the market. Not factory farmed, though. I'm careful about that."

"Yes, I know." Harris has commented on this before and finds the subject uninteresting. "On second thought, I'll look at the mail later. I need to read an article I brought home."

He crosses over to the sofa as Lauren is standing up. They work their way around each other. Then he sits down more or less in the middle of the sofa, sets his briefcase on the coffee table and opens it. Next he takes out a sheaf of papers, held with a paper clip at one corner, gets out a yellow highlighter, which he sets it to one side on the table, takes his reading glasses from his inside coat pocket, and puts them on. Methodical.

Lauren goes to the kitchen door, but pauses and looks back.

"Would you like a glass of wine?"

"Do we still have any of that chardonnay from Asoleada?"

"Yes."

"Okay." And he addresses himself to the papers at hand.

Lauren returns shortly with a glass in each hand and sets one glass on the coffee table beside Harris's briefcase. As she is setting down the glass, the Mozart concerto morphs into a Haydn symphony.

"Thanks," Harris acknowledges without looking up from his reading. He is already on the second page.

"Is that for Asilomar?"

"Sort of. It's report from the National Association of School Psychologists on teen suicide. I'm using some of the statistics in my workshop."

"I always think of the parents. Not just the grief of losing a child, but the sense of guilt, you know, I mean how you can feel guilty about things that aren't your fault, but just the sense of having failed in some way. How can that feeling ever go away?"

"Sometimes the parents do contribute." Harris looks up at her then, warming to his subject. "Of course they don't mean to, but the point of my presentation is that adults generally don't equip children to deal with disappointment. I'm not casting blame. It's a cultural thing. Adults are always encouraging kids to compete, but don't give them much to fall back on when they fail. *Better-luck-next-time* or *just-work-harder* or *this-peer-stuff-doesn't-last.* That's about it. In other words, what are the kids supposed to do if they can't or don't live up to expectations, either what's externalized or internalized? That's the gist of the workshop—how to help kids deal with failure or disappointment."

"Good topic."

"For example, there was that kid who shot himself in Bolinas about a year ago."

"Yes, I remember."

"It apparently had to do with his going out for varsity football and not making the team, so he went home, got his father's pistol, went out to the beach, and shot himself in the head." Harris turns his attention back to the text.

"It says here that seventeen percent of adolescents surveyed have had suicidal ideation just for failed relationships."

"Youth was never what it was cracked up to be," Lauren observes dryly. "So about how many kids consider suicide for all reasons? Does it say?"

"Depends on the survey. Here it says that as many as forty-two percent will say it's crossed their mind at some time, but serious attempts are another matter."

"It must occur to almost everybody sometime."

"I suppose. But luckily, or unluckily, most people manage to cope with their problem by blaming somebody else. Unless of course they kill themselves to punish that somebody else. Any kind of loss seems to be the major factor. Loss that seems irreparable. Death. Separation. Even loss of face. Maybe I should say 'status'."

"So what can you do?"

"Not too much, since school counselors don't seem to exist anymore. But kids in general need to be encouraged to reexamine their goals, you know, whether self-imposed or external. How realistic are they? People need to discover and pursue what they're good at, or could be good at. But as for relationships…that's tricky. Telling someone there are other fish in the sea has never been very consoling in cases of what we used to call 'a crush.'" He explains all this in his workshop voice and then returns to his reading.

Seeing that Harris is again absorbed in his report. Lauren goes to the kitchen door, then pauses and turns.

"I often think how lucky we've been with David. I mean he never got in trouble, and he seemed to succeed at almost everything. Good grades. Basketball. Everything. Even love. And he takes things in stride. You know what I mean?"

"Sure. Yes, very lucky." Harris still looks at the paper in his hand. Then he adds, "How long till dinner?"

She stops to calculate. "About half an hour." Then she still hesitates and dares another question.

"Harris?"

"Yes…"

"Did you… when you were a teenager, did you ever think about suicide?"

He looks up from his reading, weighing the question. "Me? I don't think so. No. It bothered me a lot when I lost the chess tournament to a girl!" He laughs a dry laugh. "But not enough to punish either her or myself. Not that way. And I fell a lot when I was learning to ski, but I expected that. The sort of failures you expect." He laughs again.

"Same as David, huh?"

"I guess so. As you said, we were lucky." He pauses. "Say, when you take the Lexus in for servicing, can you ask them to check the windshield washer? The spray doesn't seem to be reaching the top of the window lately. I added fluid the other day, but I think there's some blockage in the line, and you know how killing the angle of the sun gets around this time of year. Right in the eye. Isn't safe."

"I understand."

"I hate that commute. Will you remember?"

"I'll write it down," she says as she disappears into the kitchen.

"Laurie," he calls after her.

"Yes?" she answers from the other room.

"Where's today's paper?"

"What?"

"Today's paper. Where is it?" He has increased the volume of his voice. "I think there was an article I want to cut out."

Lauren answers from the kitchen. "It's still on the kitchen table. Do you want it?"

"Yes. Not now. Never mind."

But Lauren is now persistent. "No problem." She appears from the kitchen with the paper in her hand. "Here it is." And she sets it down on the coffee table.

"Oh, okay. Thanks. Can you hand me the scissors?"

While Harris is ruffling through the paper, turning back the page to a certain place, she goes back to the kitchen and returns with the scissors, handing them carefully with the handle towards Harris.

"Thanks. How long did you say 'til dinner?"

"A while. About half an hour." And she goes back to the kitchen, after having uttered a completely unattended sigh.

If the furniture listened to their human speech, it might hear variations in the notation, but not much in tone or tempo. As the uninformed listeners sometimes say about baroque music, "It all sounds the same."

MATT RAMIREZ AND LAUREN HAVE PIZZA

Lauren Hamilton and Matt Ramirez followed the server into the mottled shade of the lattice-roofed patio of the pizzeria, and were seated across from each other at a small table on the far side of dining area next to the wall. He was clean-shaven, with dark, crisply wavy hair, flecked with gray. Her hair, in which gray was not allowed, was dark, almost mahogany, and cut softly to the shape of her head. They were both dressed informally, he in a green polo shirt, she in a scoop-necked knit maroon shirt, both in jeans. A handsome couple.

As soon as they were seated and handed their menus, they thanked the woman in a perfect duet, at which they exchanged a smile. "And thank you for inviting me to lunch — again," she told him.

"Thank you for accepting — at last. I was beginning to wonder…"

"It was my pleasure." She was quick with her reassurance.

They held their look for a moment and then broke it to look at their menus, which they studied intently, as though the decision were crucial.

"Well, this is a pizzeria, so pizza, I presume?" he said finally, glancing in her direction.

"Sure." Still considering the menu.

"No pineapple, please." Matt sounded serious.

"No, no pineapple, but I like vegetarian. Is that okay?" She asked as if a genuine request for approval.

"You're not a strict vegetarian, are you?" A little concerned.

"Not strict, no. Just a preference." Still asking.

"Good. Then we'll order a pepperoni without pepperoni. How's that?"

Lauren laughed. "Perfect."

"Size?"

"Medium?"

"Perfect."

Then they smiled across the table. So easily.

When the server returned and took their order, Lauren asked for a light draft and Matt a glass of the house red.

"You're beautiful, you know," Matt told her matter-of-factly when the waitress had gone.

"Of course," she answered with wry simplicity.

"I noticed that right away. But I also admired the way you stood up and said your piece at the board of supes. You're eloquent, too."

She shook her head as at a compliment too far. "Ellen Graves was supposed to make the presentation, but she was sick. Conveniently for her. So I just used all her notes about the variance for the retirement center. Sure, I was nervous, but it was pretty easy, after all. I'm afraid I didn't notice you until it came to taking the pictures, but…"

"What?"

"I was happy the paper sent you. Of course." She was flirting, but lightly, so that it would be easy to draw back. "And then you showed up at our rally."

"Of course. And it wasn't because the paper sent me. I told you that, didn't I?"

"You made a point of it. And you asked me to lunch."

"And you declined."

"Cross-scheduled," she said evenly, "but pleased," she added. "Really." Matt leaned towards Lauren with both elbows on the table, looking at her in a studied way. Not clear in whose court the ball was at that moment.

"This is idyllic," she observed, filling the space. "Not noisy. I hate a noisy restaurant. A noisy anything, really. And noisy restaurants interfere with digestion. Don't you think?"

"Of course. And kill conversation? Who wants to shout about how you spent your weekend, or what you thought of the movie?"

Lauren laughed. "Or even just the weather…"

"Which is lovely, but not lovelier than the company."

Lauren looked away, feeling for a way to both accept and contradict his outrageous and welcome flattery. Courtship, really.

Then the server relieved any awkwardness by coming back with the beverages, deftly set them down with a "Here you go," and left. Matt and Lauren pledged each other with their respective glasses and drank.

"So," he said, "the gods are smiling. I don't have to be back at the paper until two, and you don't have to go home—ever?"

"It should be so long. But at least Harris won't be back from Sacramento until around eight. He doesn't like the rush traffic, which I understand. You're the one with the schedule."

"So not your place or mine, after all. But another time maybe?" He sounded serious.

She shrugged and sipped her beer again. Finally she made an observation.

"We're married."

"I know. Unfortunately not to each other."

"That was an oversight," she teased. "So why did you marry somebody else?"

"I must have had a reason, but I can't quite remember what it was."

"Come on. Think."

"I can't. It just seemed a good idea at the time. It wasn't arranged by our families. I suppose it could've been," he added.

"Yeah, I know. In this society we marry for love." Her tone was unmistakably ironic.

"But marriage for love isn't all it's cracked up to be, is it? Maybe that's why so many couples don't bother anymore. They know how risky it is. But back then, in my barrio, you sort of had to, and no, Dolores wasn't pregnant. It was just expected. And okay, I was willing, even eager. I admit it."

"That's okay. I married for love, too. Same mistake."

"No one's perfect." Matt excused her and sipped his wine. "So how did you meet the man you married for love? I like romantic stories, even when they break my heart."

"Well, I guess I could tell you, but only if you go first. Anyway, yours is probably a lot more romantic."

Matt shrugged. "Impossible. Dolores and I grew up in the same barrio in East LA. Our mothers were *comadres*. We went to the same schools. I played basketball with Didi's older brother, Louie. We couldn't not have met each other. She was two years younger, but we were high school sweethearts, as they say. No story there."

He took another drink and waited expectantly. "Your turn."

"Okay." Lauren took a breath. "But not all that romantic either. I was working as a secretary in the school district office, not that that was the sort of job I ever planned on, but well, you know…"

"Do I?"

"Well, I supposed I'd be a teacher. I was taking a double major in English and Spanish, but I wasn't sure if I wanted to persuade teenagers that a book is as interesting as a video game. Try to persuade. Anyway, the whole question was taken out of my hands because when I was in my junior year in college, my father died. All of a sudden. I managed to graduate, but I saw that I'd have to work and save some money so I could go back and finish my credential. I didn't think in terms of student loans back then, and I don't think I would have taken one anyway. I mean, I have a thing about being in debt. A sort of conservative family trait." He gave her a sharp look that made her pause a moment.

"That's wise," was all he said, but guardedly. "You speak Spanish?" he added.

"Not really. I mean not anymore. *Me hace falta la practica, sabes*," she said.

He smiled. "Nice accent. So you need practice? I could help with that."

"*Gracias.* Anyway, I was working as a secretary in the student services department when a nice looking, tweedy sort of a guy walks in and presents himself as Harrison Hamilton. I mean, what a name! He was there to do research for his PhD in psychology, and he had a grant to examine the relationship of standardized test results with different family structures."

Matt's brow wrinkled. "Standardized test results with different family structures? What does that even—"

"*No importa*," she answered with a shrug. "Anyway, Harris seemed to like chatting with me, and one day he asked me to proof the draft of his thesis. I was flattered, of course. When I was in high school, I always wanted to hang out with the intellectuals. I had a big crush on the kid who was at the top of honor roll. Martin Jaminsky. Super brain. President of the chess club, naturally. And valedictorian. What else? I never made a perfect fool of myself by dropping my books in his path or anything like that, but I kept hoping that someday he'd notice me, and I'd be the love of his life, whether I played chess or not. He went into engineering of course."

"You kept track?"

"Not deliberately, but I saw him at our twenty-year reunion. A really nice guy. Nice wife. She's an architect. Well, so it goes..." She gave a small ironic sigh before going on.

"So anyway, when Harris asked me to proofread his thesis, I thought it was about the biggest honor I'd ever had. There wasn't that much to do really. I did catch a few typos and tightened up a sentence here and there. Just enough to make me feel like I'd made a contribution to academia. And Harris was so pleased, he not only paid me, but he invited me to dinner and the opera."

"No kidding. The opera! You must've liked it! What was it?"

"Heavens! I don't remember. Wait. Puccini, I think. I've been to so many operas since then, who knows? At the time I was enchanted because I was with Harris. The first straight-A student who ever paid much attention to me. And he was handsome to boot. Much cuter than Martin Jaminsky, who was kind of skinny and pimply, but nice."

"Harris had taste. I'll give him that."

She dismissed the compliment and went on. "Anyway, it was only a couple of months after that that he proposed. After dinner at the Grotto. We were parked in the BMW he had then, exchanging kisses, or making out, as they used to say, and all at once he said, 'I've been thinking of asking you to marry me,' and I said, 'Really?' perfectly fluttered and off guard. And he said, 'Yes, really. Would you be interested?' And of course, I told him that I would be, and he kissed me said, 'Good.' So I assumed from then on that we were engaged, and apparently he assumed the same thing. He's never been one for romantic speeches, but that's okay. I'll give it to him that he's never less than polite. Really well-bred, as they say."

"You should have said you weren't interested."

"Well, I didn't. So there. And our engagement did lead to a wedding. Usually the guy wants to keep it simple and the girl wants to pull out all the stops, but it was the opposite with Harris and me. Because, you see, it emerged pretty soon that we were from different social classes. His people were way upper-middle-class professionals. His mother was a pediatrician, for heaven's sake, and his father was the chief administrator of a hospital. They weren't wealthy with a capital

W, but they were very well off and cultured. I mean they knew every capital in Europe like I know San Francisco. Better. Where to eat, where to shop, what to see. The works. My family was the middle-est of the middle class. As I said, my father was dead by then, but he'd worked all his life at a desk job at the water district, and my mother clerked in a local pharmacy. My older sister, Meg, was married with two little kids and living in Colorado. So nobody in my family was about to throw me a society wedding. They'd do well enough to show up with some towels or a rice cooker.

"When I raised the question with Harris, he said it was no problem because his parents would love to throw the wedding. Since he had no sister, I turned out to be his mother's big opportunity. She started by helping me pick out my dishware and silver, stainless steel actually, because she said that her silver would be mine someday. Which it was. Is. She also went with me to choose a wedding gown, and even insisted on paying for it! I don't have the dress anymore, but it was a gorgeous, satin affair, embroidered around the neck and bodice with those little pearl buttons, like scattered raindrops. A scoop neck. Long sleeves. Lace. Of course I have pictures. Beth saw to hiring the best photographer and all that. I mean the best one, excepting you. Of course." She made a pleasant addendum in his direction. He shrugged it off.

"Anyway, I was flattered by all the attention. Come to think of it, I don't suppose Cinderella had much to do with her wedding either. Anyway, it was a nice event at the country club and all that. My sister came out with her squally kids, and my mom wore the predictable blue dress with a white gardenia corsage and cried, and some of my high school and college friends showed up, but it was really the Hamiltons' affair. I can't complain though. It was great." She paused for a brief moment of recollected glory or merely to take another swallow of beer.

"So you lived the good life."

"Happiness is always relative, isn't it? I mean when I married Harris, I thought it would be my joy to please him, but it really turned out to be more of a task. I had no idea. I used to think that class distinctions were for the British, but I was wrong. For example, when I married Harris, I married season tickets to the opera, and I had to learn how to give dinner parties and buffets and things like that. Harris selected the wines, of course, but it was up to me to notice when the glasses needed refilling. I learned how to make small talk with people I barely knew and be charming to people I didn't especially like. As I said, Harris is every bit the cultured gentleman, and somehow I always felt I was running to keep up with his expectations. Which can be tiring. So much for my romantic story," she ended abruptly and took another swallow of beer.

Matt nodded and seemed to ponder.

"Do you have children?" He asked as though unsure that he wanted to know.

"Yes, I have a son. David."

"How old is he?"

"Twenty. Last June. He's going into his junior year at Davis. He was home for a few days around his birthday, but he had a summer job up there."

"What's his major?"

"Computer science. What else?" She laughed a small, dismissive laugh.

"A child of the age. My son learned digital photography before I did." Maybe he said this to make her feel companioned. Maybe just the truth.

"And how old is your son?"

"Twenty-nine. And yes, he's a photographer too, but live-action. He makes DVDs for special events. Some advertising."

"A good career."

"Maybe, but pretty competitive." Matt seemed uncertain, thoughtful. "Do you miss your son? Empty nest and all that?"

"I wouldn't say so. Of course, sometimes. I don't know if I was really cut out to be a mother. Maybe it was another role I played, though I think I've been good at it. But I was never in a hurry to have children. After I was married, I kept my job, and Harris was teaching at the JC. We lived in a rented apartment. But Harris's grandfather died—dare I say 'conveniently'?—and left him a bunch of investments.

Property actually, but valuable. So he sold it, and we bought a house in Kentfield. I love the place. It has a big oak tree in front and a sunny back yard where you can look right up at Mt. Tam. We eat on the deck just about all summer. I have a vegetable garden out there. It's past its prime now, but I still have zucchini. Want some?"

He gave her the dismissive look that people give to that particular question.

She shrugged in reply, as if it was worth a try.

"After David left home, I suppose I should've gone back to school, but I decided to volunteer for the Council on Aging. Probably it had something to do with my mom. I mean when she retired from her clerking job, she went to live with my sister in Boulder, but then, about five years ago, she took a bad fall and never fully recovered. Meg and I decided that she should go to an assisted living situation. Luckily, Mom agreed because she just couldn't function like she did before, couldn't help Meg around the house or anything. Felt she was in the way. My sister looks in on her every few days, but I really felt kind of guilty about not being on hand to help out more. I got to thinking about other people in Mom's situation who don't have any family nearby to look out for them, and I figured there was something useful I could do."

"I'd imagine that anything you do…"

He didn't finish his comment because at that moment the pizza arrived, like the arrival of the boar's head at a feast, held high and triumphant. The server set down the feast, commanded them to "Enjoy," and departed. They began to eat, laughing as they pulled out the first slices, trailing threads of cheese.

"Do you know why pizza is the perfect food?" he asked her as soon as he has finished chewing the first bite off the tip of his slice.

"Perfectly fattening?" she answered with the first bite still in her mouth.

"No, no. It's because…" he paused for effect…"of its universal symbolism. You know, like bread and wine, sort of."

"Symbolism? The shape?" She swallowed. "But nowadays pizzas can be square."

"Alas! But I'm talking tradition here. The wholeness of the circle. The completeness."

"Tortillas are round too," she observed wryly.

"So they are," he conceded. "Yes, very true, but I was thinking of the broader picture. The colors of the topping. Green for life. Red for passion. The brown mushrooms for the earth. That sort of thing."

"That's good. I like that. But what about the cheese?"

"Ah yes, the cheese. How could I forget? Well, let's see… that's for the sun, life itself. How we came to be here. Now."

Lauren laughed, was about to bite again, then paused, slice in mid-air. "If this is so sacred, shouldn't we say a blessing?"

"Good thought. It's not too late, even if the circle's a little diminished. Go ahead."

She pondered a moment. "Okay. So let us give thanks to the gods for this holy pizza. For the fattening food we are already eating, may we be truly grateful. Is that okay?"

"Very apt," he assured her.

"I haven't had a pizza in a long time," she observed after the consuming the last of the slice. "Maybe because my pizza-eating son doesn't live at home anymore. I don't need the fat of the land, not in this form, I mean."

"No, my dear. The fat will do you no harm. It's my good wife who shouldn't be eating pizza." He chewed thoughtfully for a moment, then swallowed. "It's not her fault," he mitigated immediately "but she really has gone to fat in the last few years. Probably from unhappiness. It's pathetically easy to marry the wrong person, even if you do marry for love. No, not her fault." He seemed to mean it, but the comment drifted off as if unfinished.

Lauren said nothing. She had already admitted her own mistake.

Feeling the rightness of silence, they addressed the pizza with a good appetite, while other patrons came and ordered and ate around them. But as the pan emptied and they became less hungry, they talked more and laughed at lesser jokes, and they both looked very happy.

Over her last slice of pizza, Lauren asked Matt how he had come to live so far from East LA.

Matt gave a small, theatrical sigh.

"I might as well explain. Dolores was really beautiful back then. Every guy in the school was in love with her. I didn't think I even had a chance at first, but when she started turning up in the hall just when I was leaving class or happened to bump into me at a game or a party, I caught on that I was in the running. I wasn't a football hero or anything, though I played basketball, like I said. Well, of course, I responded with heart and hormones. In fact, I begged her to sleep with me approximately a hundred times, but in addition to being really beautiful, she was a very devout Catholic. So there it was. I suffered for her all through my senior year and two years of community college, until I finally got a steady job in a photo lab. Then I could propose, and we could have that big wedding with a hundred relatives. But first I had to go to confession, which was a challenge because I hadn't been since I was about nine years old. The priest finally gave up and said he'd pray for our marriage because it wasn't going to be easy. He was right about that!

"Probably harder for her than for me. I don't mean I'm a bad husband, but not a particularly good one either. The usual insensitive jerk. Like Didi really didn't want to leave LA and all her family. But when I got an opportunity up here in Marin, I insisted that we move north, and like a good wife, she didn't say too much. It was a good decision—for me. Sure. I like working on the paper, and I love the north coast. I guess part of me wanted to be a nature photographer, but you don't make a living at that unless you're very, very good. Like National Geographic stuff."

"But you are very good," she reassured him.

"Not bad. But I do people. Groups and portraits. People want to see themselves, and why not? Unfortunately, the portrait business isn't what it was. Now everyone takes pictures and just tosses the ones they don't like. I've ended up doing a lot of passport photos. Big deal." It was an acid comment, but he smiled a little to prove he was coping.

Lauren hesitated over that and then thought of a question. "And your wife, is she still religious?"

"Maybe more. Time softens some believers, hardens others. It depends. Anyway, religion is wishful thinking. No harm in that. But the person who believes that stuff about the Blessed Virgin and the miracles and all that will believe almost anything. Okay. She has a right to her own mythology, as long as it doesn't hurt anyone else. I know that." He ended with a tone almost of resignation, but not quite.

The waitress stopped by to see if everything is okay. Matt and Lauren simultaneously agreed that it was.

"And your son?" she ventured. "Only child?"

"No. We had three children actually. Didi was a terrific mother. I'll give her that. As dedicated to motherhood as to the church." He paused, took a breath and went on. We lost our second child. A little girl. Crib death. We never quite got over that. Didi didn't want more children for a long time, terrified it would happen again, but finally we had another child. Stephanie. Completely healthy."

"Lucky. I admit I wanted David to be a girl," Lauren took up. "A girl would've been so much fun."

"*Menos mal.* People seem to think daughters are easier. They aren't."

A tone of closure showed that he didn't want to go any further. But then, all at once he laid his arm on the table, just beside the pizza pan, with his hand open, invitingly. She reached to take it without hesitation. He leaned towards her and whispered. "I want to see you again. But not in public…if you want…"

Lauren looked at him squarely, knowing the answer, but considering how to consent with veiled restraint. She withdrew her hand and leaned back slightly. Matt still bent towards her across the table, regarding her expectantly.

"You know," she said, "I've been thinking… maybe we could have lunch at my place. If you had time. And if you like simple fare."

"I do, but no zucchini, if you don't mind."

"I wouldn't dare. Anyway, it occurred to me that Harris is going to a conference at Asilomar. Next weekend. The weekend after this. He leaves Friday morning, so maybe Friday or Saturday. Just soup and salad." As if the menu were the deciding factor. She glanced away to allow for consideration or else to watch a couple of young women just coming in and being seated at the next table.

"God…I…of course. But I can't make Saturday. I've got an appointment to photograph a golden wedding affair. Friday maybe? I could probably carve out some time." He took out his calendar, scanned it. "Yes. For sure. Noon? I've got an appointment at three."

It was her turn to ponder. "I just remembered I have a conflict for Friday. Dammit! But probably I can change it to the next day. Sure. Noon."

"Hold on. I've got your cell, but I need your address."

"That could be useful." She grinned, picked up her purse from the floor beside her chair and took out a notebook and pen. She wrote the address, tore off the page, and handed it to him. He folded it and put it in the breast pocket of his polo shirt.

"You…" He looked at her intently.

"Yes?"

"Have a thread of mozzarella on your chin."

"Really?" Amused, not alarmed.

"Let me…" Before she could raise her hand, he brushed her chin with the back of his index finger. "What a beautiful chin you have."

"But even better now?" A smile of acknowledged flattery.

"Perfect with or without cheese topping."

JOYCE REMEMBERS

Seated in her recliner, though not reclining, Astrid Williamson looked anxiously towards the kitchen, where she heard the clink of Joyce putting away lunch dishes.

"Joyce?"

"Yes?" Joyce appeared in the doorway, dishtowel in hand.

"Where did you put my, my, you know, the thing I write on? It isn't here."

Astrid was alluding to a notepad that she kept next to the telephone on the end table beside her chair. It wasn't that she needed it at the moment, but rather that she had looked up from trying to read the local paper, and it came to her that it wasn't there. Where it was supposed to be.

"Gee, Mrs. W, I don't think I put it anywhere. Gimme a minute, and I'll come an' help you look." Joyce disappeared back into the kitchen.

"Well, it's not in the drawer," Astrid said after her testily, not sure if Joyce could hear or not, but feeling it necessary to point out that she had already looked in the one logical place, the shallow drawer where she kept her pop-up phone directory along with a pen and pencil. As she was a tidy person, it was easy enough to see that it wasn't there.

Which could only mean that Joyce had moved it. Very annoying. What if the phone rang and she needed the tablet to write a message?

More noises of dishware from the kitchen, then a drawer closing, and then Joyce appeared again the doorway with something her hand that wasn't the dishtowel.

"This is it, isn't it?" she asked, coming in with the item extended.

"Why yes, of course." What was her notepad doing in the kitchen? Astrid kept a different pad for grocery shopping, which Joyce knew perfectly well. "Why did you take it in there?"

"It sounds funny, but I just found it in a utensil drawer. When I was putting the big spoon away."

"Oh. Well, thank you." There followed a silence as Joyce put the pad back on the table beside the telephone. "Joyce, I…" Astrid looked up with a glisten in her eyes that might have been tears. "I'm so sorry! I thought it was you. I must have… but why would I…?"

"Hey, Mrs. W, that's easy! You had the pad in your hand when you went to the kitchen to, let's say, start your supper, or just get a glass of water or something, and you put it down when you went to pick up something else. I do things like that sometimes. Everybody does. Don't feel bad." Joyce touched her shoulder briefly in an awkward sign of consolation.

"No, no…It's not that! It's not sometimes. I do things like that a lot. I can't remember things. That's why I write them down. That's why I use the pad so much." She picked up the pad and considered it for a moment because there was writing on it already. "Boil eggs. You see? Did I do that? I don't even know."

"But that's it! That's how it happened. You went to the kitchen to boil the eggs, and you happened to have the notepad with you. And I made egg sandwiches for lunch. So you did boil them, didn't you? Just like you meant to."

Astrid nodded, sniffed, fished a handkerchief out of her sweater pocket and wiped her nose.

"I'll tell you the truth, Joyce. I don't know if I ever said this to anyone out loud, but I'm so scared about my mind. I'm so scared! You don't understand…"

"There now. There, there…Yes, I do." Joyce hovered in front of her chair uncertainly. "It's okay," she reassured again. "I can always help you out."

Astrid nodded slightly, but said nothing.

After a minute, Joyce sat down on the sofa across from Astrid's chair. Creamy, who was spread indolently along the back of the sofa, didn't seem disturbed. Astrid still had her newspaper on her lap, but apparently forgotten. Uncertain still, Joyce picked up a magazine from the coffee table and began flipping over the pages. "Would you like me to read something to you?" she offered.

Astrid shook her head. "Joyce, I've never told anyone. How scared I am."

"I know, Mrs. W."

"No, you don't. Don't you see? If I go to pieces, they'll put me in one of those places like happened to Maman. It's so much better just to die. If I knew the way!" Her hands were shaking a little, which in turn rattled the paper on her lap.

"Mrs. W, I do understand. But maybe it won't be that way. I mean the nursing home part. Maybe you can get somebody to come an' live with you to help out. You could live a happy life for years an' years, then maybe someday, well, you'd just sort of go to sleep, all of a sudden, and you'd never be in a nursing home at all. You know what they say. Don't borrow trouble. Me, I should know… Things don't never work out the way you think they're goin' to. They just don't," she added for emphasis.

"I suppose you're right," Astrid conceded warily, "but still…"

"You gotta stay calm. And don't ever give up." Joyce sat quiet, considering. "Listen," she said. "I never told this to anybody—I mean who didn't have to know." She took a breath. "I actually tried to kill myself one time. About three years ago. But the thing is I got so depressed an' I was so stupid. I thought that if you bought a bottle of sleeping pills, you know, just over the counter and you took the whole thing at once, then you could just drift off and die. So I took the pills and finally started to get sleepy, and then it came to me. That I didn't want to be dead. I wanted to be happy. And it came to me that if you still hope for something, which I actually did, then it isn't time to go. So I called 911."

"You did the right thing. Why ever did you want to do it?"

Joyce uttered an uncharacteristically sardonic laugh. "Okay, okay, I know some people got it harder than me. I mean born in a terrible slum or sold into slavery or something. But the plain fact is that I never really had any good luck. It makes you wonder, you know, about fate. Like is it in your stars or something? Not that I believe that astrology stuff, but I guess it's the reason some people believe in reincarnation instead of heaven or hell, because, well, maybe what you really need is just another chance. Like if you did your best an' it just didn't work out."

"I know. But you must be happier now. You seem so, well, cheerful."

"Sure. I'm happier now." Joyce smiled her crooked-toothed smile. "It would've been a big mistake. I'm really good at mistakes. So maybe my life was just a mix of bad luck and bad choices. How can you tell?"

Astrid shrugged. "How can you tell?" she echoed. "That's a big question, isn't it? Some choices are given and some aren't. Like Maman would never have decided to get, what do you call it? Senile. No, not Maman! That was surely bad luck. So sad…" Her voice trailed into the past.

"That's it! That's the problem." Joyce folded the magazine and set it back on the coffee table. "I keep goin' back to it. I did dumb things all right, but I never really had much luck either. From the start. I never really had a family at all. Sure, I had a mother, but she didn't want me. I figured that out when I was still pretty little. I guess my mom got pregnant by accident, but instead of getting an abortion like she should of, she decided to have the baby. I mean me."

"Oh, Joyce. Don't say that. Some abortions, yes. But not you!"

"Naw, it's okay, Mrs. W. Maybe my mom thought it'd be fun to have a little baby, sort of like a new toy. Who knows? Only she prob'ly forgot that you gotta get up at night with babies and take 'em for shots and change diapers and wipe their runny noses and all that stuff. Anyway, she left me with my gramma when I was about six months old and went off with some guy, but prob'ly not my father."

"How terrible!"

"Yeah… one day when my gramma was at work, my mom took off. Left a note and me. My gramma told me she called my mom's friends and all that stuff, but she never got a lead, not even a postcard. When I was little, I'd look at pictures of her in my gramma's album. Just a blond teenage kid squinting into the camera, not ugly and not beautiful. Sort of overweight. Like me." She managed a small crooked smile.

"So your grandmother raised you." Astrid surmised.

"Yeah. For a few years actually. My gramma didn't really want me either, but she took care of me the best she could. When she was at work, she had me stay with a neighbor, until I was in school. You see, she was always a waitress, though not always at the same place, but she worked pretty steady. She could never afford to have my teeth straightened, but she did take me to the dentist once in a while. Basic stuff like that. I don't think raising another kid was exactly what my gramma had in mind, but she was always nice to me. I'll give her that. I mean, she'd raised three kids already, all gone off in different directions, and only one of 'em ever sent her a Christmas card." Joyce paused and reflected.

"People think of grammas as sweet little old ladies" she went on, "but my gramma was still fairly young. Around fifty, I guess, and not bad looking. So she had a few boyfriends, off an' on. I suppose she would've liked to get married, but that never worked out. So we sort of struggled along. Gramma was home in the morning, but she needed to sleep late, so she'd get me ready for school and then go back to bed. By the time I got home on the bus, she'd be gone to work, but she always left somethin' for supper in the fridge. She still had some kind of deal with a neighbor. I was supposed to go there if there was an emergency, or dial 911 if there was a fire. Luckily, I never had to. So there is such a thing as luck, I guess. You don't really notice luck very much, unless it's bad.

"Anyhow, we got along pretty good until Bud came to live with us. He was the first boyfriend who actually ever lived with us, because our place was really little.

Two tiny bedrooms and a bath was about it, except, of course for the living room and kitchen. Most of the time Bud was okay. He'd go off to work early, most days. I think he was a carpenter. Anyway, he made good money when he was working, so we had more stuff. I even had some clothes that didn't come from the thrift shop.

Once in a while he'd bring me an extra little present, like a bracelet or something. And yeah, he paid to get my ears pierced so I could wear earrings. He got me some that were kind of pretty. But I don't wear earrings anymore. Hate 'em actually 'cause they make me think of Bud. At the time, I didn't like him all that much, but I thought he was okay. I mean I was a kid. I should've known...but how could I?"

"My daughter loves earrings," Astrid put in absently. "She has lovely taste."

Joyce sighed, entangled in her own reminiscence. "Well Bud, he did drink sometimes, especially if he wasn't working, and then he'd get kind of noisy, like swearing an' stuff. Then Gramma would send me to my room and tell me to shut the door and stay there. Eventually he'd quiet down and fall asleep, and I could go to the bathroom and brush my teeth an' all. But that didn't happen too often. We lived in San

Leandro back then, and his work was pretty regular. But you can never tell about people," Joyce added sagely.

Astrid nodded. "How true," she concurred.

"Maybe I shouldn't tell this right out, but the fact is that one day when Gramma was at work, something happened I never even thought of. Bud was hangin' around the house, watchin' TV, an' I was home with a cold. In my room making some new clothes for my paper dolls. Okay, so I was almost ten, but I liked to design clothes out of wrapping paper or magazines. It was kind of a hobby. "

Astrid nodded as if to say, "Why not?"

"Well, anyhow, Bud, he came in and said I should come and watch TV with him 'cause there was a pretty good movie on. Somethin' about dinosaurs that he thought a kid would like it, so I went in. The movie seemed okay, but almost before I knew it, he had me on his lap an' then he started stickin' his tongue in my mouth—you know— frenchin' they call it, an' I was struggling, of course, cause I was scared an' gaspin' for breath, 'cause I had this cold an' all. An' he stopped an' told me that this was the way grown-ups kiss and I should learn it, 'cause I was so damn ugly, I needed all the help I could get. Then all of a sudden, he acted kind of mad and yelled at me to go back to my room, which of course I was plenty happy to do. I would've locked the door if there's been any lock on it.

"I was back at my dolls again when Bud hollered for me to come back in the living room because the movie wasn't over. I told him I was busy, but he said to come out or he'd come an' get me. So hell! I put down my stuff and went back out, an' sat at the far end of the sofa, but Bud, he reached over and dragged me over to 'im an' jerked down my pants. See, all I had on was my underpants and bathrobe. Well, I guess I don't have to tell you what he did to me, an' I was screamin'. I couldn't help it. On account of the pain, an' wet blood runnin' down on him an' me an' the sofa. But Bud, he didn't even seem to notice. Jus' kep' heavin' 'til he got done, and then I guess he started to think it over what he did to me, 'cause he told me to go clean myself up an' if I said anything to Gramma about this, he'd hurt me worse, so I better think about it. After what happened with Bud that day, I dunno how I could of got suckered again, but that's another story…"

"Oh, my dear…" Astrid murmured, as if even her reaction was too private and too painful to utter aloud. "Oh, my dear. Did you tell your grandmother? Surely you did." It was almost a whisper.

"Later on. I just ran to the bathroom, hurtin' every step and cleaned myself up with a washcloth the best I could an' washed the blood out of the cloth and threw it in the hamper, and I guess Bud must of thrown my underpants away an' took the sofa cushion out in the back yard to wash 'cause I could hear the hose runnin' out there. So I guess everything looked pretty normal by the time Gramma got home from work. It was late an' she was tired, an' I was just lyin' in bed in the dark with the pain still burnin' and scared to death he'd come and get me again. So when I heard Gramma come in, I was really glad, but I was too scared to tell her anything. Only she stuck her head in the door, like she always did when she got home.

"'You asleep, Jolly?' she said real soft. She always called me that. Jolly.

"'No, Gramma.' Maybe I sounded a little quavery like. I prob'ly did.

"'You okay?'

I just told her I didn't feel too good.

"An' she goes, 'Your cold isn't gettin' no worse, is it?'

"'Yeah, maybe.'

"Well, Bud he was standin' kind of behind her in the doorway and heard what I said, and so he goes, 'Yeah, she ain't feelin' right 'cause she threw up on the sofa a little while back.' An' he tells her that he had to wash off the cushion an' that's why it was kind wet and for her not to sit on that part of the sofa for a while.

"Well, I dunno exactly why I came apart just then. I don't think it was the pain. Or even what he did to me. I think it was bein' blamed for what he said about the sofa that wasn't my fault. Anyhow, I started in to cry. Even though I was plenty scared of Bud, but I couldn't stop then, and I jumped up and held onto Gramma around the waist and told her it was his dick messed up the sofa 'cause he made me bleed, an' I just screamed until I thought sure she was gonna hit me, but she didn't. She turned around an' started yellin' at Bud to get out in the hall an' laid me down on the bed an' looked, well, between my legs. I guess she could tell right away that I was hurt.

"Then she went back out and started hollerin' at Bud about how the only thing she could trust him to do was get a beer outta the fridge, and she'd give him five minutes to get his stuff together an' get out, which I guess he did 'cause pretty soon I could hear his pickup goin' outta the drive. Meantime, Gramma, she called up one of her girlfriends an' they talked for a while, an' then she called the police."

Astrid sat, wordless, shaking her head slightly.

"I sure didn't mean to get into all this," said Joyce apologized.

"It's all right, Joyce. Really. So I suppose the police came," she prompted delicately.

"Yeah. The police came around and took me to a clinic, where there was a nurse or somebody examined me again, an' finally a social worker came in and started askin' me an' Gramma a bunch of questions about Bud an' how we lived and how much I was alone in the house and all that, and I guess they just figured she couldn't take care of me right. I'm not sure how she took that, but maybe she was actually kind of relieved 'cause she didn't put up any arguments, except to say she did her best, which I agreed with. It was kind of funny, though, after all those years that we lived like that, how they took me away all of a sudden and wouldn't even let me go back with Gramma, except to get my things, which she put in a couple of cardboard boxes and an old suitcase, which she later came and took back because it belonged to her. I don't know if they ever caught Bud or not, but I sort of doubt it. I think I would've heard."

"They took you away from her? What do they call that? I should know."

"Foster care. Yeah, but the people they put me with, they were okay, really. I mean they never hurt me or anything like that, and the house was warmer than Gramma's, an' the meals were more regular because Annie, she didn't go out to work. O'course I had to go to another school, which was where they started calling me 'Fatty,' 'cause new kids always get stomped on. But I sort of got used to that, and in most ways it was okay.

"Anyway, Annie an' Jack—that was her husband—just kept me and another foster kid, who was about two back then. Foster parents don't get carried away bein' affectionate 'cause it's only temporary, after all. I know some foster parents are pretty awful, but the Potters were okay. Just not chummy, if you know what I mean.

"So anyway, I stayed with them until I finished the sixth grade. A couple other kids came an' went an' some relative came and got Charley, the little kid. My gramma actually stopped by at Christmas with some kind of present, and she'd send a few dollars for my birthday, and sometimes I'd send her a postcard, which was cheaper than a letter. But otherwise I never saw her, an' after I left the Potters, I lived in a different part of town, an' I guess she lost track, 'cause I didn't hear from her ever again. I think about her once in a while, just wondering what might've happened. Maybe she got married or just moved away. Jeez, maybe she even died! But somebody would've told me…or maybe not. Anyhow I don't blame her. I mean she took care of me when she could."

Joyce gave a singularly human sigh of acceptance and trudged on into the rocky landscape of her memories.

"I dunno why the Potters decided they couldn't keep me anymore. It's true I had a lotta trouble with my teeth, an' the dentist said I should've had orthodontia, but there wasn't money for that, not back then. An' I was gettin' grown up too. I even got my period when I was with them. And Annie, she always said she preferred little kids. Maybe they stopped takin' foster kids altogether. Maybe Jack retired an' they went off into the sunset in their new camper, which was really nice. Anyway, I went to another home, the Duggins, which meant another school, but the new school wasn't bad, and it was the fall semester when I changed over, not the middle of the year. I asked the kids to call me 'Jolly,' which they mostly did. The same when I started high school two years later.

"I admit I didn't do too good in school, but I didn't do too bad either. I mean I never flunked any classes, except I got a D in algebra, but I did okay in my other classes. For some reason, I really liked world history, an' I got an A in that class because I did my homework and wrote a pretty good report about human migrations. I put in a big map with arrows, you know, showin' which way they went when they wore out their resources an' all, an' how they came to America, even way before Columbus. Anyway, the teacher really liked it.

"But it didn't take me too long to figure out that I was never gonna be much good at anything, an' let's face it, not much to look at either. When I was a junior, one of the counselors at the high school told me that before I graduated, I should sign up for the nurse's aid class that they gave at night school, so I could get a job at a convalescent hospital, which was actually good advice, except that I didn't finish the course, but I did start it. That was the year I started goin' around with Coop.

"Cooper was really his last name, but he liked it better'n George, which was his real first name. Anyhow, Coop was new that year. He came from Bakersfield, actually. Anyhow, I knew how that felt, bein' new I mean, so we sort of..."

Joyce and Astrid both startled when the phone rang. Astrid stared at it a moment, then reached over and picked it up.

PATRICK IS BORN

Hello?…Yes, this is Astrid… Just fine. And how are you?…That's good… Yes, what is it?…Oh, I see. Well, no, I guess it wouldn't matter…" She consulted her notepad "but Saturday will be fine. I might need groceries….Yes, that'll be fine…No, really… Yes, I'll write it down…Yes, I understand. Saturday instead of Friday. That'll be fine. And thank you for calling…You too. Bye." She set down the phone and explained to Joyce that Laura couldn't come on Friday, but Saturday instead. She picked up her notepad again and pencil from the side table drawer and wrote down "Laura Saturday" in large printed letters.

Astrid set the pad and pencil aside and looked up. "I wish she hadn't… it's just that I get used to a certain day and then well, once in a while something happens. It's not often. I know that, but it kind of upsets my routine. I know she can't help it," but she sounded disappointed.

"'Course I understand. Everybody's the same about their schedule, but you feel it more when you have to depend on other people. Only just for one day. Luckily. Luck makes me think of when I met Coop. I felt so lucky, but maybe I wasn't. I'll never know. I mean how can you tell what's luck and what isn't?"

"Coop? Who's Coop?"

"My boyfriend in high school. Like I said, his real name was George, but everybody called him 'Coop.' "

Astrid nodded, seemed to feel for a tactful question, but found none. "So Coop was your boyfriend…"

"Yeah, that's right. And he was great, Coop was. Nothin' like Bud, but it was like Bud said to me. I wasn't pretty and boys didn't pay attention to me, except sometimes to call me 'Fatty.' But I always had good skin, not a lot of zits or anything. An' good boobs—if you pardon the expression—an' Coop he liked that. Anyway, he started hangin' around with me an' askin' me out to the movies an' stuff, an' I could tell him stuff about my life that I never told anybody else, and he never minded. Like when he asked me to have sex with him the first time, and I told him how scared I was because of what happened with Bud, but he was real understanding about it. He goes, 'It won't hurt this time, Jolly, like it done before. We'll go slow and careful. It'll be totally different.' So I went ahead an' did it, an' Coop, he was sort of right. I mean it did hurt some, but not bad, an' Coop told me I was great an' that he never loved any girl like as much as he loved me. Sure, Coop was only a kid. I see that now, but he was a year older'n me, which seemed like a lot back then. And he was a nice kid at heart. I don't think he ever wanted to hurt me. He just wasn't too sure about his plans, like he didn't know what he wanted to do for a job, although he talked a lot about gettin' a job in a body shop when he graduated from high school. 'Course him an' his friends all liked cars and knew pretty much about them. Like, it was Coop taught me how to drive, though I never did get around to getting a license. But I do know how. Well, Coop, after he graduated, he worked in a filling station for a while an' talked about goin' in the military. I wouldn't of cared because back then I didn't know much about war and what it does to veterans, I mean even if they don't get hurt or killed. I just didn't want Coop to go away.

"Anyhow, Coop didn't decide anything right off, and we kept on having sex whenever we got the chance, like when his mom was at work. An' I really started likin' it. The sex. But mostly because I loved Coop and wanted to make him happy. Well, you guessed it. After a while I got pregnant. We weren't stupid about sex. Coop, he did use a condom, but I guess it only takes one time if it doesn't work. But Coop, he always said it didn't matter if I got pregnant because if it happened, we'd get married. I'll say this for Coop, when I told him I got one of those pregnancy tests and it was positive, he said it was okay. He didn't act all that happy, but he wasn't mad or anything either. He said not to tell anybody, especially his mom, an' he'd take me to Reno an' we'd get married an' he'd get a better job, which he intended to do anyhow.

"That really made me so happy. 'Course I didn't say anything to the Duggins either. They knew I was goin' around with Coop, but they never knew about how we were havin' sex. I think they really pretty much liked him. It was more of a problem that his mom didn't like me. Really didn't," Joyce added for emphasis.

"Well, I guess if there ever was a happy time in my life, it was when Coop n' me were plannin' to get married and for a few months after that 'cause we did get married in Reno, an' then we moved down to Bakersfield because his dad knew somebody there who'd give him a job in a wholesale nursery. Even if his mom never liked me, his dad wasn't so bad about it. Only his mom and dad were split up, an' his dad lived in another state. Anyhow, the Duggins never seemed to care one way or another when I said we were married. I was almost of age anyway. But Mrs. D did give us a set of towels for a present, which was nice. In fact, I still got one of 'em.

"Anyway, Coop wasn't too crazy about the work in the nursery, but he said it was okay. We had a little duplex that we rented, and even though the weather was stinking hot down there, I felt good, an' I was gettin' real big by then, an' when I had a check-up at the clinic, they said everything was fine. I felt really proud. Sure, I was dumb, but that was about the first thing in my life I ever felt proud of. I mean I was seventeen an' I'd never learned to do anything very useful. I mean in the way of earnin' a livin', except for that CNA class I started. An' Mrs. D taught me to cook an' do a little sewing, so I knew useful stuff for being a mother. I really thought it'd all work out.

"God! It makes me sad sometimes just to think how happy I was. I mean, there I was and never guessed I was as happy as I was ever gonna be for my whole life. I guess that's kind of usual, not knowing."

"It is, yes." Astrid confirmed. "But it's as well we don't know."

"Yeah. Anyhow, it all changed one night about a month before the baby was due. I got up to pee an' it was only when I was gettin' back in bed I realized Coop wasn't there. At first I thought he got up extra early to go to work, only it wasn't even light yet and that was in August. So I turned on the light and looked around for him, not that there was many places to look. An' then I stuck my head out the front door and seen the car was gone. Coop had this used VW that he bought off a friend just before he graduated. I was scared then, but not as scared as I was gonna be later on. I went back into the kitchen and decided to make me a cup of coffee, and when I took down my mug from the shelf, I found a piece of paper in it. It was note from Coop. It said that he'd got laid off from the nursery two weeks ago 'cause they were cuttin' back an' he was new, but he didn't want to say anything to me 'cause he thought he'd pretty soon turn up another job. I remember that he said, 'Jolly, I'm really, really sorry. I thought I could support a family. Only I can't.' He said it'd be better for me to go to welfare and say he ran out on me, so I'd have something to live on. He said not to worry about the rent for the rest of the month, and he'd left me some cash in an envelope in the refrigerator. That was about it. In his note he never did mention the baby.

"Well, after I got over cryin' for a while, I got to thinkin' that what he did sort of made sense—from his point of view, even if it wasn't right. I looked in the refrigerator, and in the meat keeper I found an envelope with a hundred dollars in twenties.

"The baby kicked to remind me that I had stuff to do. So I looked up the address of the county welfare office in the phone book, and later on I took the bus over and waited in line, like everybody, and made an application. It was pretty sad, but I knew I had to. Anyhow, the clerk said that just for the time being, all they could offer me was food stamps. In the meantime, she needed to know where was Coop, which I assured her I didn't know, but I did give her his mom's address and phone, though I was pretty sure he wasn't there. Well, she said they could start the paperwork for my benefits, but in the meantime maybe I could go to Catholic Social Services to get extra stuff for the baby and maybe a month's rent, if it came to that. Which it did, for a while. The social worker was really pretty nice, but everything she said scared me more.

"I guess I don't hafta tell you that Coop never did come back. In fact, I never seen or heard from him again. 'Course I tried callin' his mom from the pay phone down at the market. Those days I didn't have a cell. Anyway, there was never an answer except once when his mom picked up and she goes, 'George ain't here. He's lookin' for work up in Washington, him an' a buddy,' an' that was all she knew, or anyway pretended. I dunno. She said he told her that we broke up. Maybe it was even true, I mean that he said that. It was a nail in my heart all the same. I mean if he really said that. I'll never know…

"Well the next Monday after I tried to get on welfare, that was the day I went into labor. Late in the afternoon. So I got my purse and stuff for the hospital an' went to the bus stop, an' finally got a bus. I knew pretty much about the buses because, of course, Coop always took his car to work, and anyhow I didn't have a license. Believe me, that was the longest wait an' the longest bus ride I ever took. I was thinkin' I'll never get there in time. 'Course when I finally got to the emergency check-in, the first thing they asked me is if I had insurance, but I told them to call welfare about Medicaid to straighten it out. I knew that somehow they'd have to take me in, which was all I cared about right then. But the waters broke right there in the waiting room an' I was cryin' an' I wanted Coop so bad! Or Gramma or almost anybody.

"Lucky for me, everything went pretty smooth after they got me in the labor room, an' it really didn't take much more'n an hour for him to come. A nice big boy.

"Eight pounds, ten ounces." Some residual pride crept out in a small smile. "Screamin' his head off. He didn't have anything wrong with him at all. It was a miracle to me to hold him against my belly, even if he was red an' funny-lookin' like all babies. Maybe that was the happiest moment of my whole entire life.

"Only, like I kinda said before about happy moments. They don' last. I stayed in the hospital that night an' felt really peaceful, an' I nursed the baby. I decided to call him Patrick. I dunno why exactly. It wasn't after anybody I knew, but I just liked the sound of it. Patrick Cooper. It kind of flowed together. And it kinda sounded like a movie star's name. Don't you think?"

"Patrick Cooper," Astrid repeated, smiling a little. "Yes, that's nice. It does remind me…but I don't remember his name."

"Anyhow, when I looked at him I felt so proud. I mean of myself. He was so perfect. I never felt like that about anything else I ever did. So anyway, even though I was really, really tired, I laid awake in bed just about all night. Maybe I dozed a little, but what was creepin' into my head all that night like termites was how was I gonna take care of Patrick? Sure, I knew that some single mothers who had nothin' could find a way so they didn't actually starve. But I had less than nothin' and just survival didn't seem good enough. Not for Patrick. There was Coop's mom, but she didn't have much herself and wouldn't take good care of him. If she took him at all. I mean my own gramma tried, didn't she? And failed. And welfare? There was a time limit on that, and if you didn't get really lucky, you wound up in a homeless shelter, maybe on the street. I seen that in Oakland. The best you could hope for was a minimum wage job, with no high school diploma an' all. I could go back to school or get a GED, which I did later, but who was gonna look after Patrick while I did that? An' anyway, I just felt like I was hangin' on the edge of a cliff an' it's startin' to give way, and there's no point in screamin' for help 'cause there's nobody to hear you, so I just started to cry. It was gettin' on toward morning an' a nurse brought Patrick back for me to nurse him, which I needed to anyway 'cause my breasts were really bulgin'. I remember that he didn't seem to get it at first, about nursing. Then all of sudden he just chomped on an' sucked an' sucked an' it was all so natural an' quiet except for that little suckin' noise. An' I loved him so much that I cried again, but it was like, you know, with the pain of loving, like you feel maybe only once or twice in your whole life. It 's so beautiful and scary at the same time. You know, he wasn't old enough to know anything, but he sort of knew that his momma was there to look out for him, an' it come to me like an answer to prayer—not that I actually prayed—that I had to look out for him by givin' him away.

"I had to give him a family. He needed milk, sure, but not just milk, but a mom an' a dad an' maybe a dog an' even a brother or sister. A warm bed with slippers parked by the side of his bed and his own bike in the back yard. 'Course, no life's perfect. I knew that. I knew he'd fall down plenty of times and skin his knees, but there'd be somebody there to pick him up. An' maybe he'd fail a test at school or somethin' disappointing, but somebody'd say not to worry too much. Just try again. An' he'd get the flu or an earache, but sombody'd be there to give him medicine and sit by the bed and read to him or put on his favorite DVD or somethin' like that. God! he'd even have orthodontia, if he needed it. He'd grow up so good lookin'!

Joyce beamed again for just a moment.

"I knew it then, while I watched a little thread of milk run down his chin, that I could give Patrick a normal kind of life like I never had, an' maybe he'd have a chance to grow up to be a success. I don't mean famous or anything like that, but just to have a good job somewhere and someday a family of his own. So after he finished nursing on both sides and gave his little burp and dropped off to sleep right there against my boob, I looked at him with all my heart, an' then I rang for the nurse, an' when she came I told her I needed to see the social worker as soon as she came in. 'Course I cried some more after she took him away, but I was calmer too. Even a little bit hopeful.

"I told the social worker that I lied about bein' married to Coop and that Coop didn't want anything to do with the baby an' that was why he went off. I told her I was sure about givin' Patrick away, but only if he was gonna be adopted and not lost in some tangle of foster homes. I'd try to keep him if it was gonna be like that, but she said I could sign a release for adoption and that there were lists of qualified people who really wanted to adopt a newborn. All checked by the agencies. She could see where I was comin' from and a little bit she tried to encourage me to keep him, but I said no. And it wasn't about not enough love. It was about too much love. So I signed the papers and never saw Patrick again. She told me that I could arrange to see him, but I didn't have the heart to say yes. That was a mistake, but I didn't know it then. I was just too broken up.

"You see, even if I did the right thing back then, a lot times I just want to see him, just to be sure he's okay an' maybe explain to him about what happened, and tell him that I loved him and still love him and will always love him, because love doesn't change. Know what I mean?"

Astrid may or may not have been following the story by now, but she nodded.

"So anyhow, I went home from the hospital later that day. Back to that crummy little duplex where I thought Coop an' me was so happy an' sat down on the bed an' cried some more. I really cried a lot, just about the whole time, for about a week, but I made myself say over an' over again that Patrick was better off. An' I took the baby stuff back to Catholic Charities and cried some more, right there in front of the clerk, an' I guess she thought my baby died, but I didn't say anything. An' finally I got myself together enough to buy a paper an' go out lookin' for a job 'cause o'course I had to. Like I said, I didn't know how to do much of anything except keepin' house, but I finally got on as a chamber maid at a motel not too far away. It was even on the same bus line.

"The manager, he didn't want to hire me at first, I guess because I wasn't Hispanic like most of the girls, but I told him I was a good worker an' really needed the job an' gave him Lucy Duggins's phone number for a reference 'cause I knew she trusted me and knew what I could do. So anyhow, he said he'd give me a try.

"Well, 'course it wasn't much of a job, but as long as I qualified for food stamps, I could pay my rent. An' I was good at the job, fast, and I got on okay with the other maids, though they were all Hispanic. They were nice to me, but I never did figure out much Spanish, so I was pretty lonesome. 'Course I never stopped thinkin' about Patrick. I was even scared I'd see him sometime on the street and want to grab him an' run away. I would've left Bakersfield, which I hated anyway, but I didn't have the money, so I was kind of stuck."

"But you live here, in Marin." Astrid sounded a little confused.

"Sure. Fact is I got out of Bakersfield sort of by accident. There was this guy who stayed at the motel pretty often, and we chatted a little one day when he came back from breakfast before I got his room done up. He wasn't anything to look at, not like Coop. Kind of short and starting to get bald. But he was nice to me and even took me to dinner a couple of times. Not fast food. I mean a real restaurant. He told me he sold farm equipment up and down the Central Valley, and I guess he did okay. Well, one thing led to another, and I admit that I slept with him. I was that grateful. It happened more than once. A bunch of times actually.

"Pete—that was his name—he never meant to get me fired, but he did. I mean somebody told the manager, and that was that. As if stuff like that didn't go on all the time. Well, when Pete was in town again, he called me, an' I told him what happened, an' he did feel bad about it. He asked if he could make it up somehow, and it came to me that he could get me out of Bakersfield. So I have to say that Pete came through. When he went back north, he took me with him, up to Richmond. He owned a kind of rundown house there 'cause his dad used to work for Chevron, y'see, an' Pete, he inherited it sometime an' said he was going to fix it up and get a good price someday, only he never got around to it, an' the place wasn't in a very good neighborhood anyway, but, well, I lived there for about four years, got a job in food service at one of those assisted living places they call them. You know, where they have a dining room for the residents, so they don't have to cook.

"Pete, he was usually pretty nice to me and used to bring me little presents when he came back from his trips down the valley, like a piece of jewelry or something. But one time when he came back from a trip, there was no present and he acted really mad. He said I was messing around when he was out of town and that I gave him, well, the clap. That was stupid, but he made me go for a test, and—wouldn't you know it?—I had it. 'Course I got it from him, but there was no arguin' about it. He said he didn't believe me, an' he basically threw me out. I, well, sort of think there was another woman an' he wanted to get rid..."

"Joyce. I have to go to the bathroom," Astrid broke in suddenly. "I have to go right now. It just came on me. You know how it is..."

"Oh sure! I'm sorry I got so carried away. Lemme help." Joyce got up from the sofa and went to Astrid. Creamy looked up from her snooze, but didn't move.

Joyce put a hand under Astrid's arm to steady her as she stood. The newspaper slipped sideways from her lap to the floor.

"I have to go right now," Astrid repeated, starting for the hall door. "I don't want to…make a mess. Don't come with me," she added at the doorway. "I'm all right!"

She disappeared through the door to the bathroom, which she didn't bother to close. A serious hurry. Joyce could hear the sound of urine in the toilet. Made it in time. Good.

It was the sound of urinating that reminded Joyce how she lost her job at the next place she worked, that nursing home in San Rafael. After Pete threw her out, and she had to give up her job, she stayed with a friend from work long enough to find out about an opening in food service at a new skilled nursing facility over in Marin. When Joyce got that job, she thought how lucky she was because she had more hours and the pay was better, but that didn't last long either. She knew Astrid had a thing about nursing homes and realized it was good she didn't go into all that business, but it came back to her anyway, like an image on a screen. Like she was right there.

She was out in the hall, gathering up trolleys after the lunch meal, and she heard someone calling from one of the rooms. Not unusual, but it sounded serious, so she put her head in the door and saw there wasn't anyone in the bed. She went in then and found the old lady on the toilet, begging for someone to get her back in bed. Joyce reached for the call light and saw it was already on. Went out and looked up and down the hall, but no staff in sight. So there came the mistake. She knew better than to touch a patient, but she went back in and told the old lady to put her arms around her neck, and she'd help her up. And did. And that was when the nurse came in. Not a CNA, but the charge nurse. And she fired Joyce right then and there, with the old woman still in her arms. The whole thing was as clear as yesterday But no, she thought, I won't talk anymore about how I decided to kill myself. Even if back then I didn't know what else to do. Too depressing.

Astrid came out of the bathroom then and resettled in her chair, looking satisfied.

———— ⬥ ————

"I remember when I met you," Astrid took up, pleased at remembering. "At the coffee shop. Do you like it? I mean the work — not the coffee." Astrid was pleased with her small joke.

"It's okay. I mean I'm grateful I got a job. The boss is nice, an' the work's regular. I'm up around four so at five I can start the coffee makers and the dough mixer. We open at six an' the pastries have to be set out in the display cases an' all that. There's pretty good business right from the start every day, 'til there's a lull in mid-morning. Another girl comes in at eight an' stays till three, which is when we close, but I leave at one. Most days, anyhow… So by puttin' in extra time now an' then, I can sort of make ends meet. Not that I save anything. Lucky I don't smoke or gamble or anything like that." Joyce gave a small unhumorous laugh. "All I wish for now is if I could find my baby someday," she couldn't stop herself from adding, "Really, not a baby, of course. He would've turned eight last week. Patrick," she ended reverently.

"Have you tried to find him?"

"Yeah, sort of. You gotta understand that I never had any thought about tryin' to take him away from his adoptive parents or anything like that. But it's bothered me a lot that Patrick might grow up thinkin' I didn't want him, when it wasn't anything like that. Really, like I said, I just wanted the best for him. That was all. So anyhow, at one point, back when I was with Pete, I wrote to the Kern County social services people, an' they said that, since I gave up all my connection to the baby, they couldn't release information. They said if a grown child wanted information about a parent, it'd be different. Well, that was as far as

I got. I could use some help on that. Hire some kind of investigator, maybe, if I had the money, but you know how it is. I keep thinkin' someday I'll figure it out. Like I could learn to use a computer to do searches an' stuff. I could at least take one of those night classes at the JC, but I'd sort of need a car to do that. Anyhow, I'm almost glad I haven't found him just yet 'cause I want Patrick to feel good about me when he sees me. I mean like I really wish I could get my teeth fixed and drop about thirty pounds and look nice for him. So he's not ashamed of me to be his mother. I just want it to be right.

"But I've learned, in this world, it's a fact that you can't do anything without money, an' I guess that's why everybody wants it so much. It's the nearest thing you got to security, an' you can't blame people for that. I mean I sure don't, 'cause a bank account with nothin' in it is the biggest zero in the world."

Joyce smiled a little, as one satisfied with a philosophical statement, even though it isn't humorous, and reached back to pet Creamy. Creamy stirred and produced a faint, deep purr.

Astrid sat very still for a while, looking at Joyce.

"I have some money," she said all of a sudden. "You've been so good to me. Maybe I can help you out, I mean to find the little boy."

"Oh, Mrs. W, you pay me already! I didn't mean! That's not why I told you—"

"I know, Joyce. Really. Charles and I were never exactly rich, but comfortable, as they say. He was a professor. Did I tell you that? He taught history at the university, you know, the one in San Francisco. Well, Charles and I, we were always…thrifty. We saved up. We bought this house. We put some of our money into…" She stopped to feel for the word. "Investments. That was it. I didn't get any money from my mother because we had to spend it all, well, just about everything, on that place she was in." Astrid's gaze shifted momentarily, then back. "Where was I? Oh yes, the money. I have some money in the bank and those investments. My attorney, he knows about those."

"I see." Joyce concurred cautiously.

"Anyway, I have something put away. Now this house will go to Lydia someday. My daughter. I don't know if you've met her."

"Yeah, but only one time."

"Well, this man, my attorney, he knows how much money I have. He drew up a, uh, contract, for Lydia and her children. That's not the word. A way to give them money later on, for their education. A trust. That's it! But I could still afford to help you out, maybe… What's his name?" Astrid's forehead wrinkled with effort.

"Patrick?" Joyce suggested, not sure of the reference.

"No, no! I mean my attorney. His name… I think it's Ed. I've got his number in my…where I keep phone numbers. Only it's under his last name, and I can't seem to think…"

"We'll find it, Mrs. W. I'll help you look."

ASTRID'S STORY

Turning the pages of her directory over one by one, they found Ed's name, luckily, early in the alphabet. Under D. *Duncan, Edwin.* Astrid immediately lifted the phone to make an appointment, but Joyce reminded her that, unless she went by taxi, it would have to be on a Friday. Maybe she should consult with Lauren first.

Then Joyce suggested that, while she went to make tea, Astrid write herself a note.

Accordingly, she wrote: *Ask Laura about appt with Ed D.* But why? Oh yes…*to help Joyce. Friday, but next, not this. look at calender*

After Joyce came back with a cup of tea and went off to fold some laundry, Astrid got to thinking about her mother. It was the tea, of course. The family ritual.

An image came to mind of herself, sitting on the sofa by her father and her mother at the piano and her older sister, Edith, playing the violin. So warm. So secure. And then gone. Astrid would have been glad to tell Joyce something about Maman, as her mother liked to be called, but Joyce wasn't at hand. Nor could Astrid have gathered from all the welter of a tangled mind a coherent narrative.

She did understand that she, unlike Joyce, had been lucky. The father of Mrs. Charles Williamson, née Astrid Adams, was a professor of classics at Berkeley, and her mother was an educated lady who had grown up in France, the daughter of a diplomat, and a translator of academic articles from French into English. Maman also wrote poetry in both languages, played the piano with considerable ability, and was known for her charm. Astrid's older sister had married a businessman and moved to Argentina a long time ago.

The Adamses sent their daughters to private schools, took them on European holidays, and gave them everything that might be expected of a scholarly couple who took parenting seriously. But they were not snobs and constantly reminded the children that a successful life is largely a matter of luck. Like Eumaeus in *The Odyssey,* one could be born a prince and wind up a slave in another man's farmyard. Life was like that. Your character was the only thing you could really command, and even character was sometimes not of one's choosing.

Astrid was also fortunate in her marriage. She met Charles Williamson when they were both students at the university, he being a TA in a graduate course she was taking: England in the Early Nineteenth Century. When the course was over and the situation proper, Charles invited her to a concert, and since she was already in love with him, she readily accepted. One year later, give or take a few days, they were married in a small, but elegant June wedding in her parents' garden in Berkeley.

The Williamsons lived happily together, studied together, traveled together, exchanged ideas constantly. For five years Charles had a position as an instructor in a private college in southern California. But soon after their daughter, Lydia, was born, Charles was hired at San Francisco State University, and when Lydia was old enough to start school, they bought a house in San Rafael, and Astrid took a job teaching Latin and English at a parochial high school. When Astrid's father died, Maman sold their house in Berkeley and moved to a condo in Larkspur to be near them. She kept working as a translator and gave occasional poetry readings. She still played the piano and spent time teaching Lydia to speak French.

Of course Astrid and Charles did for Lydia what their own parents had done for them, sending her to good schools, giving her music lessons, taking her traveling. Not only did she learn fairly good French from Maman, but after spending a year with Aunt Edith in Buenos Aires, she spoke fluent Spanish, though with an Argentinian accent. She had so many interests and abilities that it was difficult for her to fix on a college major, but eventually she chose art.

Since Lydia knew she wasn't going to make a living as an artist, at least not for a long time, she prudently went into commercial advertising, in which she got a job with an agency in San Francisco. Like any young person, she rented an apartment with a friend and began to gather her own life around her. Although she visited her parents from time to time, they didn't see much of her. Of course there were phone calls and e-mails when one or the other needed to talk about something specific. Lydia got along well with her parents, but kept her private life in a separate compartment.

Those subtle faults that thread our human lives began to crack apart that summer when Astrid and Charles were vacationing in the Lake Country, having one of the best European trips they had ever had. It seemed a good time to go. Maman had been slowing down a bit but was in good health, and Lydia encouraged them to go with that parental attitude that grown children are so good at. It was Lydia who called them at their hotel in Windamere to let them know that Maman had taken a fall and was in the hospital with a broken hip.

Of course they flew back as soon as they were able, barely stopping at the house to drop off their luggage, and then on to the hospital to see Maman. According to the staff, she was "resting comfortably," and indeed her smile was encouraging, although all at once and for the first time, she did seem frail and crumpled and emptied of her *joie de vivre*.

When Astrid and Charles returned to their house, they saw a shiny new BMW parked by the curb and two people just walking up to the front door. It was Lydia and a man. Of course Lydia had never lacked for boyfriends, so they were hardly surprised, and this man was both handsome and expensively dressed and visibly older than she was.

Lydia introduced them on the porch.

"Mama," she said, beamingly, "I'd like to you meet Al Shaffer, your son-in-law." Then she giggled and patted her abdomen. "And your grandchild, er, Junior. I trust it was okay that we decided to make him—actually her—legitimate. I mean, however quaint."

"Really..." said Astrid, stunned into nothingness. Fortunately, Charles had the presence of mind to shake hands with his usual firm handshake and wish them both much happiness.

"And how's Grandmaman?" Lydia asked them then.

"Resting comfortably," Astrid answered in a thready voice.

Lydia was as cheerful as a candle at Christmas, twitterpated, as Astrid described her to Maman later on. In her heart, she thought of Al as "our dear Wickham," but did not say so. Lydia and Wickham? Oh my god! But Lydia Williamson, unlike Lydia Bennett, understood that Al was not their kind of person, and therefore advanced him with a sort of bravado. He was, in fact, a real estate broker from the city, divorced, with two children to pay support for. He had gone to business college, married young, produced the children, and while that marriage was still breaking up, started dating Lydia, who was working up brochures for his firm. Al wasn't a bad fellow, after all, but there was something about his smile that enraged Astrid, like a white hunter who traps the noblest leopard in the jungle and has his picture taken next to its cage, grinning. Unfortunately, Lydia was grinning too. And so her parents could only give their belated blessing, and besides, there was their grandchild. Wendy.

That was nine years ago. Lydia and Al were now living in Citrus Heights near Sacramento. He was still in real estate, doing well with a big company, they said, but still living beyond his means. And Lydia had produced three more children by then; the youngest, the twins, were about to start kindergarten. Of course, she hadn't intended twins, or even the third pregnancy, but fate and carelessness had triumphed over intention. She still wanted a career in art, she said, but how and when was currently buried under motherhood. She never mentioned divorce, but a tightness had gathered around her mouth that probably constrained complaints.

After all, she had chosen her fetters and knew it.

Pauvre petite Lydia! Pauvre petite Maman! If we didn't have false dreams and expectations, how would we live?

Astrid learned that her mother had gotten hurt by falling on the back steps of her condo, a mere slip on a dewy morning. The doctor said the break should heal nicely with proper care, and he turned out to be right. But he also said that the fall was possibly caused by a slight stroke, which might affect her "functioning," at least for a while. Of course Astrid noticed at once that Maman had a tendency to call Charles "Edward," her husband's name. Corrected, she would say, "Oh yes, of course," but a few minutes later it would be "Edward" again, and other names gradually became shuffled as well.

When Maman was transferred to the convalescent hospital, Astrid tried to be chatty with her mother. She talked about their trip to England and tried to be funny about the goose that had terrorized them at a bed and breakfast. But Maman's response to chitchat was a perfunctory, "That's nice" or "I'm glad to hear it." She stayed in a convalescent hospital while her hip was healing and she was learning to use the walker. Then she stayed with Astrid and Charles for about two months.

Lydia would come some weekends to visit her, and one day when she was gone, Maman remarked, "What a lovely girl she is," as if not quite sure of her name. Could you forget the name of a granddaughter whose name you yourself had suggested?

There was, increasingly, a hesitation to speak at all and a look in her eyes, frustrated and hurt at the same time because of the barrier between her thought, which might be clear enough, and its expression, which simply flew away from her like the fruit from Tantalus. Gradually, she even stopped asking what something or someone was called.

More than anything else, Maman wanted to go home. That much was clear, and they finally consented, given that she had a live-in housekeeper, a Filipino lady, who was well recommended. But every time Astrid went to visit, almost daily, Alicia hinted that Maman was deteriorating. Of course Maman was glad to see her daughter but was vague about everything and everyone else. Mostly she became more and more withdrawn, so it was hard to tell what shreds of memory she still held onto. At Christmas Astrid wrote her cards for her, not a small task, giving out that her dear "Maman" was "unwell," but sending her sincere greetings.

Maman began to get lost in her own condo, to drift from room to room, looking for the bathroom or for something lost. She wasn't sure what. And so she drifted away like a cloud evaporating after a rainstorm, silent and unnoticed. A ghost that animated her body came to replace the missing mind, a ghost that had no purpose, but to restlessly move the body from place to place, not even telling night from day. Alicia had no days, or nights, off.

The ghost wasn't even interested when the body that it moved so restlessly from place to place was taken to another dwelling, to a single room with its own bed and dresser and closet and easy chair and family pictures on the wall. It looked at the pictures from time to time through the eyes of Maman and found the faces pleasant and even vaguely familiar. A new picture appeared among the others. A baby. The ghost knew this baby was special because they told her so over and over.

"Wendy" they told her, and "Wendy" she repeated until the name faded again.

There was one day in the warmth of summer when Astrid and Charles and Lydia and baby Wendy all went to visit Maman because, they kept telling her, it was her eightieth birthday. And they took her in a car to a park where there were tables, and the weather was warm and clear, and the air lay on her arms and face like a second skin, and the ghost and its body were both pleased.

While they were eating their dessert of carrot cake, Lydia threw a scrap to a hopping jay, and the ghost for just a moment forgot to close the gate to the old mind, and Maman said, "Look, there's a jay!" Everyone in the group turned to stare at her.

Then the ghost remembered to close the gate. It was the last complete sentence they ever heard her say.

So the ghost continued to wander about the building from which it could not escape, nor did it want to. Where would it go? It merely wandered around inside its own space looking for any sign in this desert for an oasis of meaning. Astrid came every day with pointless books to read from and CDs to listen to, but they were only a scramble in the sterile room. Why did she come at all? Both reason and purpose had drained away.

Astrid and Charles gave Maman's piano to Lydia and sold the rest of her furniture and most of her books, though there were quite a few that Astrid could not part with and took home to their own overcrowded shelves. Some children's books went to Lydia for Wendy. Then it came down to the boxes of albums and trinkets and knick-knacks and, yes, the manuscripts of Maman's poetry, both finished and unfinished. They were probably not in any condition to publish, nor would any publisher be interested in the work of someone unable to give public readings. Astrid read some and sighed and put them in manila folders in her own file cabinet, knowing their fate was probably recycling. Let Lydia be the one to commit the murder.

It wasn't on account to Maman entirely, though it was in part, that Astrid resigned when the school decided to discontinue Latin, on the grounds that it could not afford computers and frills at the same time. Understandable, she concluded, but not acceptable. It wasn't the language, exactly, which was itself a kind of ghost. It was the farewell to the sophisticated world of her father and the knowledge that every empire is doomed and that only the details are different.

For Maman the years went by in present time. The ghost had no idea how many. Even Astrid began to lose count. Wendy walked and ran, and Jeffrey was born and walked and ran. And Maman's stairway continued to go down without any light at the bottom, without walls, without reason. For nearly seven years of calendar time, Maman descended the stairway. On the way down she stumbled a couple of times on merely "medical" problems. On those occasions Astrid and Charles both sat by her bedside, saying good bye with a mixture of misery and relief, but a day or two later, Maman was sitting up in bed again, her vacant eyes directed at a television screen that gave neither information nor entertainment. When the ghost did finally consent to leave Maman's scrappy body, it stole away in the night, and Astrid had no chance to say "*Adieu, Maman*" or even "*Bon voyage.*"

There was nothing much left to memorialize. Maman had been gone for a long time, and most of her friends had either forgotten her or had gone themselves in more dignified exits. There was no need or reason for a memorial service. There were only ashes placed in the same grave as those of Astrid's father and a small gathering of family to see that the grave marker was correct.

"I want my epitaph to say, 'DIED HEALTHY,'" Charles remarked on that occasion with unconscious prescience.

Maman's estate was nearly as exhausted as her body. It had been used to provide a semi-private room with enough wall space to hang some unrecognized family pictures and to fit in an extra chair for an unrecognized visitor. What little remained of the estate Astrid gave to Lydia, who gave it to Al to help pay back child support to his first wife. Astrid and Charles saw that the only way to give Lydia anything permanent was to put it in trust with strict conditions. Though Lydia wasn't twitterpated anymore, she was soundly and legally domesticated.

When Astrid went through her mother's few belongings one more time, she had to decide again what to save and what to sell and what to achingly convey to the garbage bin, something like disposing of the art of a Sunday painter that has cost so much time and effort and which no one really wants. Among these remnants of personhood, she found a card that Maman had given to Astrid's father "On the occasion of our 30th anniversary," with a calligraphic handwritten note inside.

> *When we are dead and there is nothing left*
> *of our good love, may someone find these words*
> *at least, and not be stricken by time's theft,*
> *which, hand in glove with death steals every light,*
> *but rather think of brilliant-colored birds*
> *who dropped these few bright feathers in their flight.*

Astrid shivered over these few lines, recalling her parents, whose gentle marriage was so like her own with Charles. Naturally, she couldn't bring herself to throw that card away, but stuck it in an album of family pictures. Maybe someday Lydia would find it. Or Wendy. A sad, happy, romantic thought. Over the next few months, Astrid and Charles tidied up a life as best they could and planned a trip to Greece to recuperate, but three weeks before their departure date Charles died "healthy" of an aneurysm. Lydia came at once with the children—just two at the time—but with the children hanging onto her, she couldn't offer much more help than shared grieving, while her mother—and Ed Duncan—had another life to tidy up. Fortunately, since Charles was ever methodical, the settlement of the estate was relatively easy. But the darkness in the house could not be illuminated, and Lydia, who helplessly understood, gave her mother a white kitten for company.

Some of this Astrid still remembered, but in tattered bits like remnants of a dream that seemed too vivid to lose at the time, but scattered all the same, until sometimes something recalled the vision to mind and then let it trail off again. Astrid always remembered that Lydia lived in a distant city, more distant than San Francisco, and that Charles was dead, leaving a great emptiness. And she remembered pieces of Maman and her slow final years, and she knew, wherever all that had happened, she did not want to go there.

THORNY VISITS ASTRID

Thorny never bothered much with street addresses, at least not once he'd been to a place. Having grown up in Marin, having worked in dozens of neighborhoods, he essentially never got lost. So now he pulled his pickup over to the curb with perfect recognition of the solid bungalow, even though he hadn't worked there in some years. He turned off the engine, got out, and paused on the sidewalk to consider his handiwork, the low brick wall with patterned coping, just high enough to define the property line, but not high enough to seem excluding. He still liked it and, better yet, remembered how Charles and Astrid Williamson had been so very pleased.

The front yard of the Williamson house was shaded by a pair of serene sycamores that were beginning to lose their thick-fingered, velvety leaves. He might not have noticed the leaf fall but for a scattering on the sidewalk, then a few more beyond the fence in the yard, waiting to be raked. A good thing he recognized the place so easily, because the house next door on the left would have been no help as a landmark, having been remodeled in the interim. It seemed that the owners had decided, logically enough, that since no one sat on the porch anymore, it might as well be included in the living room, with a new, smaller entry porch tacked on the front. Not a bad idea, but somehow contradictory to the original design, less sociable. But people didn't turn their faces to the street anymore. Television had accomplished the end of neighborhoods that the mobility of automobiles had started. Too bad. And the house on the right, which hadn't changed much in appearance was now repainted and converted to a modest office building with a nicely lettered sign suspended over the porch. Ritter and Associates. Meaning?

As he opened the front gate, Thorny could see Astrid Williamson herself sitting on the porch in a stout wooden rocker, an antique. So the use of porches was not quite dead, after all. She was rocking, very slowly, but stopped and peered at him, not quite suspiciously, but questioningly, as if she supposed he was lost and about to ask directions. Or selling something she had no use for?

"Hello, Astrid," he said from a discreet distance, halfway between the gate and the porch steps. "It's me. Thorny. The mason. I know it's been a long time." He advanced to the foot of the steps and stopped again, seeing that she still didn't recognize him.

She stared at him uncertainly for a moment, then smiled. "Thorny, how nice to see you. Come and sit down." And then, seeming to realize there was no chair for him, she apologized. "I used to have another chair. You could bring one from the kitchen," she added helpfully.

"No, no. That's okay. I'm just here for a few minutes. I'll sit on the top step here." But before sitting, he made an explanation. "Listen, I brought something for you. Maybe I should get it now. It's in the back of the pickup."

Before she could assent or refuse, he turned, went back down the walk to the pickup, and lifted a small, stout cardboard box out of the bed. With this box in his hands, he paused at the foot of the steps.

"Any special place you'd like me to put this?"

"What is it?"

He went up the steps and held the box out, as Astrid craned her neck to see what was inside.

"I know these rhizomes don't look like anything now," he remarked needlessly, "but you won't believe it when spring comes." Without further comment, he set the box down by the wall next to the front door and returned to the front edge of the porch.

"Oh, Thorny, that's very nice of you! I love… you know… iris." She found the word with only a stumble of hesitation.

"Sure. I know. It's a dozen rhizomes from Clare's collection of October Blues. Maybe you remember. They won a prize in the iris show five years ago. I figured she'd like you to have some. I know she gave you a couple of those melon pinks not long before she died. You know. The ones I planted around back for you."

"Clare's dead?" Astrid exclaimed. "You should have told me. I'm so sorry!"

Thorny startled too. "But I thought… Weren't you at the memorial?"

"Clare's?" Embarrassment shook her into silence for a moment. "Oh, Thorny, I'm so sorry. Why yes, that's right. I was there. My mind. It's… I'm so sorry! It was a lovely service. At the Garden Center. Yes, I remember now."

"Clare had a lot of friends." Thorny sat down on the top step, a few feet from Astrid's rocker, and leaned his back against the supporting post. "Anyway, I understand. How you could forget. A person gets other things on their mind. I, we, were sorry about Charles too. A fine gentleman. How long has he been gone now?"

Astrid thought and shook her head. "It seems forever, but I guess… five years, maybe? I don't seem to remember dates anymore. I was still driving then. I do remember that I drove to Clare's memorial. I think Molly… what's her name?…a friend went with me. I had to give up my car, you know. Too old. Too much traffic."

"I don't blame you. But how do you get around these days?"

"Taxi, if I have to. But I'm lucky that way. There's a lady from…what do you call it? That organization." Thorny shook his head slightly, not knowing. Astrid continued. "Anyway, someone comes once a week to take me shopping or to run errands. Appointments. That kind of thing. She even took me to a flower show at the…Garden Center, not long ago." She considered for a moment. "Maybe June. She likes to garden. Come to think of it, maybe she'd like to have those iris…bulbs—not that I don't love them—but I wonder. I mean about myself. How long can I go on taking care of things? You probably don't understand what I mean. About getting so discouraged."

Thorny nodded. "Sure I do. Why d'you think I'm giving things away? I don't think I'm gonna hang around too much longer. So I figured I oughta give things away now. You see, I've decided… well…I've realized for a while that I'd have to get rid of my house someday, and I don't have any kids to leave it to. Clare and I did all that landscaping together — for years. When she was alive, our place was kind of famous — I mean locally. And so I dithered around some, and then I was at the Garden Center the other day, and I saw a notice that the Native Plant Society was looking for a place to have a permanent exhibit, and I thought, well, hell, what about my place? They could have their meetings in the house and develop the garden to show off native plants. Only Clare's plantings were mostly non-natives, so I knew that if I did that, well, they'd have to tear out a lot of stuff and start over. But not the coast live oaks, of course, or the native fuchsias, but a lot of other stuff. The native plant people, they know all that kind of thing. At least they'd make a nice display."

He looked straight ahead as one looking at a screen.

Astrid nodded. "That's good idea. I have a daughter. Lydia. She'll inherit this house someday. I doubt she'll live here, of course. She lives in… where is it? Near the capital."

"Washington?"

"No, no! The state. You know…" She sounded accusatory.

"Oh, you mean Sacramento."

"Yes, yes. Sacramento," she confirmed, at once relieved and amiable. "My daughter has her own life, you know, and four children. And I'm in no condition to help her out. I want to be a good grandmother, but really..." She paused, either struggling for the right word or the right thought. Thorny had no idea how to lead her to it, but he waited. In the end, it was the sort of confession that she had probably known how to say all along but couldn't bring herself to say it aloud.

"It's not good to get old, is it, Thorny? Your mind, your body. Everybody says so, but you don't realize it until it happens to you, do you?"

"Well, that's true, but," Thorny made an insincere effort at optimism, "at least you've got this lady to help you out. That's good."

"Oh yes, I know," Astrid rejoined. "Joyce. Did I tell you about Joyce?"

"The woman from that organization you mentioned?"

"Oh, my no! That's someone else. That's... ah... Sarah...no, that's not her name. No, wait. Laura. She's older than Joyce. Joyce doesn't drive, you see. Anyway, I sold my car. Well, maybe I should've kept it. I don't know." Astrid struggled to regather her lines of thought.

"It's Joyce who comes around after work and does things for me, like housework and cooking. Of course I pay her. She doesn't make much at the coffee shop. And she's a very sweet person," she added.

"Well, that's good," said Thorny. "That you have the help."

"Yes, Joyce is wonderful. And Laura too. But she only comes on Fridays."

"So she's coming today. Then I better..." Thorny learned forward as if to get up to make way for another visitor.

"Oh, no. Don't go!" Astrid stopped him "Please. I mean, I thought she was coming today, but then I looked at my notebook, and it said that she couldn't make it until tomorrow. It was all right with me. The change. I don't have anything important, and she said we might have lunch together tomorrow. We have a place we like to go."

Thorny leaned back again, relaxed.

"Clare an' me, we used to go out sometimes, but not too much. She really did love to cook. Never used a cookbook—hardly ever— because her mom taught her. Old-fashioned Portuguese lady. Clare always said, 'Why go out when you can eat better at home?' Was she ever right about that! But for me, now that I'm alone, I mostly open cans or make myself a sandwich. You know how it is."

"But Thorny, where will you live?"

"What do you mean?"

"If you give your house away? Did I make a mistake? Is that what you said?" Astrid sounded worried. For herself or for Thorny?

"Oh that. Yes, well, a retired guy like me, he can live about anywhere, y'know. A mobile home park or even just a camper. Travel around, y'know. I dunno yet. There was a little town in the Sierras where we honeymooned, up the Feather River. A friend of Clare's owned a cabin up there, overlooking the river. I could go live up around there, maybe. Nice granite," he added wryly. "No good for statues, but nice for walls. A little brittle. I always seem to remember the rock from places I've been, for some reason." He chuckled, but she did not join in.

"But you'll be away from your friends."

"I'm not real close to anybody. Not really. A couple of guys I used to work with. I never made friends easy like Clare. " He looked up at Astrid and shifted his weight against the post, which persistently pressed a corner into his back. "I guess it was a natural mistake," he added.

"What was a mistake?"

"I mean only being close to one person. Like I was to Clare. But it's so rare, to find a person you can tell anything. How you feel about things. Or admit some dumb mistake. Be yourself. And when you do, you trust them so much. More than some people trust God. Way more. Fact is, I don't trust God at all." A flat statement, with no hint of bitterness.

Astrid nodded. "I felt like that about Charles, you know. Sometimes I'm so lonely without him that I just think that the only friend I have left is death." She continued to nod just slightly, as if her head were on a switch she had forgotten to turn off.

All at once Thorny said, "The fact is that I agree with you. About death. I agree so much that I really think the only place left for me to go is out. No cabin, no camper, no living some pretend existence until you die. What's the use?"

"Oh, Thorny, you are so right!" Astrid leaned forward in the chair and ceased nodding. He might have expected a denial, but as he didn't get one, he went on making his case in a firm, plodding tone of voice.

"What's a guy like me supposed to do anyway? Sit in front of the boob tube every day, lookin' at nothing? Yack it up in the corner bar? Wait for people who used to be friends when Clare was alive to ask me for dinner? Which they don't. Not unless they want to set me up with some widow." Thorny paused and took a breath. He wanted to tell someone, and Astrid probably wouldn't remember what he said anyway. Maybe she'd even agree.

"The fact is, it happens that I know this guy who really *is* dying, I mean, terminal cancer. This guy, he plans to die in an accident. He's got it all figured out, but it's gotta look like a real accident. Do you see? and if someone goes with him, it makes the accident look, well, more accidental. That's where I come in. I guess I didn't tell you that this guy's a retired pilot so the accident would be like a flying accident. And this guy, the pilot, he says that the weather in the Sierras can be tricky this time of year. He could figure out a way to make it look like the weather was responsible. I suppose that idea shocks you." He turned his head to look at her directly.

She seemed to ponder his argument for a time. Finally she said, "No, I'm not shocked, Thorny. Not at all. But you have to be sure. You have to be very sure."

"Just what I said to him. Of course. But the way I look at it, your life is something that should belong to *you*. You've always got a responsibility not to hurt other people, but when there's no one left around to take care of and no useful work, then why not call it quits? If you want to. Know what I mean?"

"Of course I know," she answered sharply, almost as if he had just asked a stupid question.

"I'm not religious," Thorny persisted. "I don't think God cares about any of this, whether you stay or go. That's just stuff made up by people who don't want to face the responsibility. They want someone else to decide. The church. The doctors. Whoever. But I say, why hang there like a tattered flag, just flapping in the wind? No use at all. Of course my life has been really good a lot of time, so why not leave it there? Like gambling. I mean quit while you're ahead, before sad memories bury the good ones. But that's just me," he added as a kind of apology for having gone on at such length.

"No, it's not just you, Thorny," Astrid concurred in a surprisingly clear and rational voice. She rocked her chair back and forth a time or two, then stopped and learned forward. "I'm so scared, Thorny. Every day of my life I'm scared. So scared about what stupid mistake I'm going to make next, like if I'm going to set the house on fire or something. I worry about things like that all the time because I just can't remember. When I call my own daughter I have to look up her number. Every time. I write down the names of her children so I can ask how they are." Astrid paused as a recollection came. "I made a mistake one time about that, and it made Lydia so mad. She thought it was because I wanted her to name the second child after her father, and she didn't do it. It wasn't that. I just forgot his name. My own grandchild!"

Thorny was dismayed when her voice broke and he looked up to see tears in her eyes because he felt somehow responsible. "I'm sorry, Astrid. I shouldn't have… that was so dumb of me."

"Oh, no, no, no. It's not your fault I can't remember anything. I can't find anything. Yesterday, it was time to feed Creamy. That's my cat, the one Lydia gave me. I looked and looked for the cat food, but it wasn't anywhere. I finally opened a can of stew—for people—and I picked out some of the meat to give her, but she didn't want it. But then when Joyce came later on in the day, she found the cat food right where it belonged. She's good that way. Joyce is. But it made me feel so stupid. And I do it all the time!" She wiped her eyes clumsily with the back of her hand.

"Well…" Thorny could think of nothing comforting to say. He let out his breath, a little sorry now that he'd given her Clare's special iris, only because he realized that she couldn't deal with them, but not feeling that he could ask to take them back.

"That's what I'll do!" Astrid announced rather abruptly.

"What do you mean?"

"I'll give Creamy away. Then I won't have to worry about how to take care of her. I even think I know someone who'd like to have her."

"You mean your helper? This Joyce?"

"No, no. I'm thinking of the other woman who helps me. The one who drives me places. It's, uh, Laura. She likes Creamy a lot. She has a nice house and garden. She took me there one time. Very nice."

"Sounds like a good idea to me. Like me. I'm giving a lot of stuff away. Besides my house, I mean. I just came from giving a bunch of tools to Gus Morales. He used to work for me when he was a young guy. Before he went into business on his own, up in Sonoma County. A good mason, Gus. It's the personal stuff that's hard. The photo albums an' all that. I haven't looked at 'em in a long time anyway, but you can't just put the record of the good times in the garbage. Can't even recycle that kind of thing." He stopped, pondering how he'd saved the hardest for last, not unnaturally. Maybe it was best to leave the personal stuff behind for somebody else, someone who didn't give a hoot, to get rid of. Just a nice neat box, like he was getting ready to move, which he was, of course, one way or another. "About those rhizomes I brought over…"

"That was very nice of you," Astrid said, having been reminded. "But you know, maybe Laura, for her garden… If it's all right with you."

"Sure, of course."

Astrid sat still then, looking straight ahead, at the street. She watched a car pass by, slow, and park in front of a house down the street. Then she looked back at Thorny.

"I want to go with you," she said abruptly. "To your accident."

Thorny answered with an open-mouthed expression that was both startled and pained. "I should never have…"

"Don't look that way!" said Astrid. "I've thought about death a lot. I've thought about it every day since I lost Charles. But I really don't know how. I would have been scared to…but it's how to do it. You don't want to end up hurt, in a wheelchair. There's a story about that by…well…I don't remember, the name but it'll come. A woman. It was about a couple… Well, anyway, I can't stay and end up empty like Maman, sitting in a chair, staring off at nothing. And that's exactly what has me so scared. I know what she had." She looked at him pleadingly. "It was…" She felt for the word.

Thorny searched a while, then said, "Do you mean dementia?"

Astrid nodded. "It's terrible. Not being able to speak because you can't remember where to find the words. Just to ask for water. Or go pee. Or tell someone where it hurts. You, you have no idea!"

Thorny looked at her crumpled face and did know, even as the post at his back reminded him how small discomforts can turn into pain, and he was glad he was going and wouldn't have to come back to see Astrid again. Clare might have been able to, but he couldn't. She was too pathetic. He didn't even know how to take leave.

"Could you ask him?" Astrid demanded suddenly, quite composed.

"Ask who what?"

"Your friend. You said you had a friend who'd take you with him. Ask him to take me too."

"Oh, Astrid, I don't think…no, absolutely not. I should never have mentioned that." He needed to get out of there, but couldn't just stand up and go, run away, leaving her like that, but he did stand up and took a step down, then turned, hesitating on that step, holding the post lightly.

"I'm sorry," he blundered. "I've got another delivery."

"But it's the right thing, you know. As you said," she persisted. "My daughter… she needs my things more than she needs me. A lot more. This house. What money I have. Then I wouldn't have to spend it on some expensive—what do you call it?— nursing home. This house is valuable. It's old, but it's solid. Not even a crack from the, uh—" She fumbled for the word.

"Earthquake?"

"Yes, of course. She could use the money for the children. For their education. It's the only thing I can do. Can't you see why I want to go with you?"

"Yes, but you can't…" He was stumped because he did see, although he didn't want to admit it. His own logic had come back to bite him. "It's not up to me."

"Thorny, just ask him! Ask him to listen to me. If I could only explain myself! I can't explain things very well, but I only want to try. When is he going? I can get ready."

The human urge to answer any question, no matter how strange, caused Thorny to answer, as if it were an ordinary discussion about an ordinary excursion.

"We haven't decided the exact day, but probably a Saturday. He's the one to figure it out because he has to put in a reservation to use the plane. Doesn't matter much to me. I got most of my affairs in order. Just a few things. Look, I should get going 'cause I've got this other stuff to deliver and some recycling." It was what he should have said when he first got there.

Astrid leaned forward, somewhat like a bird on the edge of a nest, preparing to take flight, taut, resolved. "Just ask him," she called after him. "It can't do any harm to ask!"

LAUREN CONTEMPLATES A BED

So to strip off the sheets. Too bad. You lovely deep blue sheets. Five hundred and fifty threads of the best percale,bought specially brand new that day. Should I say "virgin" until a couple of hours ago? but now lovingly deflowered? Rumpled. "A nymph in waves," he called it when he took the picture. Then he said I was "beautiful." Beautiful! Me. Did Harris ever…? Maybe on our wedding day, but everyone said that. Were supposed to. "You look nice," he used to say when we were going out somewhere, to the opera especially. Had to dress for that. But if he ever thought beautiful, he never said it. I would've remembered. But when Matt, like inspired, asked if he could take those pictures—of me naked. Only a second or two reluctant. Was I bashful with him? What a question!

Top sheet off. Too bad. Seems warm with us. A faint imprint on the bottom sheet, or do I imagine? But there I lay the way he asked me to, like the *Venus* of Velasquez, back to the viewer. Said he liked that pose best of any, the curve of the hips and back and shoulders and all that, very erotic. "Like the leaf of a jonquil," he called it. Told him I'd seen the original. Loved it. "Where?" almost as if he didn't believe me. In the National Gallery in London, I told him. Then he said all that about my having so much money, as if it was a failing. Startled. Told him I couldn't help it if Harris is moderately wealthy, liked to travel "for David's education." Not to mention mine. Sometimes a reluctant Galatea, but I tried. Did I need to apologize? But he sounded so mad! "Money! Hasn't anybody ever told you that it isn't the love of money that's the root of evil, it's the *lack* of it?" Maybe so, but can't shake how he said it. "Please don't!" My only defense at the moment. Thank god he stopped. And that was that.

No, the important thing was just us. We both knew it. The wine and the glasses he brought in his carryall, not expensive, but when we touched them together, that was like our compact—to be lovers now and, just maybe, always. Didn't need to say it. "Don't let *him* drink out of them," he told me. Could I hide them somewhere? Of course. Already done. Behind that antique gravy boat that I never used anyway. Did I ever use it at all? From Harris's grandmother. I think. Maybe. Don't remember. And this bed, of course. Ours. Only ever a guest bedroom, I told him. Harris and I never slept here. We still sleep together? He had a right to ask me. Well, yes, I admitted. But why? Habit, I suppose. No sex for a long time. I think it was good sometimes, especially when I wanted to conceive—David, as it turned out. But no, not for…a few years? When was the last time? Do you ever notice when is the last time you do anything, unless it's like a ceremony, like a last goodbye, like the final locking of a door? Like that? Like the last time I ever took Mom shopping, before she moved to Colorado, I thought as I was driving her back home, *This is the last time*, but it wasn't painful, just kind of regretful. Like reading the last page of a good book. Well, Harris didn't ask for sex, and I didn't offer. Just turned my back, but not like Venus… so I'm sorry, Harris. My fault really. I suppose for never offering my real self, not quite daring. Never liked to be a disappointment, did I? Sorry, Harris. But I did the best I could.

So off it goes, bottom sheet on the floor like a crumpled letter. Like a love letter you give up on because however you try, the words can't fit the feeling. Can never capture it—not longing, not love, not even sex. So many have tried it. Only in music—sometimes. Rarely. Like Wagner, my praying for the opera to be over, but then all of sudden he nails it. Like the immolation of Brunhilde. I wanted to cry, but didn't. So when Matt followed me into the bedroom, kissed the back of my neck, it was like I was drowning in that climax of music…but about to be rescued. *Matt, don't wait.* I begged him. Shameless really. But all that time I'd waited—hours, days, weeks, yes, years. Enough, dammit! All that about a glass half-full or a glass half-empty at least has something in it, but I didn't have anything, just plain empty. Just waiting, didn't realize it until then, and then knowing it was for Matt.

Oh Matt! Matt Ramirez! What have you done to me? What have you done!

Sorry to bundle you up, you beautiful sheets, wreck your scented memory with ordinary soap and water. As if sheets could remember… or a bed. But why not? Whatever happens can never be undone, can it? What happened here happened forever, on this bed, like the center of the world, like Delphi. Yes, beloved, I've been there too, and I shivered because it was so ancient and so numinous, like I can still feel it, while Harris was immersed in a guide book about the history of the excavation. And David was bored.

THORNY MAKES A DONATION

So Thorny, you're famous again, eh? I wouldn't have expected it of a modest guy like you." Matt was inclined to humor, even though the world in general hadn't changed, and this event had its unhappy aspect. Still, he felt like a man standing on the remembrance of the best holiday of his life. Moreover, it was a soft, warm afternoon with just a cooling, gauzy drift of fog. Marin County at its most photogenic.

"It wasn't my idea," Thorny returned dourly. "It was Carolyn's. From the Native Plant Society. You know her?"

"I've met her."

"Well, she said something about arranging an article for the paper, and I said okay because it was important to them, but I didn't think both a reporter and a photographer were gonna show up, for chrissake. No offense," he added.

"None taken. Anyway, you've got to admit that donating a piece of property like this is big news. Around here especially. Like giving away a diamond mine almost. No wonder the editor wanted to make it a feature story for Gardening. I think it should've gone on the front page of the main news."

"I wasn't in a mood for it," said Thorny with a wave of his hand. "I'd rather just be anonymous. That's what I should've done. Wasn't thinking fast enough, I guess. 'An anonymous donor' like they say."

Matt nodded, not taking a position. He had met with Thorny's proud modesty twice before, once for the garden section and once for a special on a new city park, for which Thorny had done the flagstone walks and fountain. The small encounters and easy conversation had led, not quite to friendship, but to a friendly acquaintance, a recognition of mutual liking. When Matt saw the obituary notice for Clare Thornton in the paper, he thought of going to the memorial service, but a job came up, and then he set her death to the periphery of his consciousness.

"Well," he observed to Thorny, "since you won't let me take your picture, that's anonymous enough. I guess the artist is revealed in his work, eh?"

"Something like that. This is Carolyn's show anyway. You could snap her in front of a manzanita. Her shape sort of matches the flower," he added wryly. "But she means well," he mitigated his meanness. "I've known her for a while."

Carolyn Biggs, chairperson of the local Native Plant Society, was deep in conversation with Rachel Glenn, who was tall and spare by contrast, the paper's garden editor. Rachel was making notes on an old-fashioned clipboard as they talked. Probably they were discussing the future of the property, what needed to be torn out and what planted, to make it reflect the aims of the society. At least everyone had agreed to leaving any plants that were native and of course Thorny's terraced hillside masonry.

"There's a place in the wall behind the house that looks solid," Thorny volunteered, "but it's really four rocks set together, fitted so close they look like one rock from a little distance. I did that to make a space inside, and that's where I put Clare's ashes. So as she'd always be in her garden. But I'm sort of thinking now of taking the ashes out and scattering them in an another place, a place where we vacationed one time. Why not? Since I won't be here anymore anyway."

"Sure." Matt could see a kind of happiness, in spite of the pain, that lay in the affirmation of an unusual love. At least there was that.

"She was very smart, Clare was, even though she never went beyond high school. I mean she understood things. Like once we went whale-watching off Bolinas, and she said that, although the whales had to live in water, which was kind of like an economy, they had to come up for air. That air was like human love, she said. And she was right. By the way, she took an accounting class at the adult school so she could keep the books for my business. The billing, everything. She was just plain intelligent."

Standing with his hands casually in his pockets, Thorny might have been discussing the soil conditions of their plantings, but his voice had the slow, painful and yet happy nostalgia of an exile reminiscing about his homeland.

"Is there some way I could get a shot of the layout from above?" Matt asked him suddenly. "Something that shows the patterns of the beds a little more?"

"Sure. Why not? Since you're here an' all. We could go upstairs. I look out my bedroom window all the time and sort of chat with Clare about the gardening we used to do. Maybe that sounds stupid."

"Sounds natural to me," Matt responded with honest reassurance.

So they went up through the back door and the kitchen and up the inside stairs and into a sparely furnished bedroom with just a couple of landscapes on the wall and photographs of Thorny's wife and son on his dresser. Matt wondered if keeping pictures like that eased pain or intensified it. Like the pictures Didi kept of themselves and the children on her dresser. Except for Marilu's.

Thorny opened the unscreened window that overlooked the west side of the house, so they could look down on the garden with its irregular but balanced pattern of steps and terraces. "A few years ago," Thorny told him, "every bed had something colorful in it, either massed colors or a nice combination. Clare saw to that. I've kind of let it go. But there's still liliums there." He pointed. "And over there some salvias. I didn't put in any annuals like petunias. Not since Clare died. I wasn't the gardener of the family, just the hod carrier, but it still looks pretty nice. I mean you can sort of see how it was."

Matt could. He unslung the digital camera, went down on one knee next to the window and began to feel for the winding sweep of the construction. Then he started taking pictures, absorbed in process. Thorny stood to one side, silent, unobtrusive. When Matt had taken a dozen shots of various areas, he stood up.

"Well, with or without colors, this is the best arrangement I've ever seen. Perfect composition."

"The terracing wasn't my idea. Not to begin with. It was on account of Greg that we started the terraces. Clare, she wanted a level place for him to play when he was little. For the swing and a sandbox and that stuff. The whole thing just grew out from there in bits and pieces. Over years. It was pretty much done by the time he died."

"Yeah, I heard about that. But it was before I met you." Matt didn't remark that he was sorry, though he was. He knew what it felt like to lose a child, but he thought it too late for condolences. "About how long ago was it? But if you don't want to," Matt fumbled.

"Just over twenty years. He'd be thirty-seven now. A grown man, probably with his own family, maybe a mason like me, but who knows? I wouldn't have cared what line he wanted to follow, but I always think it's good to work with your hands, to make something you can feel proud of."

"Does photography count?"

"Sure. Anything you can look at and admire and say, 'I made that,' even if you only say it to yourself. Greg, he used to help me out now and then when he was a kid, so I always thought he might grow up to be a mason. But it wouldn't have mattered to me, so long as he was happy."

"I know what you mean. Of course I was pleased when my son went into photography, though more technical in a way. He makes DVDs, like for special events. There's art in that, too, of course."

They both looked over the garden as they were talking, parallel spectators, looking at the same view from different minds.

"Greg's ashes aren't here," Thorny explained suddenly. "Maybe they should be, but at the time he died… I don't know if we could've stood it. To have him so close and so lost at the same time."

"I can understand that." In his mind's eye Matt saw Marilu's small grave in the local cemetery, though he hadn't visited it in a long time. Why drive a thorn into your flesh on purpose?

"Greg's here in a way, though. Just about every one of those retaining walls has a rock in it that Greg picked up when he was kid. We used to go up to the Eel River when he was little and camp out at a spot where there's a bend, and the water's low in the summer, and the rocks are interesting. All kinds, water-polished. And when Greg was just a little tyke, he'd get an ordinary pebble in his fist an' he'd say, 'This a good one, Daddy?' an' I'd say, 'Sure, it's great, just the kind I was lookin' for,' an' I'd get him to try to toss it up into the bed of the pickup, which he usually missed on the first throw, but then in time he'd get it in. He'd never give up till he got his rock into the truck. Maybe that's when he really developed his throwing arm, up at the river, throwin' rocks and skippin' stones. We'd have contests to see who could skip it the most times. Greg got really good at that. Way better'n either of us.

"You wouldn't know this, but he was a great varsity pitcher in high school. But in my heart I guess I really wanted him to be a mason like me an' my dad. I never knew how many generations it went back. Into the slates of Wales. When you come from a rocky land, I guess you've got stone in your body. But…" Thorny permitted himself a sigh. "The walls stop with me." He gave a shrug of unwilling resignation.

"Greg wasn't perfect" he went on, "but as good a kid as you could want. He made good grades, and we never had to scold him about his homework. And he helped around the house and the yard if we told him. Kids don't ever volunteer to work, do they?"

"No, not in my experience," said Matt with dour acknowledgment.

"So you know, then. You have kids?"

"I do," said Matt, "but not kids anymore, of course." He offered no other information.

"Greg would rather have been off with his buddies, shootin' baskets or playin' catch. But when he got older, he did odd jobs around the neighborhood because Clare taught him a lot about gardening and looking after yards when people went on vacation. I mean, how many kids can even tell vinca from English ivy? And people liked Greg because he was dependable and polite. And he put his money in his own bank account. Sometimes, I wish he hadn't done that 'cause then he wouldn't have been able to buy that goddam motorcycle. But the accident wasn't the fault of the bike. Or Greg's either. He was a responsible kid. License. Insurance. The helmet. The works. That was the damnedest part. We didn't have anybody or anything to blame, so you can't even feel anger. Or at least, you can't admit you feel it, y'know?"

"I do." Matt confirmed the sentiment.

"It never seems to get any less," Thorny said. A bleak observation. "Whenever he left for school in the morning with that helmet on, he looked like a cross between Marlon Brando and Darth Vader. I told him that one time, but he didn't think it was all that funny. Like, who was Brando, anyway?" They both laughed. "But he did know who Darth Vader was, of course." Thorny smiled a reminiscent smile.

It wasn't only a name or an image, but an era that rose up in Matt's mind out of Thorny's comment. All those Saturday matinées he used to go to when he was a kid, then Saturday nights, necking with someone, usually Didi at first, then always with Didi. He pulled his thoughts back from East LA.

"So if it wasn't the motorcycle...?" Matt ventured, feeling he shouldn't open the wound, but knowing it was open already.

Thorny nodded. "Memory's a mean closet to get into, isn't it? Whenever you open the door...well you can't tell what's gonna fall out. They don't call 'em 'skeletons' for nothin', do they?

"He was never reckless, not Greg. It was on a Saturday. He said he was gonna take a friend out to the coast—and—I dunno—we never even asked him who it was or anything. We trusted him, y'see. The CHP guy said he wasn't speeding, but just hit some loose gravel from one of those little slides that come down once in a while. Any time of year really. On a curve. Couldn't have seen it before he got there. That sandstone breaks off like crumbs off a cake, and he just skidded into the path of pickup. It wasn't the other guy's fault either. Nobody's fault, like I said. When we got the call we rushed to the emergency, thinking he'd be okay. We kept saying, 'It's gonna be all right. Even if he's really hurt, even if he can't play ball anymore.' You know stuff like that. But he was already gone before we got there, and they said something about the girl who was with him was in intensive care. A girl? We didn't know he had a girl. Anyway, when we went in to look at him, it was like part of his face was screed off by the asphalt, cause the helmet got knocked off. All bone and torn bloody flesh, and I told Clare not to stay there. To wait in the hall.

"After she went out, I just stood there. I didn't believe this could've happened. Not to Greg. Always so careful. And I was standing there— like I can see him now—and I could never tell Clare how much I hated him. Yes, I hated him. You probably wouldn't understand," Thorny added in a ragged voice.

Matt wasn't sure if he should answer or if Thorny was only pausing to control himself. "I think I would," he ventured.

"I kept thinking what a stupid idiot he was, and I couldn't stop myself. 'Why did you do this to us? How could you? You bastard, bastard…' like that, on an' on. Not out loud, of course, but like I was screaming at him inside myself. I never yelled at Greg. Ever. And I wanted to go to Clare, but I couldn't go feeling like that."

"Yes, I do understand. Absolutely." The image gave Matt a sorrow he hadn't expected. Rage pushing against love and momentarily winning.

"And then the other hate started," said Thorny. I mean hating myself for hating him, which made it all the worse, and then I just started to cry. I cried my way just about down to the floor, I was so bent over. For a little while I thought I was gonna die with gasping, but I caught hold of myself somehow, thinking about Clare out in the hall by herself.

"There wasn't anything I could do then but to straighten up and go out to her, an' take hold of her. An' when I did, she just cried and cried, shaking like a building in an earthquake. She never asked to go back in the room. She said she didn't want to remember him dead. So we just stood there and held onto each other, crying and shaking."

Matt remembered the way he and Didi held each other in the hospital when Marilu was pronounced dead. Hell, they knew she was dead when Didi lifted her out of the crib. At first he'd been too shocked to cry, and Didi only screamed. He nodded his understanding when Thorny paused, bereft of voice.

Thorny went on, finally. "After a while a woman came out of a room a few doors down the hall, alone, sniffling like she'd been crying too. I would've ignored her, but Clare, she let go of me and went over and asked if she was the mother of the girl on the motorcycle and the woman said yes, and Clare asked if the girl was gonna be okay, and her mother said yes. It was mostly a broken elbow and lacerations, but she'd be okay, and Clare said, 'Oh thank God, thank God!' like it was the best news she'd ever heard, and then for just a minute I hated her, too. But then I was proud of her at the same time. Clare always had so much class. Like a natural genius for doing the right thing. So she hugged the other woman for quite a long time. And never said a word about losing Greg.

"We had him cremated and took the ashes up to the river where we used to go camping, an' we scattered them by the river, knowing the winter storms would slice through and carry them away. It was the best thing we could think of. And then we drove home without talking much and never went there again."

Matt saw the pointlessness of words, so he only said, "Yeah" in a low voice and again he nodded. It helped him not to look towards Thorny, but out the window at the garden. Thorny also looked straight ahead.

"Of course we staggered on with our lives," Thorny said, as if addressing the window, "even though it didn't seem like we had that much to do anymore. People say time heals grief, but it doesn't. It just buries it, layer on layer, like sediment. But it's still just as much there. They say to remember the good times. Well, of course we did that, and sometimes that made the pain worse. The remembering. Clare couldn't seem to have more than one child, but we always thought we'd have grandkids. I think maybe that's what makes it so hard. When you have a child, it feels like a whole life lays out ahead of you. You've created this child, and when they're born, it feels like that creation will just keep unfolding for the rest of your life. But when you lose a child, you lose a past and a future at the same time."

Thorny's voice was steady now, but when he paused, Matt glanced at him again and saw tears on his cheeks. Standing helpless and rigid by the window, Matt had to wonder how he would have felt if Dan had died in an accident. Inexpressible pain, of course. He resented Dan a little less to remember his unqualified love, but then the resentment resurfaced. Children! A mixed blessing. But he couldn't say so to Thorny.

"I guess I met you and Clare about ten years ago," Matt observed, groping for anything to say. "When I did the first story on your garden. Clare was sure proud of it. The garden. She had good reason."

"You bet. When it was in full bloom anyway. I admit that working on it did us good, as much as anything could. Anyway, we stuck together and went on with our lives. We even went out more'n we used to, y'know, like to movies and exhibits and lectures at the college. And flower shows, of course. Yes, it was around then that you came over to take pictures for the paper. 'Farewell to Spring' was the heading because of the clarkias."

"Are those clarkias down there, in that corner on the right?" Matt waved his hand in the direction.

"No, no. Those are cosmos. The clarkias are early, like I said. Long gone."

Cosmos, Matt repeated to himself. That cluster of tall pink flowers at the front of Lauren's house. Cosmos.

"We never missed the Greek Festival or the Renaissance Pleasure Faire. And we took some great picnics up to Mount Tam or over to Bolinas or up the coast to Mendocino. You can't beat the views on a sunny day just after a storm has broken up and you still have those massive cumulus drifting away. You can't get any more beauty than that. Sometimes we thought that life was still pretty good. I guess it was something like having a leg cut off and after you get used to the artificial limb, you might say it's not so bad, but you still can't help wishing every step that you had your real leg back again.

"We spent fifteen years or so like that, kind of limping along, so to speak. Of course, I still liked my work an' I worked hard, an' Clare still kept the books an' looked after the house and garden. You might've said that nothing much had changed…if you didn't know. And then Clare started to lose interest in the garden and more and more often I'd come home from work and she'd be watching some silly thing on TV, which wasn't usual. Of course she'd be knitting while she watched, because she never did like idle hands, but she wasn't exactly active and sparkly like usual. I dunno why it took me so long to figure out that she was sick or why it took her so long to admit it. I guess it was denial, like they say, and that she never liked to complain about anything. It was strange. She was never sick before.

"But one day I took a good look at her and saw how thin she was, and I didn't like it, and I remember saying that it was time we both had a check-up. We went to the doctor, and I checked out fine, but her… The doctor said she was jaundiced and he'd like to run a few tests at the hospital. And believe it or not, I didn't worry too much, not even when they said she had a liver disease. But in fact, it was cancer. I guess I thought, well, there's treatment for that, and we'll just do it, and part of me didn't believe that fate could be so mean. So we did the chemo and the radiation part and she got through all the sickness that it gives you, and seemed better, and it still came back. They did more tests and the result was really bad. There was nothing more to do." Thorny paused, thinking of Richard Young. The deadly prognosis.

"Well, Clare, she was calm. She didn't complain. All class, like I said. I just cut down on work so I could be at home more, and she stayed inside and watched TV or videos or read, and when I wasn't around she was writing farewell letters to her friends. I found that out later.

"I remember one day I came home from work and saw her stirring a pot of stew, holding onto the edge of the counter for support an' I felt so mad I almost hit her. I mean because there was food in the pantry and the freezer, but she always wanted our meals to be fresh cooked. I guess you saw where the vegetable garden was on the other side of the house. Well, anyway, it was kind of like how I felt that day about Greg, like 'How can you hurt me like this?' But I just took a breath and went over and looked in the pot and told her how great it smelled, which it did, of course, but then I cried and so did she. It was one of the few times.

"Well, after one of our appointments with the doctor, he said we should get in touch with hospice because it didn't look like there was much time left, and it was gonna be 'difficult.' The doctors, they don't use the word 'hell' much, do they? Joan, she was the lady from hospice, and she said that feeling angry was normal. She said it was okay. Clare liked her and so did I, but of course Clare liked just about everybody.

"One day I remarked to Joan that our fortieth wedding anniversary was only two weeks off, and she said, 'Why don't you celebrate now, while Clare can still enjoy it?' And it hit me then that she really meant 'while Clare is still alive.' I guess I'd almost gotten used to Clare being sick in bed. At least she was there." Thorny paused, swallowed and went on.

"So anyway, I got a bunch of cut flowers the next day. Must've been the first ones she didn't grow herself, and some really nice perfume. She never went in for perfume much, but I thought, why the hell not? It was called Maja or something like that. When I gave it to her she said, 'Oh Thorny, you're a prince! Put a little behind my ear. Just a dab.' So I put a touch of it on her. Her hair had grown back by then, dark and curly, like it used to be. Only her face was way too thin. Her Portuguese eyes that always looked like pools of dark chocolate were now so sunk they looked more like mud holes after the rain.

"Of course I threw that perfume away, straight in the garbage after she was gone. I didn't even want to see it. Anyway, she made it until two days before our anniversary, just kind of slept away. Joan was there and a guy called Dutch, and they stayed on for a while after the undertaker came, and they told me to go ahead and talk about how I was feeling an' not to worry if I felt like crying. Well, of course I cried. I never minded about crying. But I'm not sure what good it did. They gave me a book to read. Something about stages of grieving. Hell, I already knew about grieving! And all the people who came to her memorial, it didn't help any for some of 'em to tell me she was with God. It almost made me laugh. There's no damn God. My work was God. Our family was God.

Our marriage was God. Period." Thorny stopped and was silent, staring down at the garden.

Matt would never have put his feelings about God so bluntly, but now he felt that Thorny was absolutely right. It was refreshing to hear someone say it in so many words, even if the statement came out of grief. If Matt had a god at all, it was beauty. It was nature. Or it was the right color, the right light, the right composition, the right moment. The indrawn breath of wonder that you can't stop. Lately, his god had extended to Lauren. So for him god had to be whatever is the absorbing reality. What else? Too inexplicable and too personal to go into with Thorny. Into the silence, he merely murmured his agreement.

"It's a funny thing about death," Thorny went on in a philosophic tone. "I mean that when it comes for most people, they'll do anything to escape it, but when you really want it, it's always busy calling on somebody else. I mean my door's been open for the last two years now... I never meant to carry on like that," he concluded suddenly, irritably, "but everything's changing, y'see. Of course it's hard to let go of something you've got used to, but it's good too. Life is change, like they say. Even granite breaks up and marble wears in time."

"You're right. About everything," Matt told him, distracted now. He saw that Rachel, with the clipboard under her arm, and Carolyn of the Native Plant Society had come around from the other side of the house and were standing in the garden below them. Carolyn wore a colorful visor and looked like a spectator at a tennis match. He saw Rachel glance at her cell. Checking the time?

"I guess we better go down," he said. "The girls seem to be winding up the interview. Do you plan to move out of the area?" He asked as they turned away from the window. He was giving his house away, for heaven's sake, so there had to be a Plan B.

"Like I said, I've got options. One guy I know about, he bought himself a nice camper and just went traveling around the country, stopping here and there, wherever it suited him, state parks an' places like that. He could pick his seasons.

"I've never traveled much, but maybe it's time. I mean, I don't have any ties here to speak of. I've got this friend, Rudy, who keeps trying to set me up with a new girlfriend, keeps sayin' I shouldn't be alone." Thorny shook his head. "I don't want any of that. I just wanna get away. Know what I mean?"

"Yeah, sure." Matt did wonder if a man who still lived in the house where he was born would be happy with life on the road. There was something about Thorny's proposal that hovered between optimism and denial.

Thorny led the way downstairs. On the back landing they both paused, and the two women came toward them smiling like bridesmaids.

Rachel, the gardening editor, was effusive. "Thorny! This place is such a treasure! Of course I've seen it before, but I didn't remember the fountain."

"Sorry it's turned off. I should've thought," Thorny apologized.

"No, that's fine. I can imagine how it would murmur through the ferns."

"Your fountain definitely stays," Carolyn assured him.

"Thorny," Rachel went on, as though she'd just thought of it, "you don't happen to have any of Clare's iris rhizomes left, do you? I still remember that one with the lavender standards and the purple falls."

"Actually, I gave most of those away the other day, but there are a few of the Parrish Blues and maybe a Holiday Sunrise in a box in the shed. I was just gonna leave 'em, for anybody, but if you want some, that's fine. So if you're interested, go have a look. They're labeled."

Trailing gratitude behind her, Rachel strode off towards the garden shed, a small frame building that had weathered along with the house so as to be a natural part of the garden, while the other three stood there, no longer with any particular business at hand.

"I know the bearded iris isn't exactly your thing," Thorny said to Carolyn, "but there's the wild iris."

"Of course. It's all beautiful. And the season is so short. Like the checker lily. Almost like a secret, like morel mushrooms or something. You have to know where they are."

Matt, who was gazing around the garden like an idle stroller suddenly felt sorry that Thorny was moving away. You don't often meet a person so genuine.

"Listen," he said, "why don't you let me buy you a beer somewhere or even some supper. Nothing fancy. My wife's helping to serve dinner at some doings at her church, so I was thinking of eating out anyway. What d'you say?"

Thorny considered. "Yeah, I guess I could do that. Why not? Just need to lock up."

Rachel was coming back to them smiling, her clipboard tucked under her arm, her cupped hands full of what looked like flattened clods of dirt. "You wouldn't have a paper bag, or something, would you?" she asked Thorny.

"Sorry. Wasn't thinkin'. Just a minute…I'll get you one." And he hurried back into the house.

"Wonderful place," said Carolyn Biggs for the seventh time that afternoon, still helplessly euphoric over their bit of luck. "Exactly what we needed!"

"Yes, who would've thought it?" Rachel concurred. "Maybe there's a God, after all, eh?" And she laughed.

MATT TELLS PART OF A STORY

After they had left Thorny's house, Matt stopped at the paper to file his photos. Then he drove on a few blocks to Brooks and Books, a locally-owned cafe favored by most of the newspaper staff. Consequently, the servers there knew all the staff and so were prone to make passing comments, such as "What's stirring in the inkwell?" as if anybody knew what an inkwell was anymore. Or maybe more specifically, "I read about that new height code for buildings. How'd they ever get that through the city council?" As though a mere reporter knew—or could comment if they did. Even other patrons sometimes joined into the nattering, as they once did in country stores in small towns.

But in the late afternoon the place was relatively quiet. Matt and Thorny went to a booth near the back, where a shelf of used paperbacks, not completely tattered, justified the second half of the shop's name. Ignoring the books—though Matt often paused to check them out— the two sat down and considered the unremarkable menu.

"So what's up at the propaganda factory?" Mary, a brisk blond waitress in her forties, asked Matt, order pad in hand. "Propaganda factory" was her favored sobriquet for the paper and not bad, as Matt conceded.

"Well, beautiful, where there's an ad, there's a paper," Matt returned the ritualized answer, "which simply demonstrates the freedom of the press."

"That, at least, is true," she affirmed. "Now, what I can I bring you?"

"Make mine a Reuben on rye and a dark draft."

"And your good-looking friend?" she asked, scribbling.

"A sandwich sounds pretty good," Thorny concurred, after a brief consideration. "How about a roast beef on wheat?"

"Sure thing. And to drink?"

"Oh, the same. No, make it a pale ale. Okay?"

"You got it."

Matt leaned forward, elbows on the table, forearms crossed in front of him. He seemed relaxed. Thorny leaned back with his arms folded loosely, also relaxed. The business of the day drifted away behind them.

"I just remembered I shouldn't be eating meat," Matt observed unexpectedly.

"How come? Your doctor…?"

"No, no. I'm just… I'm practicing to be a vegetarian. The advice of a friend. A lady, actually. Never mind," he added. "I won't tell her. About the Reuben."

"Ah, well, I guess everybody needs a few guilty secrets. No problem."

"At least my wife, she doesn't care whether I eat meat or not."

"Good cook?"

"Oh yeah. Like I said, she even volunteers at her church to help cook for special dinners. That's where she is now, at least I presume. A spaghetti feed or something. She's a good baker too."

"You're a lucky guy."

"Yeah, I guess. The only problem is she eats too much of her own stuff, though I can't blame her exactly. When it's so good. I just… when you were telling me about you and Clare, I couldn't help wishing …I mean Didi and I get along okay, but we aren't close anymore. You know how it gets with some couples. The coupling sort of loosens up, like the knot of a shoelace but not enough to split apart. So we sort of dangle along. Too bad. I know. But *asi es la vida*." It was more painful than that, but Matt realized that further comment would be pointless.

Thorny nodded his commiseration, if not exactly empathy.

Mary came to the table then with a frosty glass mug in either hand and set them down.

"Thanks, hon, you're the greatest," Matt said.

"Yeah, I know." She smiled at the practiced exchange. "Tell the boss." Then she turned to wait on another couple, two booths away.

Matt's eyes followed her for a moment, then returned to Thorny. He picked up his mug and sipped past the foam. Leaning forward, Thorny did likewise. It was a companionable act set in a companionable silence. Setting down his mug, Matt rubbed the bridge of his nose for a moment, as someone does who relieves the pressure of glasses, though he wore glasses only for reading.

"What you told me over at your house, about your son," he began, out of the quietness, "it got me remembering. Some days I don't think about it, or hardly, and some days I'm obsessed. I dunno why. But you see… we lost a teen-ager too, only in a completely different way."

"Sorry. I didn't know…"

"Of course not. And it wasn't a death, but sometimes I think it feels the same. She's our second daughter. Stephanie. We lost our first little girl in infancy. A crib death, they call it. But with Stephanie, I don't quite know what went wrong, but I can't help but blame myself sometimes. I really don't know. Never will, I guess." He took another sip of beer, looking only at the mug.

Thorny didn't know if Matt wanted him to ask, so he was tentative, casual. "She ran off or somethin'? You don't have to say…" he softened the question.

Matt sipped again before answering, then nodded a very slight nod. "I guess today is one of those days I get to thinking about it. About my family. Not a complete success, though you would've thought so at the beginning. My wife, Dolores, was considered a beauty in the barrio where we grew up, and she was, too. All the guys were crazy about her, and I guess everybody was puzzled that she decided to marry me and agreed to move up north instead of becoming a model or something. She could have. But she really wanted to be homemaker, and that was fine. People should do what they're good at, if they can. And we got along well, except that Didi—I mean Dolores—was always really religious and seemed to get more so as time went along, especially after we lost our baby girl."

"I'm sorry about the baby." Thorny almost said he was sorry about the religion too. Clare wasn't religious, but her mother, who was a sweet old thing, had enough religion for the whole family.

Matt acknowledged the condolence with a nod. "The baby we lost, she wasn't our first child. Didi had a baby in the first year of our marriage, when we were still in LA. That was Danny. Dan, now that he's grown. A strong, healthy boy. I don't know if I was ready for him so soon, but like I said, Didi was religious and only believed in the rhythm method, which didn't work. But the minute I saw him… it was like it'd been my idea all along. He was a great baby and a great kid. He grew fast and seemed to do everything a little earlier than average, which of course all parents think is wonderful. I took a million pictures of him, and Didi was on the phone to her mother or one of her sisters or sisters-in-law all the time, telling them what Danny did that day. At least she didn't have a cell phone then," he added wryly.

"But anyway, when Danny was three, Didi had another baby, a little girl. We named her Maria Luisa after Didi's mother. We called her Marilu. It was our dream to have a daughter, after Danny, and she was unbelievably pretty. But she died when she wasn't quite two months old.

"I've never really stopped thinking about it. Even now. You see, that night, the night she died—well, Didi and I hadn't had sex in quite a while—on account of the pregnancy and birth. Marilu was in a crib in the corner of our bedroom so that Didi could get up to nurse. Anyway, we just sort of decided… Afterward, we both slept, really sound. Early in the morning I woke up early, just like I always do, and I picked up my clothes from the chair and sort of sneaked out of the room to dress so as not to wake Didi or Marilu. I was thinking how great it was that Marilu slept through the night, though I should've realized it wasn't normal. I just went into the kitchen and made some coffee and started out to the garage when I heard Didi screaming. Marilu wasn't breathing. We called 911, but it was no use.

"The doctor said it wasn't anybody's fault but I knew I should have looked at her at least. I was wrecked inside. And Didi was completely traumatized. Went into such a depression that some days she couldn't get out of bed, couldn't even take care of Danny when I wasn't around. So we had her mother come up to stay for about three months, until Didi got some help from one of those support groups." Matt didn't add, but remembered, that a sign of her recovery was starting to take an interest in those dreary Mexican soap operas again. No need to go into that.

"Well, I started thinking maybe we should have another baby, but Didi said no because she was scared it would happen again, even though the doctor said it was really unlikely, and there were new monitoring devices to prevent that kind of thing, but I understood the way she felt because I partly felt it too. She even started believing in contraception. But finally, almost six years later, we decided to take the risk, and Didi conceived again and had another baby and that was Stephanie, and she was perfectly healthy. No problems at all. Of course we hovered over her like crazy and really loved it when she cried in the night because we knew it meant she was okay.

"And she was a sweetheart. Not just pretty like her mother, but a very sweet child. Mama's little helper an' all that. She did well in school, had lots of friends. She had some talent, too. She played Celia in *Much Ado About Nothing* when she was only a sophomore, and everybody said she was great. It wasn't just us. Dan, her brother, even though he was almost nine years older, he was great with her. He never seemed jealous of all the attention we gave her. Sort of looked after her like an uncle. They spent a lot of time together until he left the JC and went to live in the South Bay. Maybe it wasn't a good time for him to go, just when Stephanie was starting high school, but I didn't think about that until later on. Anyway, for Dan, it was time for him to move out. He was restless and needed to get on with his life. I understood that."

Matt broke off his account because Mary was coming over with their sandwiches on a tray. Potato chips and a pickle on each plate.

"A Reuben and a roast beef," she reviewed, setting down Matt's plate and then Thorny's. "Anything else?" She looked from one to the other.

"No, that's great," Matt answered for them both.

"Enjoy," she enjoined them and went.

"Is he still in the Bay Area? Your son?" Thorny asked as he picked up his sandwich. Maybe Stephanie wasn't quite a safe subject. Unless Matt wanted to talk about it. When you start a story, sometimes it seems to beg completion, and sometimes it wants to back away.

"He lives in the city now. I think I mentioned that he opened a video business a few years back. DVDs now. When he was a kid he liked photography, like me, but like we all know, life moves in the currents of technology. Anyway, it's a good business to get into. If I was Dan, I suppose that's what I would've been doing. He's not getting rich, but doing okay. Not bad, considering all the competition." He paused, took a bite of his sandwich. "They do a good Reuben here."

"Good beef, too," Thorny observed.

When Matt had swallowed and taken a shallow sip of beer to wash it down, he went on. "As for Stephanie, by the time she hit high school she was at least as pretty as Didi ever was, only taller. We used to say that she had pixie eyes, eyes that laughed, eyes that looked interested in everything they saw. When she started dating, I tried to keep track of the boys she went around with. At first it was mostly school events—games, dances, that kind of thing. I practically required references before I'd let her set foot out the door, but by the time she was a junior and getting into theater, I'd about given up. There were too many. I told Didi to keep her confidence, but as she pointed out, teenage girls don't confide in their mothers, they confide in their girlfriends. It seems like it's just that modern girls have more stuff to confide about. It's sort of like boasting. Now they even do it online, so it's not confidential at all. It used to be that the boys boasted. A macho thing. But now, everything's different." He shook his head, picked up his sandwich again, took a bite, and chewed it thoughtfully.

"Maybe different, maybe more of the same," Thorny tried to be consoling and realistic at the same time. "You know how it is. Every generation thinks that the next one's going to the dogs."

"I suppose you're right. But things went seriously wrong with Steph. I don't know how the hell it happened, but one evening just after we'd gone to bed, we got a call from the local police to say that Stephanie had gotten busted along with some other kids during a drug raid. A drug raid! Jesus! I couldn't believe it. I pulled myself together and got down to the station to cover the bail, so I could get her home the same night. And honestly, I thought what the hell, it was only a little pot. I smoked some grass myself when I was in high school. It seemed like all the kids did it sometime or other. So maybe not such a big deal. But that didn't mean I thought it was okay.

"On the way home from the station, Stephanie didn't have much to say except that the kids were having a party at somebody's house, passing a few joints, nothing unusual. Some agents came in, looking for a particular dealer, who it turned out wasn't there. Anyway, I wanted her to think I understood, and I certainly didn't want to lecture. I told her I knew the drug laws didn't make sense, but as long as pot was illegal, she should knock it off. Don't tempt fate, and she said okay. Well, it turned out that she got off all right. You know how it works when some of the kids have important parents, and Stephanie was lucky to be in good company. Anyway, somehow the charges got reduced to drinking underage, and all they got was some community service. And I told her to take a lesson from that experience, and she said she would.

"Only nothing was quite the same between us after that. We hardly ever knew where she was when she wasn't at home. She was good about telling us where she was going, but we weren't quite sure it was the truth. She wasn't doing theater anymore, so it wasn't rehearsal. She just sort of came and went, blank as a plank. Even the pixie eyes seemed to kind of shut down. Her grades went down, but she wasn't failing anything, so I kept my mouth shut." He sighed slightly, reliving his defeat.

"Twice I missed money from my wallet and started being very careful about where I put it down, but still I wasn't sure enough to confront her. I thought maybe I lost the money somewhere, maybe forgot what I spent it on. I guess that's what they call denial. I'll tell you the truth. By the time you learn to handle something like that, it's too late to make any difference." He sighed again.

"Are you saying she's in jail?" Thorny asked cautiously.

"No. I don't think so. If she were, at least we'd know where she is. She did get into serious trouble, though. It was in October of her senior year. I got a call from Didi at work. I was working late that night because of having to process some pictures after the county board meeting. She said Steph was in the hospital from what looked like an overdose of some kind. So I went down there and stood by her bed and just cried. And of course Didi cried. And prayed. Steph was unconscious then, but she came out of it later that night, and the next day we took her home. The lab reported that she'd been given chloral hydrate, the rape drug. Of course, she couldn't remember anything.

She did seem more subdued for a while, and she promised to be more careful.

"About that same time, Dan was starting up his film company in the city. Of course he was busy, but I appealed to him to come up and talk to her. Have a chat, at least. They'd always been close, and I sort of thought they still were. So he did come for a weekend, and they hung out together and had fun, but when he was gone, I wondered if anything was different, and when I asked Stephanie what they talked about, she said, 'Nothin' much. Why?' I stayed casual and dropped it. Of course, I talked to Dan on the phone, and he said not to worry because she'd come out okay. She wasn't on meth or anything like that. He said it was a phase, and she was too smart to go under.

"Fine. But in the meantime, here's my beautiful daughter, barely making it in school, mostly partying, and my wife wearing ruts in the pavement that leads to the church. As I said, Didi was always religious, but when Stephanie was in the hospital, she started to pray like a real maniac. She told me that Steph had survived the overdose because of prayer, and she was just thanking God and the Virgin for their mercy. But I kept thinking, what about Marilu? Where was God's mercy when we lost her? And what about Stephanie herself? She didn't seem to thank God for anything. For once in my life, I wished she'd been more religious, like Didi.

"I was at work a lot of the time then, but one Saturday afternoon, it was the week before Christmas, I was home, replacing a piece of cracked floor molding in the hall, and Stephanie came out of her room with a purse slung over her shoulder and went by me like I wasn't there, heading for the front door.

"'Hey, where're you goin'?' I tried to sound casual.

"'Just out for a while. I gotta date.'

"'Oh yeah? Who you goin' out with? Frank?' I couldn't stop myself. At least Frank was a name I knew. I'd even met him.

"'No, Mike.' She was at the door, starting to sound impatient.

"'Mike who?'

"'Just Mike.'

"'Look Steph...' I stood up. 'I just wanna know...' Later on I found the hammer where I put it down in the hall, but I sure don't remember doing it. Only I'm glad I did because I dunno.

"'Daddy, quit it, will ya?' she said to me. 'I'm late. He's waiting out front.'

"I tell you, the back of my head prickled like I was about to get ambushed by Indians. I followed her out onto the porch and when I saw the creep who was leaning towards the passenger window of a dirty blue, scratched up sedan, I couldn't believe it. If we'd been in Hollywood, I would've guessed this kid was made up for a part in some hoodlum movie, but around here, if a guy can't comb his hair or put on a clean shirt for a date, you'd question his judgment about everything. Know what I mean?

"I told her, 'I don't know this guy. I just want to talk to him for a minute, that's all.' Her back was to me, but I knew she could hear me.

"'Oh, just leave it!' she said without even looking around. 'I gotta go!' She just kept on going down the walk and me trailing behind her like an idiot.

"So I was talking to her back, but I told her I had to know where she was going. That she couldn't go until I knew. Her answer was that she was going to Mike's place for a party. She was at the curb by then.

"'I'm sorry,' I told her, 'but I gotta know where he lives.' I guess I was about ten feet behind her." Matt lowered his voice, realizing he might be heard beyond Thorny. "Anyway, she turned to me by the car and looked square at me and said, 'Who the fuck cares? So just stick it up yours, shitass!' My daughter said that! I couldn't believe it. I mean we'd had quarrels before, but not with that sort of language, not on either side. Never.

"Then that punk put in his two cents. 'Yeah, why don't ya, Daddy? Huh? huh?' Like that, sneering. I guess he knew he was safe in the car.

I don't know if I could've taken him, but he knew I wasn't about to try, not with Stephanie just getting in and the neighbors watering their lawn next door and craning their necks to see what the hell was going on. So I was beaten. And then out came good ole Dolores, standing on the porch behind me, crying her head off and pleading with God to make Stephanie come back. But at the moment, I didn't want her back. I was too pissed off and, of course, humiliated.

"'Okay,' I said, 'go with this sonavabitch. Go ahead, but if you do, you don't come back here. You got that? You go and you're gone. You understand?' 'Cool,' she answers. 'Fine with me.' And then something that sounded like, 'Let's get the fuck outta here,' to the punk. She never even hesitated, never paused a second to consider. Those were the last words I ever heard from her. The very last."

Matt let out a final, terminal sigh like someone who's just set down a load of bricks or sheetrock. Exhausted. "Christ! I never told anybody that story before. I got carried away." He took another long swallow of beer.

Thorny nodded. "It's okay. That was a stab smack in the heart."

"Sometimes I wonder if she answered like that so she could say I threw her out of the house. That it was all Daddy's fault. That was the way Didi explained it to everybody. That I'd chucked our only daughter out of the house just when she was getting better. Threw her to the wolves and so forth. That was five years ago, and she still blames me. So much for Christian charity. Anyway, she doesn't have to keep saying it. I know I lost it. I know I shouldn't have said what I did. I guess my tongue got tangled up in my machismo or something. I don't think I've made a lot of big mistakes in my life, but that was a doozie, and I can't get clear of it because I don't believe in a forgiving God. Only people can forgive. Either themselves or each other. But I can't forgive myself and Didi won't. Only what's the use of the blame? What's the use of the guilt? It's just so much slow poison." He looked away towards the wall.

Thorny nodded a quiet acquittal. "Yeah, I see what you mean. At least Clare and I stuck together. I've thought about that a lot. I know that in a sort of odd way at least we were lucky to have each other." A slight pause, while Thorny studied Matt's averted face. "I'm really sorry, man. I mean it." Thorny had drained his beer and now contemplated the empty mug for a moment. He looked at Matt again, taking a chance with a question. "You never heard from her again?"

Matt looked back at Thorny then. "About a year after she ran away she called. Didi talked to her. She said that Steph sounded a little vague, but talked about coming home. Said she'd call again. Said to talk to Daddy about it. Well, it was fine with me. I was more than ready to have her back, but she never called again. Then about six or eight months ago, Didi heard from a cousin that Steph had turned up in East LA, living with a Salvadoran guy and looking reasonably happy. Didi says it's the answer to prayer. Sure."

"So you'd take her back?"

"Absolutely. No matter what. If she wants to come. But I mean, at least she's gotta call or something. I'm not gonna go down looking for her. And I wouldn't even know where to begin."

Thorny nodded again, supportive. "I got a feeling you'll work it out with her someday. Or she'll work it out with you. One way or another."

"I used to think so too, but it's kind of like waiting for your lottery number to come up. Look at the odds. I mean, if you win it's a miracle, and I don't believe in miracles. I think maybe the time for happy reunions has run out."

"I know what you mean. About giving up." Thorny looked thoughtful, as though about to say something desperately personal. Not a mere walk by the shore, but plunge into deep water. "I've given up. In a manner of speaking," he said. "I just got a few ends to tie up, and I'm outta here."

"You did a good thing with your house. But you'll miss this area, you know. You've put so much of yourself into it. And it's the best spot on earth."

"I know…" Thorny seemed about to go on and then took another bite his sandwich instead.

Their conversation drifted to a local development, a retirement home. Matt wanted to know what Thorny thought of it architecturally.

Thorny pondered the question. "It's fine, I mean a nice building. I kind of like that way the wings are angled, not like so many shoeboxes stuck together. Nice landscaping, looks like. But not for me, if that's what you're wondering. No long days in front of the boob tube. No card games or Scrabble. Not for me." He lowered his voice, leaning closer across the table. "I wouldn't say this to anybody else, only I know you wouldn't be too upset if you heard I'd died. You'd understand."

"Of course I'd be upset," Matt responded. Conventional, but honest.

"No, I mean it. If you knew it was what I really wanted. I'd want someone around who'd say 'Good for Thorny! He went out the way he wanted, not crumbling away like so much sandstone.' You see, that guy I told you about, the one who knows he's dying, well, we've a plan to go out together—in a private plane—because he knows how to fly, y'see, so as to make it look like an accident."

Matt stared at him for half a minute, brown eyes looking fixedly into pale blue ones, amazed, and then less amazed. Finally, he nodded. "I'll try to remember that. If I can. 'Good for Thorny.' I know I'm supposed to say, 'Don't even think about it!' but maybe I've learned not to tell other people what to do. Leave 'em alone. Even Didi and her Blessed Virgin. Who am I to tell anybody anything? Sure, I've got opinions. That's human, but I mean let's not try to play God, huh? That's all I know."

He trailed away as if confused about where to go from there. He looked at his mug, nearly empty, picked it up and drained it.

"You're okay. You really are," Thorny reassured him, relieved now that he had said what he did and had been understood. "You ready to go?"

"Sure." Matt sidled his way out of the seat and picked up the check. "My treat, of course." he said. Without arguing, Thorny followed him to the register.

When they walked out of the cafe, Matt didn't know whether he felt more relieved by their conversation or more mired in remembrance.

MATT CONSIDERS PHOTOGRAPHS

I had more fun with those pictures than I ever had with any portrait in my life. Even my children. Using the Canon, not the digital, opened the curtain to get in some natural light. Bright pink flowers out there. Cosmos? How apt. I switched on my photographer's eye. The lighting, the composition. Turned her into a subject. I admit it. For a moment she's not Lauren. Then she is. In and out, like image and ground. Three shots from slightly different angles. Pile up the pillows to enhance the curve of the back. *Look to the left. Chin up a little. Good, good. Perfect.* Those shoulders, back, curve of the hips. Yes, perfect. No, spectacular. I told her so.

I snapped another one.

"Now something coy. Turn towards me, rest against the pillow, pull up the sheet, just under your breasts. A little smile just over my shoulder. Nice. Giaconda. Nice sheets, by the way." I snapped another shot, two.

"You're a natural model," I told her. She really is beautiful. "Only don't you dare pose for anyone else." Would I really care? Yes, maybe.

"I was thinking of making my fortune. After all, I need a profession."

"No, you don't. Being you is enough. Plenty." I meant that.

She smiled. Pleased, I hope. Reassured? She almost believes in herself, but not quite. She needs to know.

I folded the neck strap and set the camera on the dresser. Then I just looked and admired. It really killed me, having an appointment, having to take pictures for the garden section, of all things. But there it was. I had to apologize again.

"But I like the garden section. I read it a lot," she assured me. "Just call me soon."

"I'll try. You know that. What's your number?" I couldn't help teasing her.

"You've got my number, you… you… unconscionable seducer."

"Interesting, but not precise. I have a conscience." Which is true. "And you're more seductive than I am by a long way. "

"Let's not get into who's sexier than whom."

I love her grammar.

"So when can I call you?"

"I gave you my cell number, so whenever you think of me."

"Can't."

"Why not?"

"I'll think of you all the time," I told her. I'm sure a lot of the time. "I'm sorry, but my schedule's different every day. I'll get you somehow. Now give me a parting-is-such-sweet-sorrow kiss."

She did that, and the pleasure almost hurt. Shakespeare knew all right.

So it was then or never. I had to finish dressing, get my cell and camera stuff. I told her not to see me to the door. One sweet sorrow is enough.

—⸪—

So here I am again. Didi not here to cook dinner. Okay, but I had dinner. Didi was always a good cook. A good mother. Good housekeeper. Good Christian. Did I say a good wife? I know she tried. So what's the matter with her? Nothing, I guess.

With me? Nothing too serious. So what is it? I'm not perfect, but a man's supposed to manage his family. I tried to—or maybe tried too hard. Dunno. I'll never know.

If you were young again, Dolores, eighteen, pretty as a monarch butterfly on the lilac blossom, with those terrific bowl-shaped boobs and a waist I could almost put my hands around, and I was twenty, trying to figure out how to conceal my erection every time I got near you, would I press you up against the wall again and ask, "Will you marry me, Didi? Will you please, please marry me? *Te amo, Didi, por dios, te amo!*" And would you finally say, "Yes, Matt, yes," like Molly Bloom, so innocently cunning? And would it be the same all over again? Would we get married and learn the art of living with and around each other, and would we have Dan and Stephanie and go to all the school programs and parent meetings, and would we lose our children just the same, through bad luck or stupidity, or maybe some of both? Jesus Christ! I suppose we would.

Matt was looking at the image of Dolores beside an image of himself in the wedding picture she kept on their dresser in the bedroom. He had set his wine glass down next to it while he got out and put on a pullover sweater against the cool of a foggy evening. And there they were, staring at him, thirty years more innocent. She was over made-up and buried in piles of white ruffles, a cheap (if expensive) fashion of the time. He in a tux that concealed neither his skinniness nor his embarrassment.

All he wanted to do was to get this determined virgin into the sack and make her his beyond all marriage licenses and religious rituals and unending mariachi music. All he could think of was the jingle:

> *Yo te hago suave*
> *Tu me haces duro*

Y así unimos
En un encanto puro.

No soft, no hard, no union. No enchantment anymore. More like a desert landscape without even a rain cloud on the horizon. He couldn't have summoned an erection for her now, no matter how he might have tried, which he sure as hell wouldn't. He thought briefly of Maddy, the pretty intern at the newspaper. Who seduced whom? But it was only a brief affair. And years ago. *We were both needy. Just that. After Stephanie was born, Didi and I pretty much forgot about sex, so maybe I looked around a little. Didi never asked anything about anything. But she insists on keeping that dumb picture on the dresser as a reminder that we'd married "for love" many forgotten years ago.*

He kept staring at the photograph on the dresser while he emptied his glass, but he wasn't seeing Dolores now. He was seeing a series of pictures drying in his darkroom. Among them was a form like a jonquil leaf, the graceful lines that only nature offers. The curves of her shoulders, spine, hips, thighs. He flipped snapshots of her through his mind. No flounces, no make-up. No suffering Jesus on the wall. A real marriage this time. Shared thoughts, shared jokes. Like the reunion of old friends from the same hometown. No cajoling into bed or in bed. They simply led each other, like children looking for shells on the beach. No pretenses or pretensions. Of course, there was some reticence. Lovers can stay strangers in some ways, and strangers can be surprisingly intimate. He hadn't yet told Lauren the painful things about Stephanie that he had, to his own surprise, just shared with a mere acquaintance. But someday he would tell her. He'd tell her everything, but not in bed. Not there. Maybe on a walk somewhere, on a golden afternoon by the Marin headlands. Or deep in a redwood grove where slanted light filters the silence. Or on Mount Tam after a storm with mounded clouds all over the bay, high white hills of floating water that cast gray-green shadows on the water below.

A swirl of thoughts and images converged and scattered like motes in the low sun at the end of a long, beautiful, sad, and altogether very strange day. Mostly, the words they had so lately spoken to each other overflowed his recollection. Sometimes words are just so much hot air. Yes, usually. But sometimes they coalesce like vapor into clouds and clouds into the rain that rescues a parched land.

ASTRID HAS VISITORS

On the wide porch of the sedate two-storey bungalow, Thorny noticed the cardboard box of iris rhizomes that he had left four days ago, he hoped not entirely forgotten. Maybe I shouldn't have brought these over, Thorny was thinking, as he and Richard paused by the front door. *Kind of a waste, but a present's a present. I'm not about to ask her to give them back.* He pulled his gaze away from the box and pushed the modest white button next to the door. It seemed the kind of dignified door that should have a brass knocker, but it had fallen, by chance, into the era of electricity. A faint buzz responded inside.

"This place must date from the twenties," Richard observed, filling the waiting space between them.

"Maybe. Or even the teens. Right after the earthquake. There was a lot of building back then. That'd be my guess, but before the bridge went in and opened everything up. My granddad was a young fellow then, seeking his fortune, as they say, and wound up here. Couldn't have chosen better either. At that time…"

The front door opened a little, a tentative slit, and a narrow piece of face appeared in the crack. Then a little more. An upright rectangle of pale skin and gray hair above it.

"Who's that?" the rectangle said. "Is that you, Thorny?"

"Yes, Astrid. It's me."

"I thought maybe. I wrote it down. That you were coming." And she opened the door wide enough to show her whole height and width, but paused without asking him in. "You brought someone with you," she added with a hint of suspicion.

"Well, yes. I told you. I meant to tell you." He knew he had. "This is my friend, Richard. I wanted you to meet each other. I thought you said it was all right," he added as a prod to her recollection.

"I suppose I did." She either remembered or pretended to. "Come in." She stood back to let them pass. They all paused just inside the door, as if each one was waiting for some instruction from the other, as for a director who hadn't yet arrived on the scene. "Did you tell me your name?" she asked Richard, as they hovered.

"Just Richard. That'll do."

"Richard. That's a nice name…English…?"

"I guess. Anyway, it was my grandfather's name. I'm sure of that much." He offered a tentative smile, which she did not return.

"Think of Richard the Lionhearted," Thorny offered. "Is it okay if we just visit for a few minutes? Richard has an appointment downtown, but I kind of persuaded him to stop by to meet you."

"Yes, of course. How nice…" And Astrid preceded them into the living room, where she sat down in her accustomed chair. "I like to sit by the telephone," she explained. "I used to think I had to, but my daughter, she bought me one of those phones you can carry around. That's handy, but I lose track of it sometimes. So I just sit. And this chair is comfortable."

The two visitors pondered their choices. The cat was stretched at length in the very middle of the sofa, thus occupying most of it, in the way of cats. There was another occasional chair across from Astrid's, an upholstered armchair that had probably been recovered a few times during a long life. Thorny and Richard exchanged uneasy glances, but it was Richard who saved the awkwardness by taking notice of the expanse of books occupying the wall that separated the living room from the hallway.

"You've got quite a library," he observed. "Do you mind if I have a look at your books?"

"Of course not. If you want to." Astrid turned her head to follow him as he strolled over to the tall shelves. "There are a lot more upstairs. My husband was a professor. He needed them for, uh, reference. He had hundreds of books. Are you a book dealer?" she asked abruptly. "They aren't for sale. I don't read much anymore, but I'm keeping them for my daughter and her children."

"No, no, I understand that. I'm just interested. That's all. I like to read."

Thorny took the opportunity to sit down on the available chair, prepared to chat with Astrid, if it seemed in order.

"I used to teach myself," Astrid offered to neither in particular. "Did you know that?"

"No," Richard answered, his back partly to her, as he scanned the titles.

"What did you teach?"

"Different things, but English mostly. I knew French, but I didn't teach it. My mother grew up in France. In the capital. In Paris," she added, recalling the name.

"Yes, I see you have quite a few books here in French," Richard noted.

"Do you speak French?" Astrid inquired. "My mother spoke it very well."

Still scanning, Richard said, "All I know is a little Spanish. Like most Californians," he added in self-explanation.

"My daughter knows Spanish," Astrid said proudly. "She lived with my sister for a while in…one of those countries. In South America." She clearly fumbled for the name of it, but it eluded her. She struggled helplessly into a lengthening silence.

Richard and Thorny looked at each other, but neither could help her.

"I was never a great reader," Thorny noted, trying for a new direction, "mostly magazines. But my wife, Clare, she loved to read, especially when our kid was little. She read to him a lot. And to me too. She was a good reader. Sometimes she read mysteries, like Conan Doyle or Agatha Christie. We had our favorites. It's nice to think that some writers are still popular. They make their stories into TV series or movies, usually mess them up, but still sound, like good masonry." He pondered this partly to himself.

Thorny got to thinking about the longevity of stones. Unfortunately, it was mostly the people who put up the money, not the craftsmen, who got the credit, got something named after them or even went down in history books, as if they'd ever picked up a hammer or a chisel. The pyramids. The cathedrals. The Parthenon. Jesus! What a lot skill went unrecognized! But the truth is in the thing itself, not history books or plaques or monuments. The workman's secret pride. The truth is in the product, not the ownership. Thorny smiled grimly to himself.

"You have a lot of poetry," Richard noted while Thorny pondered the question of workmanship. "I was never a great reader of poetry, but I remember some of these from school days, believe it or not." His eyes grazed over Browning and Chaucer and looked in vain for any titles or authors that he most enjoyed and did not find them. No Arthur C. Clarke. No Isaac Asimov. He liked both fiction and non-fiction about the possibilities of the stars. But mostly hard science. Not fantasy. He moved on along the shelf. No Carl Sagan except *The Demon-Haunted World*. A fine collection, but the wrong landscape. Savannahs instead of mountains.

Richard turned away from the shelves, and contemplated the slightly bent figure of Astrid Williamson. He wondered what to say, what he was even doing here.

Thorny had persuaded him to meet 'the old lady.' But she wasn't old. Her hair was going gray. Yes. And she was a little stooped. Yes. But her face was unlined, except for some worry lines on her forehead and finely wrinkled skin and shallow pockets below her eyes. Everybody got those, sooner or later. She was forgetful, clearly, but that too was not unusual. Getting him here was a well-intentioned mistake on the part of Thorny. Richard worried now that if she had an understanding of their project, she wouldn't remember that it was entirely secret.

Richard walked over to stand uncertainly at the end of the sofa, where the cat still occupied much of the usable space. Not polite to dislodge a pet in someone else's house. He folded his arms briefly, then put his hands in his pockets. At a loss what stance he should take. Clearly it was time to leave. But how?

"This is a nice house," he observed neutrally, though it obviously needed to be redecorated. But not his problem.

"Thank you," Astrid said, looking up at him. "I've lived here a long time. Joyce, she helps me take care of it. She comes here every day after work." She picked up her notepad, looked down at it, and then back to Thorny. "I did write down that you were coming today. 'With friend,'" she read. "I write everything down, just in case I forget something, and then when it's past, I cross it out or tear out the whole page. Like it says, 'Lauren on Sat.' She usually comes on Fridays, but she couldn't. Was it last week? I made a mistake here. With a small flourish, she tore the dated page off and set it aside on the table next to the telephone. "Joyce can't take me shopping, because she doesn't have a car or a license. She knows how to drive, but she never seemed to be able to..." she added obscurely.

Richard took his hands out of his pockets and glanced at his wristwatch. Uncertain. How to get out of here, he kept wondering. He looked at Thorny.

"What we came to talk about, partly," Thorny began hesitantly, "was about a trip I mentioned."

"Trip?" Astrid looked at him blankly, her notebook idle on her lap.

"The trip Richard and I are planning. But it doesn't matter." He wasn't sorry for a chance to back away, since his remark showed that she didn't remember.

"Oh, the trip, of course." She gathered her thoughts together suddenly. "Of course, you told me. But does he know about it?" She inclined her head slightly towards Richard.

"Oh yes. He's the one, the one who's making the plans." Thorny was troubled now that she had remembered.

"Then he knows that I'm going too," she offered with a certain relief. "But you mustn't tell my daughter," she added firmly. "She wouldn't understand."

"Of course not. We wouldn't think of telling her," Thorny assured her.

Richard still stood there, a frown gathering on his forehead, hopelessly trying to look casual.

"We haven't worked out all the details yet," he said conversationally, giving another opportunity for disengagement. But Astrid only stared at him expectantly.

"Well, actually we have, for the most part. But you understand that I can't take anyone along who isn't completely sure. Completely. Because we aren't, well…We aren't coming back." He added, seeming a little short of breath. "Not ever," he persisted. "I mean I don't know if you really understand." He paused again. "We're going to die," he concluded brusquely when she showed no immediate reaction.

Even Thorny wondered for a minute if she did indeed understand, as she sat staring at Richard, noncommittal as a cat in a windowsill.

But her mind was not asleep, after all. "Of course I understand!" she said abruptly. "I'm not stupid! If I stay here, before long they'll come and take me to one of those…nursing home places. And they'll use up all my money, the money I plan to leave for my daughter and her children. Don't you think I know what will happen? Don't you understand that?" she added like an accusation.

Richard nodded, took in a deep breath and let it out slowly. "Okay, I'll tell you what we're planning. But it's like you said about telling your daughter. This is absolutely secret. You're not to tell anyone—anyone at all—about what we're planning. Not your helpers, your neighbors, your attorney. Anyone. You and Thorny and I are the only ones in the world who even have a hint. Do you understand that?"

He surrounded her with repetitions.

"Of course I do! I'm not a…a blabbermouth!" she finished triumphantly, looking over to Thorny for approval. He gave her a faint smile.

Without further comment, Richard told Astrid when and where they would be boarding the plane. It would be a week from next Saturday. The eighteenth. Nine in the morning, at the latest. At the county airport. Thorny would come to pick up her up at a time they agreed on. If they agreed. All this was important to remember.

Astrid knew that and wrote the date and time and 'Trip' on her pad painstakingly. Thorny got up and went to her side to look at the notepad.

"Yes," he confirmed. "Trip.' Good. Nothing else. 'Eighteenth.' Right. Let's say that I'll come here at seven o'clock. Sharp. Can you be ready?"

"Of course." And she wrote "Thorny/Th."

"I'll give you a call every day, in case you think of something I can help with," Thorny offered. "Or if you change your mind. You can, of course."

"I know," she answered impatiently, "but first I need to see… I can ask, uh, Laura to take me. I need to see, what's his name? The one who does legal things?" She strove vainly for the word,

"A lawyer?" Thorny prompted.

"Yes."

"But you can't tell him about the plan! Do you understand?"

"Of course I do!" she answered abruptly. She made a further note on her pad and then put it down. "I feel better now." It appeared that in a way she did. "I can't stay here, you know. I don't want to. Not anymore." She sounded perfectly calm, perfectly resolved.

Richard nodded, drew his right hand from his pocket with his car key in it. "I have to go. I've got an appointment downtown in about…" He consulted his watch again. "…about thirty minutes, and parking may not be easy. With a plane you know where to put it," he added wryly. "So anyway, I've gotta go. Thorny has his truck out front, so he can stay on. Anyway, it was nice meeting you," he said to Astrid, with oddly formal finality.

She nodded in response, but as Richard stepped towards the door, she stood up from her chair. "I have a picture to show you," she announced, and walked past them to an end table at the farther end of the sofa. "Here," she picked up a wood-framed portrait that was set just in front of a lamp and held it up in front of her for both to see. Richard turned from the door for a better look. It was the portrait of a young woman with short, dark brown hair in three-quarter profile, a classic portrait of a very pretty woman, confident in her particular beauty. "This is my daughter. My daughter," she repeated. "I think I told you…" But the picture wavered in her hands. "I can't seem to… she has four children. But I can't…"

All at once she dropped the picture face up on the sofa. Although it did not hit the cat, that prudent animal slid to the floor and walked away towards the hall door, its tail flowing behind it.

"Go away!" she ordered them unexpectedly. "I didn't ask you to come here. Leave me alone!" she followed up when neither of them moved. Thorny stood rooted by the other end of the sofa, amazed and uncertain. Richard took a step back to the door. "Go away! Just go away!" she ordered them again, angry and yet glassy-eyed with tears. Then she stooped, picked up the picture from the sofa, and threw it angrily face down on the floor at her feet. Thorny winced, but the frame was stout and merely thunked as it hit, mocking her useless rage. "I just want it to be over!" She looked at Thorny accusingly. "Don't you understand?"

Thorny, for the moment, was more concerned about the fate of the picture than with whatever it was that she expected him to understand. He was imagining that her next attack would be to smash it with her foot, so he stepped forward, stooped quickly, and picked it up. Then, not sure what he should do with it, he put the picture face down on the coffee table in front of the sofa, where he realized it was still within her reach if she should make another assault. But as he had done the best he could think of, he let it lie. No, he did not understand why she was enraged at her daughter. And why had the rage hit her so suddenly? If Astrid Williamson had been a close friend or relative, he might have tried putting his arm around her, but there wasn't that sort of familiarity between them. So he wavered, embarrassed for her, for himself, and particularly for Richard, who could hardly be expected to do anything, but stand as he was, one hand on the doorknob, exchanging an equally puzzled and helpless look with Thorny.

All at once Astrid sank down on the sofa where the portrait had been moments before and bent her head into her hands and shook with crying. She hadn't looked especially thin before, but now her shoulders seemed bony under her dress, as if over the frame of a wooden hanger.

"There now." Thorny took out his pocket handkerchief and, taking a step forward, held it out to her, as one might offer a treat to a dog that might or might not prove to be friendly. "It's clean," he added, but she made no move to accept his offer, did not even look in his direction. "Everything'll be all right," he tried to sound encouraging, as he returned it to his pocket. "Things'll work out. Can I call someone for you?" He clutched at new thought. "You told me you had a helper. Should I give her a call?"

"No, you don't understand! You don't!" She looked up then and accused him with her eyes, frantic as a rabbit running at a fence. Her cheeks were wet.

"I really have to leave," Richard said from across the room. "I'm sorry you're upset, but I don't know…" Thorny looked at him and nodded. "I have to go," Richard repeated, while Astrid bowed her head again, rejecting them both.

But when Richard pulled open the door, there was someone standing exactly in front of him, clearly about to come in, a heavyset, blondish young woman, carrying a bulbous shoulder bag.

"Excuse me," were her opening words, pronounced at just the same time as Richard's own excuse. And then, "What's the matter with Mrs. W?" she asked, as she saw Astrid bent over like a wilted flower beyond him. Thorny backed away from the sofa, glad that someone seemed to have come to the rescue, but not sure who it might be.

Richard stood back to let her pass by.

Ignoring Thorny, she went to Astrid, sat down beside her and put one arm around her.

"There, there, Mrs. W. What is it? You can tell me."

"My daughter…" She looked toward the newcomer, her cheeks glistening. Begging and ashamed at the same time.

"You mean Lydia? Is she all right?" Joyce was instantly concerned.

"Yes, yes of course. Lydia. I remember now. Maman liked that name. You see?" Leaning forward, she picked up the picture from the coffee table and turned it over. "Such a pretty girl and artistic too. She favors Charles, don't you think?" She looked up at Thorny, smiling. "He was my husband," she went on to explain. "He was a professor. Did you know that?"

"Yes," Thorny confirmed. "I knew him. He was a wonderful man."

"Yes. He's gone, you know. Passed away last month. No, no, I mean last year."

She sniffed noisily. Now would have been the time for Thorny's handkerchief, but the newcomer, releasing her arm from Astrid's shoulder, fumbled in her bag and brought out a small packet of tissues, from which she pulled one free.

"Here you are," the young woman assured her, handing it to her and dropping the packet back into her bag. "Everything's okay now." She looked from Astrid to Thorny, as if for some direction or explanation, but unsure how to frame the question, or whether she ought to.

"I'm Thorny" he thought to tell her. "Kind of a family friend," he added. "Maybe she told you I was coming."

"Yeah, I think she did. Anyway, it was on her notepad. I'm kind of like her helper."

"Then you're Joyce."

"That's right. Yeah, I should've told you right off. Sorry."

"No problem. Glad you got here."

"Anyhow…" Joyce turned to Astrid. "How about if I make us some tea? How about that?"

"I don't know," she answered uncertainly, then more decidedly. "Yes, tea. That'd be nice. Maybe some for Thorny and there's another gentleman here with him." She looked towards the door, but that man was gone.

ASTRID AND LAUREN DISCUSS CREAMY

When Astrid Williamson opened the door to Lauren, she seemed more composed and alert than in some weeks. She was properly dressed in a print blouse and dark blue skirt and sensible leather walking shoes. There was something teacherly about her appearance, a relic, perhaps, of old habit.

"I'm so glad you could come over today," she said as she ushered Lauren into the room. "I know Thursday isn't our usual day, but Ed What's-his-name was busy on Friday, and I really needed to... It *is* Thursday, isn't it?" she added, turning and looking sharply at Lauren.

Because of Astrid's acknowledged memory problems, Lauren wasn't sure if she was joking or not.

"It is," she answered neutrally. "Anyway, it was fine because I didn't have anything else on for today." Lauren had thought of doing some gardening and had nearly turned her down when Astrid called on the previous afternoon, but something like guilt for having changed her own schedule last week urged her to assent and especially when Astrid said that she was planning a trip and needed to get something "settled" before she left. She had just made an appointment with a lawyer and needed to know if Lauren could drive her. Otherwise, she'd take a taxi. She didn't sound in the least confused, but quite determined.

As there was still some spare time before the appointment, the two women sat down, Astrid in her usual chair and Lauren across from her on the sofa. Creamy was on the back of the sofa, but at the far end, her front paws tucked under in cat-fashion, meditating with half-closed eyes.

"It's nice you're going on a trip," Lauren observed with conventional correctness, although she was somewhat puzzled. "Are you going to see your daughter?"

"No, no. I'm going on an airplane. Just for one day really. With a friend. Thorny Thornton. Maybe you know him."

Lauren shook her head, but when Astrid described him a little and said he was a ma son, Lauren recognized him as the subject of the article that had appeared in the Tuesday edition of the paper, the one about the donation of his house to the Native Plant Society. Which she might not have noticed if Matt hadn't been the photographer. Everything Matt did was important.

"No, I don't know him," she emended, "but I know who he is. Must be a very nice guy." Where, she wondered, would Astrid be going with this Thorny person?

"He isn't a pilot, is he?" she ventured. There had been no mention of flying as one of his talents.

"Oh, no. Just a friend, that's all. Anyway, there's just two things…" Astrid pressed on quickly, looking at her notepad. "I mean two other things I need you to help me with. If you can."

"Yes?" Lauren answered agreeably.

"Well, first of all, there's a box of iris. Roots, uh, what do you call them…?"

"Rhizomes? The other day I saw the box on the porch."

"Yes, that's it. Yes, by the front of the house. Thorny gave them to me, but I can't use them. They're special, so I wondered if maybe you could take them with you when you go home."

"What a nice offer! I mean really. I love iris. My garden's pretty full, but I'm sure I can find a spot somewhere. Bearded iris. There isn't anything like them." Lauren wasn't feigning her gratitude, only wondering where to fit them in. Her mind quickly toured the beds of her back yard where she had iris already, but could maybe add more by taking out some salvias. "Oh, thank you. That's very nice!"

Astrid glanced at her notepad. "And I need you to take Creamy."

"Well, I… we haven't had a pet in the house since David's dog, Rudy, died, but I suppose…Only didn't you say you're just going out for the day?"

"No, not about that," Astrid said brusquely. "I mean take her. I mean keep her. I can't take care of her anymore. Just can't. I forget things. And what will happen to Creamy if they take me to one of those nursing places?" She ended with the old question as if it were a new one.

"But Joyce, surely Joyce would like to have her."

"No," she said firmly. "Joyce can't have her because she lives in a rental place. No pets. It's the rule!" She sounded almost annoyed at Lauren's ignorance.

"Okay, I see. What about your daughter?" Lauren was at the same time asking herself if she wanted a cat, but couldn't really answer. She liked Creamy, but she hadn't had a cat since childhood. Would it be nice? She hadn't thought to ask how Matt felt about cats. "Wouldn't Lydia—"

"Oh no! My daughter, she has four children. You know that. They'd only bother Creamy. Pull her tail. Who knows? I think children should have pets, but not Creamy. She's used to me. To a quiet house. You don't have children."

"Not living at home."

"Anyway, you know what I mean. Lydia gave Creamy to me. Did I tell you that?"

"I think you did."

"After Charles died. She said I should have some company, and that was nice. But it's not working anymore. I have to put my affairs in order." She considered her notepad again. "I have to see Ed Duncan today. Didn't I tell you that? It's written down..."

As Astrid considered her notes, Lauren thought about Creamy, but her eyes wandered to the coffee table, which she noted was unusually bare. No magazines.

Only today's newspaper and an old book with a tattered leather binding. Poetry maybe?

"At two o'clock," Astrid announced.

"Yes, I remember." Lauren had, by chance, arrived quite early.

"He's my, what's the word? Attorney. I've been thinking about fixing my will. You know Joyce doesn't have much money."

"Yes, I know."

"I want to leave her something. In my will. She's been so good to me. Like a daughter almost. Of course, Lydia will have this house, and some, uh, stocks, and my personal things and all those books." She nodded in the direction of the shelves. "Some upstairs too. That's all arranged. But Joyce, she needs some money. To have her teeth fixed. You've seen her teeth.'

"Yes."

"And she wants to find her son. She had a baby a long time ago. But she had to give him up for... what's the word?"

Lauren gave her time to think, but to no avail. "You mean adoption?"

"Yes. She wants to find him. She told me all about it, poor thing. It's not a secret," she assured Lauren. "She wants to find out how he is and tell him about, well, what happened. But there's some problem.

She needs help with that. Maybe if she had one of those things, like a typewriter."

"A computer?" Lauren offered.

"Yes, of course. A computer. My daughter wanted me to have one of those, but I couldn't make sense of it. I said, 'Give it to Wendy.' But Joyce could buy a computer and learn how… She's smart enough, you know." She looked at her notepad again.

"That's a great idea. Maybe I could help her to learn it. Just the basics." Lauren had never pretended to be adept. That was where David came in.

"I have a cage," Astrid observed abruptly, looking up.

"A cage?"

"For Creamy, so you can take her with you. When we get back from my appointment. And her dish and comb. And extra food. It's dry, not messy. And there's enough for quite a long time. Creamy's very quiet, not like some of those, those yowly cats. And she doesn't scratch the furniture. She has a, what do you call it? One of those things for cat claws. You know what I mean." Astrid began to seem exhausted from searching.

"You mean a scratching post?"

"Yes! And I have one of those boxes on the back porch, for poopy, but I let her go out in the back yard. Unless it's raining. She mostly goes outside to do her business. But she doesn't wander." She was doing what she could to sell the product. "You don't live on a busy street, do you?"

"No, not very, just a neighborhood. It's pretty quiet." Lauren considered for a moment, trying to bring logic to the question. "She doesn't catch birds, does she? I have a feeder."

Astrid shook her head. "I don't think so. She brought me a mouse a couple of times."

"I see." Still pondering. Although she hadn't yet agreed to take Creamy, it was looking more and more as if she had. It came to her that she really missed their little dog, Rudy, the irrepressible terrier, and the many backyard games with ball or Frisbee. How they used to stand together on the back deck and cheer him on. Even Harris. He was at his best when David was young, but now… And at the moment, Lauren realized she wouldn't miss Harris in the poignant way she did Rudy. What a thought! But still it was thinkable.

"I think Creamy would be fine," she conceded finally. *Not a bad thing really. Harris shouldn't mind. He's not home much anyway. Matt will like her. He'll take pictures. Lady with Cat. Or how about Naked Lady With Cat? But watch out for those claws. Maybe naked isn't a good idea.* Lauren returned from her vignette. "If you're sure…"

"About what?"

"About Creamy. You'll miss her."

"No, it's fine. I'll be fine." Astrid put her notepad down beside the telephone with the relieved air of a problem finally solved and stood up. Lauren got up too, stepped to the end of the sofa and scratched the cat briefly behind the ears. Creamy was agreeably soft to the touch, and her ready purr was soothing. Why do cats purr when it's dogs who love you? Then she followed Astrid into the kitchen to start collecting Creamy's paraphernalia.

ASTRID CALLS LYDIA

When Astrid came back from her appointment with Ed Duncan, she felt exhausted, but she also felt good. She didn't think she had acted at all crazy because she had her questions carefully written down for Ed to go over. About reviewing the trust for her grandchildren and about, what did he call it? A, uh, legacy for Joyce. Astrid had written Joyce's name, address, and phone number, but seemed alarmed not to have her Social Security number. Ed said not to worry. He promised to take care of everything. She just signed where he told her to sign. It seemed to go quite well.

But when Lauren had gone, taking both Creamy and the iris rhizomes, the house seemed truly emptied, as though Astrid herself were no longer living there, like another piece of furniture, waiting to be taken away by the movers. She considered the calendar inside her notepad and counted the days to the one she had circled. Ten days. It seemed a long time, but yet she still had things to do. Above all, she wanted to see Lydia.

She made a note on her pad. It consisted of the names of her grandchildren, just to be sure, and why she wanted Lydia to visit. Not the real reason, of course. That was important. That was vital. Or Lydia would stop her. With all that Astrid forgot, she had to especially remember that the flight was not a secret, only the purpose. No one could know except Thorny and Richard. No one could know, she repeated like a mantra, except Thorny and Richard. For Lydia, she had to say it was about her will. Which it was mostly. She carefully emptied her mind of everything but that thought and the telephone.

Astrid pushed the button that Lauren had programmed for her a while back, after explaining how much easier it was than trying to remember the number or bothering to look it up for every call. Lydia would be button one, even though that wasn't a number she used very much. Joyce was button two, and Lauren button three. Lauren wrote them down and taped the note to the side of her telephone.

Astrid pushed button number one. *No one can know except Thorny. It's all about the will.* On the other end a telephone was ringing. No answer. Then…

"Hello?' the voice questioned, a little girl's.

"Hello. Wendy." Astrid had prepared. "Is that you?"

"Yes."

"Wendy, this is Grandma."

"Yes, I know. Hi, Grandma."

"Hi. How are you, dear?"

"I'm fine. I had a cold last week. I got it from Jeffrey, but now Allen's got it. How are you?"

"I'm all right. It wasn't very nice of you to give your cold to Allen, was it?" Allen, she knew without consulting her list, was one of the twins. She was doing well. She was even being a little funny.

"I didn't do it on purpose."

"Of course not."

"But maybe he deserved it for messing up my science chart with his new crayons."

"Your chart?"

"Yes, it was really good — at first. It was about where our food comes from, I mean how far away, how much better it is to eat the food from around where you live. Besides the farmers market is really fun. Mom takes us." Wendy paused, as if it has just occurred to her. "Do you want to talk to Mom?"

"Well, yes." Astrid consulted her notepad briefly. "If she's handy."

"She's in the back yard, working on some furniture, but I can take her the phone. Can you hold on?"

"Yes, of course, but…" She worried because it seemed like this wasn't the best time, but how could she know?

There was a sound of moving feet, then a door opening and closing. Astrid couldn't remember when she had last talked to Lydia, but she thought it was quite awhile, Lydia having let her know that phone calls interrupted a very busy day. Well, of course they did. She knew that Lydia and the children had come to visit her around Christmas. They brought some presents, and she had given some. For the most part she couldn't remember either what she had given or received, but she knew that Wendy had made her a collage of their family, a group picture compiled from various photographs, it being impossible, as Wendy adultly explained, to get that many people to sit for a portrait at the same time. Al's picture obviously came from a real estate brochure and looked very nice indeed, even if phony as anything.

Lauren had helped Astrid to put it in a store-bought frame, and Joyce had hung it in her bedroom. Wendy had talent, just like her mother. Pray God she doesn't throw it away.

Then she heard Wendy saying, "Mama, it's Gramma."

A somewhat anxious voice came on the line. "Yes, Mama? What is it?" As if she anticipated a crisis.

"It's all right," Astrid reassured her daughter nervously. "I just needed to ask you something. I'm sorry if I interrupted…"

"I'm painting a set of table and chairs we got for the twins at a yard sale."

"Oh. That sounds nice."

"I mean I'm busy, Mama. I haven't finished the chair legs yet. What is it? What do you want?" At the final words she seemed to soften her tone, but not her rhetoric.

"Well, I'm… Lydia. I'm sorry, but I need you to come here, just for a little while."

"What sort of 'little while' did you have in mind?" Now she was cautious.

"Oh, just an hour. Maybe two." It wasn't a question she had prepared for.

"Really Mama, I told you the last time you called that I couldn't make it down there until the kids had started school. I thought you understood that. So okay, school has started," she admitted with clear reluctance, "but Allen has a cold."

"I didn't mean… Maybe it won't last very long," she replied, chastened.

"Yes, I think it's a little better," Lydia conceded. "But what's so godawful important? Can't you tell me on the phone or write to me or something? I wish you'd try to use e-mail. It'd simplify everything, you know."

Astrid shivered a little, remembering her experience with the small computer Lydia had given her. "Just use it for e-mail," she said at the time. So simple. Later on Laura had tried to explain it, but it never seemed to make sense. No wonder Lydia was mad at her.

"It's just that… I'm going on a little trip, just for a day, but I really need to settle some things before I go. That's all. I have things to give you. And about my will. I saw Ed, what's-his-name, today. It's about that."

"Can't you make photocopies and put the stuff in the mail?"

"I need to explain. I just wish you could come for a little while. I know it's a long drive, but I do need to see you."

"It doesn't make sense, Mama, for me to spend three hours on the road to see you for an hour. Now, does it? And that's about all the time I could take, even if the kids go to the after-school program. I've been putting off things just about all summer. I mean I've got other things to take care of, and the house is a disaster. Al's boys have been here for two weeks, damn it! They just left last weekend because, thank gawd, school was starting. Fat, teen-age boys. Skateboarding, playing stupid video games, and my boys think they're terrific. They come from another planet, Mama. You don't know what it's been like!"

"No, I suppose not, but Lydia, please don't be mad. It's…it's very important. I have some things I need to give you before I go."

"When are you going?" came a voice now relatively resigned, but not happy.

Astrid regarded her calendar again with its plainly circled date. "It's, uh…the eighteenth. That's a week from Saturday. I'm going in a private plane. It's such a nice offer. And I've never done that before, I mean that kind of plane."

"Yes, well, that sounds very nice, but how long will you be gone? Maybe I can come down later."

"No, that won't work!" Astrid protested, startled. "I need to see you before I leave. There's some business about my will. I have a, uh… what do you call it? A…."

She was getting very entangled in her efforts to remember what to say and what not to say, and the words she needed fled like mice.

"A what?"

"You know, for you and the children. A legal thing."

"A trust?"

"Yes, that's it! A trust. I need to tell you about it."

"I already know about it, Mama," she said with impatient patience.

"Yes, of course, but it isn't only about the trust. I've just made a few changes. I went to see the lawyer." She faltered, as if walking in a marsh.

"Yes, you told me. Ed Duncan."

"Yes, that's right."

"What changes?" Lydia asked, or demanded.

"Well, for the children, of course. For their college. And for Joyce. You know Joyce."

"Of course I do."

"Yes, well, I decided to leave her something. And for the children, as I said. Not him…" she added, declining to use a name that she actually remembered.

Sighing with resignation, Lydia agreed. "I suppose I could come down next Thursday, not this week. I'm sure Allen will be back in school by then." She seemed to ponder. "Yeah, that should work. As soon as I see the kids off to school. I could be there by around ten-thirty."

"Maybe you could stay for lunch. If you want," Astrid added. "I mean if you have the time."

"Yes, maybe. I'll see. Is that all? I gotta go paint. My brush is drying."

Astrid's hand shook the notepad a little. "I think that's all," she concluded.

"Okay. Well, bye Mama. See you Thursday. That's the…just a minute…the sixteenth. You better write it down."

"Yes, of course I will. Yes, well, bye dear. I love you, Lydia," she added, trying to make amends for her intrusion.

"Yes, Mama, I love you too." Lydia offered the ritual reply.

"Love to the children. Please say goodbye to Wendy."

"Of course. Listen, I have to go and paint."

"Yes, I understand. Bye, bye."

Astrid didn't wait for any other word, if there was one, but set down her notepad and shakily put the receiver back in its cradle, looking to be sure it was properly set. Then she sighed a little sigh, picked up the notepad again, and turned over a page. She suddenly remembered that Friday was Laura's day, but that was changed, of course, since she had come today. But Friday of next week…she would not need Laura. Joyce would help her. Maybe she should call Laura about that. Button three on the machine. Remembering, she wrote down "Lydia, Thurs. 16th" at the top of the clean page, and then picked up the phone again. *Need to call Laura. What was it again? Button three. Button three.*

As Astrid finished her conversation with Lydia, Matt Ramirez was picking up a call from his wife, Dolores. She was almost too excited to be coherent. She had just heard from their daughter, Stephanie.

MATT HOLDS A BABY

Dolores begged Matt to come home immediately. "Stephanie needs us," she insisted. She would explain everything when he got there. But he told her that first he had to go to the district office to take pictures of a group of newly hired teachers, including a new counselor and a vice-principal. He asked for a summary of Stephanie's message and got it. It was dire enough, but didn't seem like something he needed to rush home for.

The new counselor turned out to be a young, bilingual and very pretty Latina. Matt quite naturally found her attractive, but at the same time he felt annoyed that this young woman was succeeding at something useful, while his own smart, beautiful daughter was not. He tried not to resent the young counselor for being a success. Who was her father? How had he pulled this off? Did he even have much to do with it? At least Stephanie wasn't in jail. Be grateful for small favors and all that.

The new vice-principal, on the other hand, was a pleasant, stocky, middle-aged fellow, who reminded Matt somewhat of the vice-principal at his own high school. Except more pleasant. Vice-principals back in those days were hired goons. It was part of their job description.

Thanks to Didi's call, the past and present were folding together and kept folding as Matt edited the pictures on his computer. Not much to do there. Just a bunch of people who seemed pleased with their jobs or at least happy to have them.

Didi hadn't told him much on the phone except that Stephanie had called about her baby. They were suddenly grandparents without benefit of expectation.

He reviewed their brief dialogue.

"You did say, a baby…?" he had asked her.

"Yes, a girl. She's in Boyle Heights in a duplex. She wants us to come down right away."

"She actually gave you an address?"

"Of course. Maybe we could get a flight tonight…"

"I don't see how. It's been a long day, and suddenly it's getting a lot longer. Look, I'm about to go to an appointment. Have to. It's my job. By the time I'd get home and we got to LA even if we could get a flight—it'd be…" He had paused to calculate. "Around two in the morning, and we wouldn't have a place to sleep. I presume that Steph doesn't have a guest room, and I trust she wouldn't be awake, unless she's walking the floor."

"We could stay with Raquel," Didi said, referring to a cousin who also lived in Boyle Heights. "I already called her to see if it was okay." Apparently it was. "But you're right," Dolores had conceded. "We couldn't show up in the middle of the night. But we can stay with her tomorrow night."

"Okay. I'll get home as soon as I can," he had told her. "I gotta go." Now the group picture was ready, and he'd explained to the news editor that he had to go out of town on family business for a couple of days. He said that Jim Johnson, the intern, could fill in. Jim knew his business well enough, but Matt hoped he wouldn't need to fill in precisely because Jim did know his business, which made Matt a little concerned about the day when they decided that Jim could do his work at a lower salary. He didn't think that day could be very far off. Then he accessed flight reservations on his computer and found what he wanted, not really wanting to go at all. Every thought was chaos.

Leaving the building, Matt carried feelings composed of anger and excitement. There might be a reconciliation with Stephanie, but he didn't count on it, and yes, for a moment he'd nearly forgotten that he had planned on seeing Lauren tomorrow. They were both so eager. He got in the Honda, which was hot, rolled down the windows, and dialed her number on his cell phone. What time was it? Just past five. A lot of traffic. Four rings and a voice-mail answer. "You have reached Lauren Hamilton at 415…etc. Please leave a message." Dammit.

"This is Matt Ramirez," he said in his most formal manner. "About our appointment for tomorrow. I'm afraid I have to go to LA for a couple of days. It's about my family. So I'll call when I get back to reschedule. Really sorry about the change." He didn't want to leave too personal a message, even on her cell, so he had to trust her to understand, which he did. She'd have to know that the cancellation was not his choice. That was the great thing about it. About them. Trust. You have to believe in something, and Matt chose to believe in that.

"It's an answer to prayer," was the first thing Didi said when he walked into the kitchen from the garage. Although she was standing by the counter, chopping a tomato for a salad, it was as though she had been lying in wait, and although Matt would have been willing to share her excitement, there was something about casting it as a divine intervention that turned it sour.

"Is it?" He never really intended to openly belittle her faith, but somehow it came to his mouth naturally, like the curving tail of a disturbed scorpion. I'm glad you're happy," he tried belatedly to correct himself, but just missed sounding sincere.

"Matt, don't be that way. Please!" She rinsed her hands at the sink and dried them while she was talking. Then she went to him as he stood impassively by the door. "You know how I've prayed for this, for years now, ever since the day you…well, since she left."

Awkwardly, she put her arms around his waist, and half-heartedly he embraced her around the shoulders. Didi, he admitted, was a good person. He didn't exactly feel guilty about having ceased to love her, but did feel a need, at times, to explain why. Although she had gone to fat, her face was still pretty, and although she was practically a religious fanatic, yet he accepted that she had always been devout.

She had only turned down sex when it was "the wrong time of the month," but at times she seemed more than willing, especially when she actually hoped to get pregnant. But now, all at once, he understood that it hadn't helped that she had also ceased loving him. Neither said so, but the fact stood between them like the wall that divides two countries who are not at war, but mutually suspicious.

Matt couldn't keep out of his mind the exuberant sexual experience he had had with Lauren a week ago. The sheer perfection of every step, something like remembered music. A kind of ode to joy. Yes, that was it. He had never thought of Beethoven's Ninth as erotic before, but now? One helluva climax. *Freude! Freude!*

Matt pulled his mind away from the warm bed with something like the soft tear of Velcro. Then he gave Didi a squeeze and dropped his arms. She had no option but to step away.

"I told you. She has a baby. A little girl. She wants us to come."

"When was it… she born?"

"Day before yesterday, at four in the afternoon. They kept Stephanie overnight and sent her home yesterday. She's fine. She said she would've called from the hospital, but she didn't have a phone card."

"Don't they reverse charges anymore?"

"Matt, I dunno. She was woozy, I expect. But she wants us to come right away."

"And the baby… It, she has a father?"

"Well, of course, but not the guy she lives with. She'll explain."

Matt rolled his eyes. "So what does she want from us?" Acerbic again in spite of himself. "To share her joy? I suppose she needs money."

"No, she didn't ask for money." Dolores defended her daughter readily. "Of course we should give her something. She said that Medi-Cal paid for the delivery, but she had to buy some things for the baby."

"Okay, sure," he said with mild concession. "I got us a reservation on the morning commute flight. Seven AM. So we better set the alarm. We can grab the Airporter at 5:15 and rent a car in LA." Matt circled Didi and went to the refrigerator for a beer. Dismissed, she went back to the counter and began to toss the salad.

"Couldn't you maybe cancel it? We could leave right after supper and drive through the night. We've done that. Not much traffic. We'd get there a little sooner."

Didi sounded like a cajoling child.

Matt sighed a deliberately audible sigh. "Look, it's been a long day, and I'm not up to it. Any time we drove through the night to get to LA, we were both a lot younger. Now one or the other of us would fall asleep on I-5, and we'd never get there at all. When was the last time…?"

"Okay," she answered a question that was largely rhetorical. "Angelica's wedding. I know, but you had to work Saturday that time and—"

"And I said never again."

Matt cracked open his beer and took a sip, contemplating. "So why is she so hot for us to come?" he ventured again. Apprehension was threading into his thoughts. "A christening already?"

"Well, Matt…" Didi's tentativeness revealed that his apprehension was justified. She set down the salad bowl and turned to him. "She's talking about us taking the baby. She says she can't keep her."

Matt considered the print on the label of the can he was holding: Rainier…best taste…

"What?" he said. Forewarned is not necessarily forearmed.

━━━◆━━━

The duplex where Stephanie lived on Pointer Street was predictably small and run-down, but relatively uncluttered, due to the real lack of material possessions. Stephanie answered the door in person, dressed in a loose cotton print bathrobe that oddly became her—as everything she wore became her—hugged each of them in a perfunctory way and then went back to a sofa bed that, unfolded, took up a fair portion of the single room that served as living, bedroom and dining area. The dining area consisted of a card table and four chairs that actually appeared to be a matched set. A TV set squatted on a box at the foot of the bed. The baby wasn't in the bed, but in an old style suitcase, from which the lid had been cut off, resting between two of the chairs. The suitcase reminded Matt of the one his maternal grandfather had carried into their house when he came to visit from Uruapan and never happened to go back home. They threw the suitcase away when he died eight years later. Perfect quiet from that quarter indicated that the baby was asleep.

"Thanks for coming," Stephanie conceded. "I'm glad you could."

She didn't look different to Matt from the last time he had seen her, disappearing into the car of that creep she called Mike, except that she seemed thinner and, having no make-up, seemed pale. When she looked up at them from the bed, with her dark, sleep-starved eyes, Matt had the old urge to rescue her from the net she had put around herself, and had to tell himself again that there was no point in trying. "That's an interesting crib," he observed without approaching the baby and trying not to sound judgmental, but rather appreciative of their ingenuity.

"Yeah, it works," Stephanie agreed readily. "Manny an' me, we found it at a yard sale. Don't worry, Mama. I cleaned it up really good,

160

and the blankets are clean too. I got those at Goodwill and washed them, even though they looked clean already, but you can never tell. So don't worry about germs or anything."

"Oh Stephanie!" Didi seemed to waver between addressing her daughter and going to the baby. "You'll be such a good mother. Honestly! You just have to try."

"Let's not get into that. I told you on the phone. When we found out for sure that the baby wasn't Manny's… I agreed with him that why should he raise a kid that's not even his when he can't afford to raise one that is? I mean, sure, he's willing to have a kid someday, when he gets a little savings, but he just started at the body shop, and when I get a job, it'll probably be minimum wage for a while, so who's gonna take care of the baby? Aunt Angelica's got three kids of her own, and she lives across town anyway, and Raquel works full time. I'd have to pay for daycare, and you know how that is. The system's made so you can't afford children. That's just the way it works. I mean I don't wanna starve, and I don't want the kid to starve either. Maybe someday it'll be different, but not now."

Matt would have liked to deny her logic, but couldn't. Stephanie had, as usual, managed to be both stupid and smart at the same time.

"But Steph… any baby—" Didi began.

"Mama, don't make me sorry I called you, okay? I was planning to just give her up for adoption when I thought of you guys. And I just thought maybe you'd want her and maybe she'd be better off with her grandparents. Okay, so we didn't get along, but it never meant that I didn't trust you to do the right thing. I know you tried an' all that. Anyway, I talked to a social worker and told her I wanted to see you before I made the final decision. But I can't keep her. Can't."

"Who's her father?" asked Matt. "Maybe he wants her." As a father, this fact could not escape his attention altogether.

"Well, I guess I'm not really sure. I know that sounds crappy, but there was this big party in Covina, which I guess is where it happened, because we were all pretty high and not using condoms all the time. And it could've been Miguel or Georgie or somebody…" Didi sighed. Matt growled, just audibly. "Don't get excited. It wasn't like I was raped or anything. We were just high. I didn't think I was pregnant right away because I always had kind of irregular periods, and by the time I decided to get a pregnancy test, I'd moved in with Manny, so I thought maybe it was his kid. He wasn't crazy about the baby, but he said it was okay. If it was his."

"Why weren't you on the pill?" This coming from Didi was startling.

"I was for a while, but it's not free. In fact, prescription drugs, they cost a bundle."

"Okay. And what about other drugs?" Matt couldn't stop himself from asking.

"Matt," said Didi.

Stephanie shrugged, as if it were a question beneath her dignity to answer, but finally she did. "I've been totally clean ever since I found out about the baby. I'm not as altogether stupid as you think. And Manny's clean too. Not even pot anymore. That's one of the reasons I like him. He's not screwed up like most of 'em. He's okay. His dad was an illegal from El Salvador, for crissake. He hasn't had an easy life, and I don' wanna take away whatever chance he's got."

"Do you love him?" It was Didi who asked the question.

"I guess sort of, yeah." Her tone bordered on a kind of tenderness that Matt noted with relief. Maybe she wasn't showing a maternal feeling for her baby, but he felt there was something of real caring for this boy Manny. It seemed to him that a feeling of protectiveness was always at the core of love.

"Okay…well…that's good," he approved neutrally, not wanting Stephanie to regret her admission.

For lack of further conversation, he and Didi both went to the suitcase crib in the corner and stood looking down.

"Oooohhhh…!" It was Didi who uttered the time-worn exclamation of spontaneous, irrepressible, awestruck, tender feeling. "Oh, Steph!"

Matt also stood amazed, but silent. The baby was soft to look at— black-haired and creamy in complexion, not red. Though tiny, she didn't really look newborn, but already well entered into life. She slept on her back with her small fists lightly curled, baby fashion, her head slightly to one side, her eyebrow ridges ready for their dark brows to happen, her small mouth with a glisten of drool at one corner. She was swaddled in a light flannel blanket that might have been yellow at one time, judging from smudges of remaining color.

Matt swallowed, tried to think why he felt so painfully happy, why he was so near crying. He didn't care anything about being a grandfather, had never even thought about it. Was he seeing Stephanie as a baby? No, it wasn't that. Was it just the baby's own minuscule perfection? Maybe. Maybe in part. And then it came to him. He was seeing Marilu, who was also perfect and who died for no reason. This little human looked so like her. Like a return.

He stood transfixed until he heard the sound of rustling behind and turned to see Stephanie getting out of bed, untying the sash on her robe. Her belly still bulged a little, but was already forgetting the form it had carried.

"Mama?" she asked. "How long does this damn bleeding go on?"

"Oh…" Didi turned to her, pondering. "It's kind of like a period. It just gets lighter every day, and maybe in a week or so it's all over. I don't quite remember. If you think it's not stopping, you should go back to the hospital. Did you have an episiotomy?"

"Yeah."

"Be sure to get the heat light on it every day."

"Sure, I know. Listen, I've gotta go to the bathroom, and then I was wondering if you could go shopping with me. I need some stuff. The store's only about six blocks from here." She passed the crib, only grazing the occupant with a glance as she went by, and paused by the door that evidently opened on the bathroom. "And Daddy, could you fix the clog in the kitchen sink? It doesn't hardly drain at all. Manny put Drano in it, but it didn't make any difference."

"I don't have any tools," he protested, still intent on the form in the crib.

"Yeah, right. You can ask the guy next door. He told Manny he could borrow his wrench, but Manny had to go to work. He said if that didn't work, to call Roto-Rooter or somebody. I gotta go…" And she went in and closed the door. In a minute they heard the sound of peeing.

Matt and Didi looked at one another, sharing a real moment for the first time in weeks or months or maybe years.

"She's so beautiful," Didi said needlessly, but humanly.

"Yes."

"I've never seen a baby so…"

"Yes."

"Except, you know…"

"Marilu." He hadn't spoken her name to Dolores in a long time.

"Yes," she agreed in a moment of rare communion.

And they continued to stare wordlessly at the sleeping infant.

When Stephanie came out of the bathroom, she explained her errand. "I gotta get more diapers and some stuff for us, or are you eating with Raquel?"

"I guess we'll have lunch with you," Didi answered. "Raquel invited us for supper. You and Manny too, if you want to."

"Nah. I'll see her some other time. I'll get something on for Manny when he gets back."

It occurred to Matt that they might not even meet Manny. He thought he wanted to, but he wasn't sure. He wasn't very sure about anything just then.

"You're breast feeding her, aren't you?" Didi asked her.

"Sure, but I told you already that I can't keep her, so I need to buy some formula, too."

"Yes, of course."

"Daddy, will you go see about the wrench while I get dressed? That guy's okay. He's nice. His name is Arnie. He'll be there. I didn't hear him going out, and you hear pretty much everything in a duplex. You can stay with the baby while Mama and I go to the store. Do you want to drive?" She addressed her mother. "It's not far. Or I can drive."

"I could drive," Didi answered hesitantly, "but maybe you better. Because you know where it is."

"Listen," Matt suddenly felt anxious. "What am I supposed to do if the baby wakes up? She might be hungry."

"Nah, I just fed her a little while ago. I got really drippy breasts. Mama, how long does it take for your milk to stop?"

"I don't know," Didi answered wearily, and Matt saw that she had tears running down her face. He put one arm around her shoulders.

"It's okay," he said. "It's okay. Really. Look, I'll go get the wrench."

Arnie looked a little sleepy when he came to the door, though it was late in the morning. He was a short, balding guy in a tee shirt and jeans, but sleepy or not, he was nice enough to assure Matt, in what might have been a slight Mexican accent, that he had really been awake.

"I work the pm shift over at the hospital," he nodded the direction over his right shoulder. "In maintenance," he said. "I'm not a nurse or lab tech or anything like that. Or chief of surgery." He smiled wryly. "But I can sure fix a wheelchair."

"Then you'd have a wrench. I guess. My daughter said you would."

"Oh sure. I'll give you the snake, too, if you need it. Come on in. I'll be back in a minute." He disappeared out a back door of the modest room, which was, of course, a duplicate of Stephanie's, but brightly decorated with tacky prints of desert landscapes and a striped throw over the sofa. It was one of those outrageously vibrant Mexican serapes that can't help looking cheerful. There were the usual family photos parked on any flat space. The whole room was clean and orderly.

"I'm sorry I bothered you," Matt said when Arnie came back to the door with a mid-sized monkey wrench and coiled up snake in hand.

"Nah. It's okay. Those kids, they don' know too much, but they're nice kids. I like 'em." He handed over the tools.

That came as a relief to Matt, who hadn't been sure at first if he wanted to admit his relationship with Stephanie. "They're lucky to have you for a neighbor."

"Nah. I don' do nothin' much for 'em. You start doin' stuff for kids and they pretty soon want you to come and cook breakfast and make the bed. Not your girl," he added hastily. "She looks out for Manny, and she even brings me over some homemade salsa once in a while, if she's got extra. An' it's good. *Sabrosa*. And they're quiet. That's important in a duplex. I mean they play the TV, but not loud. Me, too. We respect each other. Know what I mean?"

"Indeed I do. And Manny…" He put the question obliquely. "Is he… okay?"

Arnie smiled. "Hey man, he likes baseball. We watch the Dodgers together sometimes. But he's hard workin', that kid," he mitigated any assumption that watching baseball was all he did. "Salvadoran, y'know."

"Yeah."

"So how's the baby? She don't cry much."

"Fine. She's fine. But Stephanie… she's nervous about being a mother." Matt hadn't thought of a logical way to explain that a beautiful, healthy baby could be rejected. It wasn't something Hispanic mothers did.

"She'll do okay. Like I said, she's nice kid. But tell her I don' babysit. Okay? I mean I raised one family already. Three kids. My wife's gone and my kids moved all over the place, so I just kind of take care of myself. Y'know? Don' take it wrong."

"Course not." Matt moved toward the door. "I'll have your stuff back in *dos minutos*, okay?"

It wasn't *dos minutos* actually, but after Didi and Stephanie had left, he did get the trap off and was emptying indefinable black crud from a dishpan into the toilet, which, fortunately, worked fine. It was then that the baby started to cry. He washed his hands in the bathroom basin and went to her aid.

Even when she was crying, he didn't find her screwed up face ugly, only distressed. He hesitated over the crib. Probably wet. What else? But even in that small room, he hadn't a clue where to find a diaper. The baby cried on, but not a screaming cry, just plaintive. So small. So small in a massive world. How did you ever dare to be born? He leaned over the suitcase and worked his hands under the baby and blanket, supporting her head with his right hand, barely remembering how to hold a baby, nearly frozen with anxiety. Then he got her into the crook of his left arm and started to jiggle her gently up and down, walking back and forth in the tiny room, uttering soft sounds of adult consolation. "There, there…sh…sh…" over and over. So small. "Everything will be all right," he assured her and himself, while she looked up at him with slightly unfocused, improbably blue eyes. How could he promise anything would be "all right" when hardly anything is ever all right once you become a human being. It's all uphill from there. Okay, so joy is possible sometimes, and achievement, and hope, and love, and beauty. But like jewels found by a pathway, there's nothing you can count on, nothing you can make happen.

Walking her and surveying the room at the same time, Matt saw a plastic bag on the floor under the makeshift crib. An ordinary shopping bag that seemed flattened, but maybe not wholly empty. He bent carefully so as not to alarm the baby and picked it up. Yes, it did contain a couple of disposable diapers, the usual thing these days, not cloth like they used to be. Well, who could say whether it was better to put millions of diapers in landfill or wash millions of cloth diapers in potable water and poisonous detergent? Progress made for strange choices.

Carefully he laid the baby down on the bed and pulled away the strips of her wet diaper, raised her bottom by lifting her feet, and pulled it away. Her little nakedness moved and frightened him. All babies seemed too vulnerable, but maybe a girl baby more. The same feeling he had had with Marilu and Stephanie. How did a male gamete produce a female, anyway? Biologically, he knew the explanation and still it seemed odd. Especially how some unidentified seducer at a party had made this child a girl. But the baby seemed unconcerned with it. She had already stopped crying and looked up at him with unfocused eyes. Blue. They wouldn't stay blue, of course, but they were amazingly pretty. He gingerly slid the unfolded diaper under her buttocks. She had no baby fat yet. So small, so light. A breeze would have blown her away. Who said that? Matt wanted to put some powder or something on the redness of her pudenda, but had no idea where to find such a thing. So he simply taped the sides together, feeling how everything you do takes a kind of skill, practice at least, and he was definitely out of practice. But she made no complaint. The trust of it. Trust and distrust had to be learned. Hard lessons.

Matt looked around for a place to put the wet diaper, but found only the kitchen garbage pail, which was already stuffed full. He stuffed it some more, then returned to the baby and cautiously picked her up. He didn't have to. She wasn't crying, and she was too new to roll herself off the bed, but he just wanted to hold her. He wanted the trust to become a solid thing.

During the next ten minutes or so, Matt told her many things, and she remained calm under the drone of his voice. He told her about Marilu, how she made him feel fatherly again, which means both happy and scared to death. It came to him—and he told her—that being a father is even more amazing than being a mother. "Look," he said, "your mama grows you from an egg inside and it all seems kind of natural because she feels you there every day, but how does that teeny sperm cell that you can only see under a microscope, how does that make up the other half? That's what confounds me. I could hardly believe it—the first time I saw Dan, your uncle. You've got an uncle, how about that? And then I saw Marilu. She would have been your aunt. And then I saw your mama. And I felt all of them growing inside your grandma, under my hand, every day. But my part was already over, so it was amazing to think that they were half of me. And you're a quarter of me, and since you don't exactly have a father, maybe I can claim half of you, too. Why not?"

And so he walked and rocked and watched the small face relax little by little into sleep and didn't think she looked like the child of an orgy, but a royal child. Like Sleeping Beauty at her christening, before the witch laid a curse on her. A child at the center of the universe. Like at the end of *2001: A Space Odyssey*. Nobody's child. Everybody's child. And yet nameless. How could that be? He didn't even know what to call her. Except "the baby." He wished Lauren could see her. She'd think of something. "I wish she could be your mama, and we could be a family." Matt sighed.

He didn't exactly want to put the baby down, now that she was so warm and right in the corner of his elbow, but he had work to finish, and so he did. Back in the suitcase. "You were in a handbag?" he murmured, recalling the famous question of Lady Bracknell, and smiled faintly. "What's in a name?"

That was the first question Matt asked when Didi and Stephanie came in the door, laden with huge paper shopping bags.

"What did you name her?"

Stephanie plopped her sacks on the unfolded sofa, one clearly packed with diapers. "I didn't have a name in mind exactly because my girlfriend, Viki, kept saying I was gonna have a boy, so when it turned out to be a girl, I just told them to write down Maria Dolores. Like Mama. I don't really call her anything because I knew I was gonna give her up. When you name something, you sort of get attached. Know what I mean?"

"Yeah." He didn't add, "Like a puppy or a kitten."

Meanwhile, Didi had also put down her sacks and gone to the crib. "Did she sleep okay?" she wanted to know.

"Yes, fine. She was just awake for a few minutes." Everything a baby does, he remembered suddenly, is important information. "Anyway," he added to Stephanie, "I got your trap cleaned out. Maybe you guys should get a snake."

"A snake?"

"One of those," he said, pointing to the coiled, thick wire on the kitchen floor. "I gotta take Arnie's tools back." He picked up the tools and made for the door, but then he paused. "Maria Dolores is a great name," he assured Didi, though in fact he'd never thought much of it. *Sorrows* wasn't the best name in the world, even with Maria in front of it. "But I've been thinking that she needs a name of her own, and when I looked at her, I thought of a flower. No, not Flora. There was a Flora in my middle school who was a pain. Nobody liked her. She was loud in a class where loud applied to everybody. So anyway, I thought of 'Iris.' I mean she can have any name on her birth certificate, but I was thinking that her real name could be Iris."

Stephanie shrugged. "Why not?"

Didi considered the baby for a moment. "Iris is pretty," she conceded. "I've got a cousin, Iris. Only I don't know her too well. She lives in Palm Springs."

"So, are you guys gonna take her?" Stephanie wanted to know.

"Of course," Didi answered while Matt was simultaneously saying, "That depends," although he had also made up his mind.

"I mean this is about the most drastic decision you're ever likely to make," he warned her, "so you've gotta be sure, and we've gotta be sure. We have to know that you're serious, that you're not coming back for

Iris in a year, or five years, or whenever you think you might want her back. That won't do."

"Of course not. Why should I?"

"Why not? Birth mothers do change their minds, and the courts, well, you can never tell. So this has gotta be real, like a final adoption." It was a little hard for him to admit that he didn't trust his daughter to raise her child, but suddenly he felt very protective of Iris, even against her own mother. "So will you put something in writing? Something we can get notarized? I don't know the best wording, but we need to get something in writing and then work it out with a lawyer when we get home. Will you do that?"

The quickness with which Stephanie said, "Sure," both chilled and reassured him.

It relieved him when Dolores backed him up. "You and Manny can visit sometime, of course, but I agree with your father. We have to know."

"Fine," Stephanie reaffirmed and began looking around vaguely for something to write on. Dolores pulled a notepad and pen out of her purse.

"Where's your garbage bin?" Matt asked Stephanie before she began to write.

"Around the side of the house. We share with Arnie, so it doesn't cost as much. Why?"

"Because you've got garbage."

MATT PONDERS A SOLUTION

The solution first occurred to him on Sunday afternoon on the plane somewhere above Santa Barbara County, with the Pacific Ocean on his left and the distant pale line of the Sierras on his right and Iris, asleep next to him in the crook of Didi's arm. Sometimes the baby's mouth moved a little with its own particular restlessness, and when it moved a fleeting dimple appeared next to it. Matt watched for that dimple and loved it. He had never seen it in either Marilu or Stephanie. Iris was, after all, her own person.

He first noticed that dimple late Saturday afternoon after Stephanie had finished nursing Iris. She had been nursing the baby while she lay in bed and watched TV, flipping channels idly with the remote while the baby sucked, and Didi cleaned the kitchen. Matt sat beside the card table on one of the straight-backed chairs that wasn't in use as a support for Iris's suitcase crib. Matt liked watching Stephanie suckling the baby, but her obvious boredom made him sad. He glanced up to see Didi also watching Stephanie from the kitchen doorway and knew she was wishing that she were the one who was nursing. Whatever happened to the maternal instinct in Stephanie? Was it like some physical trait that sometimes skips a generation? Not this instinct, surely.

It also made him sad to feel angry at his daughter all over again. Every time he thought he'd stopped being mad at her, it came back, but not a clean feeling like one has at a real enemy, but a feeling weighted with regret and guilt and the exhausting struggle to reject the feeling itself, like the pain of an autoimmune disease. He hated her for making him feel that pain, and he hated himself for feeling it. And he hated his terrible disappointment at the waste.

He and Didi happened to meet Manny as he was coming in from work, and they were on their way to Raquel's. He didn't seem a bad kid. Although he was skinny, Matt noted that he had hard muscles in his arms, which he hoped was a sign of a good worker. Manny was understandably nervous, but polite, shaking hands softly in the old country way, and he seemed affectionate to Stephanie. Matt liked the way she smiled at him when he came in and the way he bent to kiss her. Maybe they had a chance at a life together after all. Someday, Manny apologized without prompting, they would have a *chamaco* of their own, but they could not afford to have one now.

By this time, Matt wasn't particularly sorry to hear that, but he had to wonder if having another grandchild someday really interested him? Not likely.

When Stephanie had finished feeding Iris, she handed the baby to Didi and flipped to another channel. After Didi burped the satisfied infant and put her down in the lidless suitcase, Matt stood beside her for some time, simply watching her with the deep attentiveness of a new father watching a baby that is doing nothing but being. Amazingly, explicitly being. Then Iris's mouth moved in a particular way that brought the dimple, which appeared, fleetingly, then faded.

As it appeared and faded now in the airplane. And Matt thought: *Dear God, help me to protect this baby, this miraculous child.* Then he remembered that there was no god. There are only other people. And who can predict them? And he knew at that particular moment, even as he knew when he looked at Lauren asleep from making love, that he was a happy man. Love expands you somehow, as a candle in a mirror expands light or a sunrise on a morning after rain. Or hearing an old melody that brings back a world of happy recollection. Didi held Iris in the crook of her left arm, while the baby slept to the drone of the airplane. In spite of his clutching anxiety, the moment glowed for Matt, as only love makes happen.

He had never served in the military, but Matt knew that soldiers learned that they might need to die for one another. But anyone could die for love. If need be.

So it came to Matt what he might have to do to protect Iris, what no one else could do on her behalf. It made him shiver, but he had to think about it. By the time they finally came to their house in San Rafael, and the sun had left its pale fan of light behind Mount Tamalpais, Matt had very nearly decided. He stood in the doorway of the bedroom and watched while Didi changed Iris and picked her up. The naturalness of it. Didi was happy now. She had her baby back, the lost one and the new one in one body. She carried Iris to the living room and sat with her in their rocking chair, with the small head in the crook of her left arm, and crooned, uttering wisps of lullabies in Spanish from her own childhood. Matt had grown up in an English-speaking household and had nearly forgotten the old music. What a beautiful tongue to give an infant. Didi had given that to Dan and Stephanie and he had never thanked her.

"I love the sound of that," he said in a constricted voice. "Sing some more."

Didi smiled briefly and went on singing. A simple thing. So easy!

Then Matt went to his studio to look for a box large enough to be a temporary crib, and while he was there, he also looked up a phone number on his cell phone and called Thorny Thornton. Thorny was in, and after an exchange of pleasantries, Matt said that there was something he wanted to discuss right away, as soon as they could get together. He would explain then. After making an appointment for the next day, he thought of calling Lauren, but it wasn't a good time nor could he, despite his feelings for her, think of anything comprehensible to say.

HARRIS FINDS HAPPINESS

There is quiet in the master bedroom of the Hamilton house. Present is the usual furniture: the queen-sized bed, the bedside tables with their matched reading lamps, two dressers, and an occasional chair. In one corner of the room are a small desk, a computer, and a filing cabinet, which serve Lauren as a home office. Creamy is dozing picturesquely near the foot of the bed.

Lauren is sitting at the desk, intent on the computer screen. She is wearing jeans and a pale blue knit shirt with short sleeves and a scoop neck. A youthful outfit, but at the same time conservative. She types a little, pauses, types again, reads over what she has written and sighs with her whole upper body.

Then Harris comes in, talking on his cell phone. Lauren pauses in her musing, inclines her head towards him without turning all the way around.

"...so I told McFarline I'd chair the committee on the twenty-third. Not that I exactly want to. Still, it's a good cause. We need to figure out how to implement the security screening of foreign students without impeding their welcome. I mean we need their talents, not to mention their tuition. Well, you know all about that. So I'll see you at the conference." A pause. "Right. So long." And he sets the phone on the bedside table.

"Another unintended consequences of 9/11," he adds to Lauren "It's not the foreign students who are a threat. Certainly not the Muslims. Did you know that over a thousand students native to this country die every year from medical conditions or accidents related to alcohol?"

"No, I didn't, but I guess I'm not surprised." She answers him still without quite looking around.

"What are you writing?" he asks then as he loosens and pulls off his tie.

"Just a note to David. He e-mailed me about a novel he wants me to send him. *Nostromo.* I wanted to let him know I'll get it in the mail tomorrow."

"Why *Nostromo?*"

"He's doing a paper on Conrad for a fiction class."

"Does he want Ian Watt's book on Conrad? I have it somewhere…"

"He didn't say. It's criticism, right?"

"You've read it, haven't you?"

"Not that I recall," she answers to the screen.

"I thought we discussed it. Years ago." With this glancing piece of reproach, Harris unbuttons his shirt, takes it off, and tosses it on the chair, a gesture Creamy utterly ignores.

"Can't David get what he needs at the library?" he adds.

"I think he wants his own copy so he mark it up. And save money buying one, even used."

"Good thinking. That's our boy." His approbation sounds sincere.

Harris seats himself on the side of the bed, pulls off his shoes, puts up his feet, but so as not to disturb the cat, and leans back against the headboard. He takes a deep breath.

"Laurie, I need to talk to you about something."

"Yes? Shall I save what I have here? I'm not quite done."

"Sure. Save it."

Lauren turns back to the computer, hits a key, then faces fully around to Harris and waits.

"It's about my trip to Asilomar last weekend."

"Yes?"

"I told you the conference was a success."

"Yes, you did."

"Well, I should have told you something else. I should have told you that I went there with a woman. She was going anyway, but we drove down together."

"Okay."

"I mean we stayed together at a motel, not on the conference ground. We planned it that way." When there is no response, he adds, "We had sex."

"I see." She shows no reaction but the two flat words.

"I don't know if you do." Harris leans forward slightly without getting off the bed. "I'm not the sort of person to enter into an affair lightly. You know that. I've been completely faithful to you for twenty-six years. There simply hasn't been another woman. And my profession isn't without temptations. There've been some, well, quite attractive and willing—opportunities. But I've always considered myself a man of principle."

"Yes, I know. And you are," she respectfully confirms.

"So you have to understand that this is important for me. That's why I feel guilty. Not about being attracted to another woman, but because I like to think of myself as being honest. Because I should have told you right away, the minute I got back. This past week has been rotten for me because I despise dishonesty, but I wasn't quite sure how to do it. I should have leveled with you then."

"Or even before you went."

"Maybe so. The thing is that Fay and I... I started liking her when she first came on the faculty two years ago. It's not like it was impulsive in any way. I just liked her. As a colleague. In fact, I've probably mentioned her to you."

Lauren shrugs. "Maybe so."

"Fay Robertson. Now I think of it, she was at the McFarlines's barbecue last July."

"Then I'm sure I met her." Lauren does not say if she remembers.

"Well, you might say that we simply hit it off. Anyway, she was in the process of getting a divorce, which took time. And then more time to get over. To adjust. And when I started feeling a real attraction, I wasn't sure if she felt anything for me, but around last Christmas it seemed like we began running into each other more and more, or she'd stop by my office just to chat. Or ask my advice about something. We started having coffee together. That sort of thing. Of course she knew I was married, from the beginning. She never pushed it. She's not that kind of person. Anyway, finally I asked her if she'd go to the conference with me and stay in a motel and she said yes." He presses on quickly to forestall comment. "We've talked, Fay and I, and we've decided that we want to be together. I mean live together. Maybe get married in due time."

"So you're telling me that you want a divorce." How indifferent she sounds!

"Well, yes. Yes I am. It's not anything against you, Laurie. I guess you know that. It's one of those things that sometimes happens when children leave home and there doesn't seem to be a lot in common anymore. I won't call it a mid-life crisis, but more of a re-evaluation." Pausing for a response and getting none, he goes on. "Should we spend our lives together when it's not authentic?" he asks. "Going through the motions when it's not important to either of us?"

She seems to ponder that and then makes a small affirmative "Uh-huh."

"It just doesn't seem to me that you and I have had much to talk about since David left for college. I didn't notice it much at first. As long as he lived at home, we were always concerned with his comings and goings. The school activities. The family vacations. All that. Then, suddenly I realized that I didn't have anything to say to you that wasn't about domestic matters. Insurance payments. Advising the gardener, repairmen. That kind of thing. A few social engagements. There's nothing intellectual to bind us. No meeting of the minds, as it were."

Lauren looks at him then and answers with remarkable aplomb, "You may be right."

Harris, eager to justify himself, gets off the bed and goes to the window, looks out, though it is getting dark, and turns to Lauren. "This isn't a criticism of you, Laurie. I hope you know that. You've been a very good partner, and an outstanding mother. In fact, I'd say you were cut out to be a mother. Maybe we should have had another child. I don't know. And you do a lot of good with your volunteer work. You're a good person."

"Thank you," she responds evenly.

"But… and I'm sorry, but I don't know how else to say it. I find our life together boring."

"Really?" she answers, as though a little surprised, but not much.

"Since David left. I know you read a lot. You're very informed, but you don't seem to express opinions. You don't *analyze* very much. It makes it hard to have a conversation. I don't know what you think. About anything."

Lauren is finally moved to a kind of defense. "We don't read the same things very much, though, do we? I mean your stuff is mostly professional. Which is natural. Me? I suppose I read more for entertainment. Or general information."

"That's not the point. You don't really seem to have opinions about much of anything. So there's nothing to discuss." Thus he succinctly confirms that she bores him.

She cannot quite let this pass without some rejoinder. "I just like to think things over before I make a comment, and by the time I've come to a conclusion about something, the conversation or event or whatever has moved on." A bit defensive, she adds, "So I'm not a quick reactor. Sorry about that."

"That's not what I mean—"

"Actually, I do have opinions," she interjects. "I've kept a journal for years. It's *full* of opinions." She doesn't elaborate on their nature.

"I'm talking about our communicating. OK, I know you're an observer. But you don't enter into your observations, as if you're afraid to commit yourself." He has no more to say on the topic, and Lauren does not respond. Maybe she even agrees with him. Or maybe she doesn't care.

"Well," she takes up after an open silence, "should I add something about this—about us—in my e-mail to David? I haven't sent it yet."

"Of course not! It's way too soon." Harris stares angrily in her direction, then controls himself, and returns his gaze to the window, looking outside even though it's gone dark by now. "We'll talk to him when he comes home for Thanksgiving. In person."

"How do you think he'll take it?"

"He'll take it all right. He's a sensible boy."

"Yes, he is." She pauses before uttering a fraught question. "So you're not moving out right away. Or am I the one who's moving out?"

"Well, both of us, in time. I'll probably go first. Fay has a tract house in Rohnert Park, so I'll move in with her and share the payments. Roomy enough. Four bedrooms. She doesn't have children, so have extra space for our offices, and I'd like a place for David to stay when he visits. And it's not far from the university, so that's handy. I won't have this stupid commute anymore. I could even bike to campus in good weather."

"Sounds great," she concedes. Harris talks like a boy about to buy his first car.

"So I stay here." She doesn't sound displeased.

"It's up to you, of course. You can certainly stay here until you find something else you like. I've considered our financial arrangements, and I realize you don't have a profession to fall back on. Maybe you could find something part-time, but don't worry about it. I want to be fair."

"I appreciate that."

"In other words, you'll get half the profit from selling the house, and I'll even swallow the capital gains. Naturally, we'll split our investments. After we sell the house, you can probably find a smaller place. Maybe a condo. Take your time. I want to see you comfortable." He sounds both magnanimous and reasonable.

Lauren stiffens. "We'll sell the house?"

"It's community property."

She nods, but makes no comment. It's one thing to lose a husband, but another to lose a house. A home.

"People do change," Harris pursues his explanation. "It's a cliché, I know, but there's truth in clichés. Maybe our interests, or at least our focus, have changed. I'm not sure. But anything that doesn't grow, dies. A fact of life. And it's not about sex," he suddenly thinks to comment. "It's about communication. Sex is only a rather small part."

She nods, half listening, then comments. "It's also about a sense of fulfillment. It's about feeling important in a world where you're taken for granted."

"I don't take you for granted," he defends himself brusquely. "I never have."

She looks at him but declines to debate that point. Then she looks at Creamy, perfectly serene in the midst of imminent change. Her lot in life seems to be as an ornamental compensation for loss.

"I guess I'll move my stuff into the guest room," he offers.

"No!" She pauses. "I want to sleep there."

"Why?"

"Just do. I like it."

"Whatever you want."

"I better finish up this email to David and send it." Lauren turns back to the computer.

"Tell David I said hello," says Harris, and leaves the room.

MATT TELLS THE OTHER PART

Matt hadn't expected to be at Thorny's house again. Thorny's plan to donate it made it seem already gone, but of course he still lived there, packing up belongings, disposing of furniture and whatnots. By this time the house no longer looked very lived-in, although some of the basic furniture remained. An easy chair, a loveseat, and a couple of floor lamps, but nothing really personal. Not even a picture on the wall. What had been a home was just a building now. It seemed cold, though actually it was not.

Thorny led Matt through the living room, out the sliding door on the further side, and onto the flagstone deck area where another man was waiting, sitting in a mass-produced green resin chair—one of four—with his back to the house. He was looking toward the garden, which was mostly under an umbrella of late afternoon shade. When he heard the door open behind him, he stood up, though slowly, and turned.

Thorny introduced Matt to Richard Young, and they all sat down. Matt was wondering where to begin, but he didn't have to. Thorny began by apologizing to Richard for bringing him up to San Rafael, but as he had said on the telephone, it seemed the right thing to do.

Richard nodded, but didn't react, as though they had been through all this apology business before. There was a sternness about Richard that Matt should have expected, but it made for a kind of concrete barrier that he needed to climb over, and he felt almost too exhausted in spirit to climb a simple stair. He had gone to the paper that morning to review a layout, but left early, claiming another appointment in the afternoon. Even telling that small lie felt laborious, as if the words had a heaviness of their own. Everything had a heaviness. Suddenly he understood the weariness of Sisyphus. But at least his own heaviness would have an end. If Richard would take him.

"So," Richard inquired. "Thorny tells me your situation is desperate. Meaning?"

Matt had rehearsed his lines and still he fumbled. "I uh… I'd like to tell you a convincing lie. I'd really tried to think of one. But that takes energy and I don't have any. So the short of it is that I've looked at every damned option, and at this point the only way left for me to provide for my wife and granddaughter is with my insurance, and they can't collect the insurance till I'm dead." Finally saying it gave a small relief to the weight, but very small.

Richard didn't comment, but merely looked at him with raised brows, as if to say, "So what?"

"I explained it all to Thorny." As if that were an explanation. "As I told him," Matt tried again, "my decision is already made. I need to die in some kind of accident. Like stepping in front of a truck or something. It's what I have to do. I'm not old, but I've had a good enough life. Like Thorny here, I always liked what I did. I think I was—have been—a pretty good photographer. Not that I'd ever be famous, but always competent."

Matt saw from the blocked look on Richard's face that he was straying, that Richard, like someone waiting at a bus stop, wasn't particularly interested in listening to a stranger recount his credentials. But Matt's problem and its genesis were part of the same thing.

"I…what happened…what I told Thorny, had to do with my family, not my work. I, we…our daughter ran away about five years ago. She had a drug problem, and we couldn't seem to get to her. She just took off one day. We did everything we could think of to find her. Checked with all her friends, informed missing persons, sent messages to our relatives. Didi was convinced that Stephanie would go to her maternal grandmother or one of the several aunts or cousins, but she didn't.

"My son, Dan, he came up with an idea. We agreed that it might be a way of finding her. He was always interested in photography, too. Mostly video work. Then movies. He went to the community college after high school and then started a small business. I loaned him some money for that, just to get him started. Actually, he never paid it back, not all of it, but that was okay. Dan began with a studio in the South Bay, making videos of social occasions—weddings, anniversaries, reunions, that kind of thing."

Richard didn't react.

"Well, Dan's work was good enough that he got a gig doing a video for a tour company, I mean a cruise down the coast to Acapulco with a bunch of people who won the trip, and the promoter wanted to use it for advertising. It turned out that Dan started doing a lot of cruises and falling in with some rich people and high rollers, which did him good professionally, but I don't know…if it was the best crowd…. I don't mean he got into drugs, but he started spending a lot of money that he didn't really have…on fancy stuff. A new car, great clothes, even art. He didn't just want to be *near* those plutocrats — he wanted to *be* them."

Richard folded his arms, like a vice principal behind a desk, waiting for a better explanation as to why the student in front of him had cut algebra for the third time.

"So, as I told Thorny, even though Dan and Stephanie weren't close in age, still they were close, and I think that when Stephanie ran away, Dan took it very hard. Now that I think of it, I'm pretty sure he felt sort of guilty about it because he didn't take her acting out seriously, maybe because he hadn't tried harder to do something to help her. But what could he have done? I dunno.

"Anyway, after months of looking for her without any result, using every lead we could think of, Dan came up with this idea. He said he wanted to make a documentary on runaways. He could talk to a lot of people that way and maybe get some new leads as to where she might've gone. He'd include her picture in the text. Maybe somebody would've seen her. He said he wanted to get into documentaries anyway, and he'd get the investment back when he sold the film to a major company, like PBS. So we thought this idea was worth a try. Of course Dan had no money in the bank. He never did, and by then he was renting an apartment in the city and a small production studio too, so he had a lot of overhead.

Anyway, he said, 'Why don't you guys refinance your house, and I'll pay you back when I sell the rights? Your house is worth a bundle now, and I haven't got anything to mortgage. But I have some talent. You know I can do it.' He said he'd do research on how much it would take to make the film. And he could get money from somebody he met on a cruise — but not enough for the whole project.

"He had a point, of course. Our house was nearly paid off. Finally. We'd scraped together a down payment, back when prices weren't so godawful high. We had a mortgage of about $250,000, which seemed an awful lot at the time, but was almost a gift. You don't see a garage for that anymore. Anyway, Dan was a toddler then, and we were determined to have a home for him to grow up in, and, dammit, we did it. The house was small, out on Pt. San Pedro Road, but it had a deep lot, so I could add a studio in the back. And we kept it in good shape. Now that house is worth…who knows? Three, four times what we paid."

Richard gave a slight nod of impatience. No one needs a lesson on Marin County real estate. "So you refinanced."

"Yeah. It was like starting our original mortgage all over again, but Dan was so sure. So convincing. He offered to pay half of the monthly payments, but you can probably guess that he rarely came across with anything like that amount. He just didn't have it. Of course he kept saying it'd all be paid off when he finished the film, and it was 'going well.' He said he was 'learning a lot' and had an experienced guy to do the editing. He'd rented some new equipment, bought a better camera, and so on. Which meant that I had to keep going into our savings to make the mortgage payments, and when the savings were about gone, I sold some mutual funds I'd been counting on for retirement. The money's not gone yet, but going. You get the point." Matt assumed he did, but Richard was completely silent.

Good ole Dan. I put so much trust in him. Like everybody who knew him. He's so good looking, charming. So quick-witted. And he takes advantage of every bit of it, the way a really beautiful woman takes advantage of her beauty. He had all the possibilities to become a real artist. Or so I told myself, anyway, but when he started doing those cruises, when he started meeting those rich dames, he probably laid them all. I dunno. You can hang out with that crowd if everybody understands you're the court jester, including yourself, but Lauren's right, of course. There is a class system and it sure works. No point in going into that.

Is he all that interested in Stephanie, anymore? Yeah, when Didi called him to tell him about her baby, what did he say? "Gee, me, an uncle! I guess I should send a present." Then he tells Didi he's off to Cancun for a week. What was wrong with me? With our family? I don't get it, but even if I did, what difference would it make now?

It's done.

Matt looked from Richard to Thorny but Thorny simply waited. Of course Matt had told him most of the story beforehand, but Thorny was too discreet to put in his opinion here and now.

"Well, the so-called bottom line turned out flat. Dan never made money on his documentary. I suppose you could've guessed that. He finished the project, yes, and it was good. Lots of interviews with kids and parents and social workers and law enforcement and so on. And he sold it to an independent channel in San Jose and another one in Portland. He got something back, but no profit. It seemed that by the time he got it done, it was like the public debate had gone to other things. The only part of the film that seemed to interest the stations was the part that had to do with drug use or homelessness in general. That kids ran away from home and hung out on the streets wasn't news anymore. The saddest part in a way was that Dan never got any lead on Stephanie at all. She told Didi later that she and this kid she went off with went up to Vancouver, B.C., for a while, before they split up, so they weren't even in the country. She only decided to turn up when she had a baby she didn't want." He shook his head in a kind of wondering despair without realizing it.

"I did one thing right, though. Just before our second child was born, I took out a life insurance policy. I have a copy of it with me. I can show you." But Richard waved a negative signal with his hand, as if to say, "Get on with it."

"It'd pay off the standing mortgage and leave around a hundred and fifty thousand. Didi could sell the house and get enough to buy a small place somewhere else, maybe near her mother in LA, she'd probably like that. Or she could easily convert my studio to a granny unit, which is what it's zoned for anyway, and rent it. Dan's out of the picture, financially speaking, but she might like to stay in Marin just to be closer to the city. I don't think she'll do anything stupid. Of course she'll raise Iris as a Catholic, but you can't have everything, and I suppose there are worse fates. The important thing is that she and Iris will be taken care of." It was all he could focus on.

"So what you're saying," Richard took up, "is that you're willing to die for an insurance policy? That's the only way out?" He shook his head, incredulous. Possibly he had forgotten that insurance was also part of his own plan.

"Bankruptcy?"

"It wouldn't solve the problem in the long run. Maybe it sounds crazy, but that baby, that child, she never asked to be born to a dysfunctional mother. Maybe a whole dysfunctional family. Anyway, I can't provide for her any other way. I've been down every alley, and there just isn't enough." The words echoed back to him in thought. *There just isn't enough!* He looked at Richard directly and waited.

Richard unfolded his arms then and rested his hands on his knees. "Thorny tells me that you know most of the plan already. I've arranged for a Cessna 310 out of Gnoss Field. I'll file a flight plan for Reno and we'll end it in the Sierras, probably in a thunderstorm. There's enough weather activity this time of year. I know I can make it work, but it'll be final. For me it has to be."

"That's exactly what I want. I could accidentally step in front of a truck, but what if I'm not killed? And why ruin the day of some poor unlucky truck driver? The thing is I don't want to blow it. I just want to provide for my family. Mainly for the baby. That's all."

"I can see that," Richard conceded then, as if he really did.

Thorny nodded, but he wasn't looking at Matt. He was looking out at the remains of his garden, Clare's garden, entirely in shadow now.

"I'm not even sure how sorry my family would be to see me go. After the first shock, after the estate's settled. Naturally, I'll leave everything in order, as much as I can. For Didi and Iris. I've got an appointment with an attorney tomorrow morning."

He had a mental image then of Didi looking so damn natural with Iris propped up on her shoulder, burping. So natural, it could've been her own baby. *She doesn't seem to mind doing all that all over again, all the feeding and changing and walking the floor. Doesn't need me. Not really. We haven't needed each other for so long. A cardboard couple. There's only one person I don't want to let go of, one person I do need, and I can't even tell her.*

"I tell you what," Richard said abruptly. "I'll think about this and get in touch tomorrow morning. If I say 'yes,' you can still say 'no.' That's understood, I trust. Do you have card with your e-mail?"

"Sure." Matt took a business card out of his wallet and handed it over.

"I don't want too much communication with too many people," Richard said, as he glanced at it. "And I don't want Thorny to go on… recruiting," he added without quite looking at either man. Maybe it was a kind of joke. Maybe not. "If we lose control of the plan," he went on, "we might as well scrap it. Only we can't. At least I can't."

"Of course not," Matt confirmed. *Of course not. I can't lose control. I can't lose control.* A mantra now. *I can't lose control.*

LAUREN PUZZLES

So what the hell am I supposed to do now? Is this god's revenge for adultery? But look at Harris. He's an adulterer and he's happy as a clam. Getting exactly what he wants. And needs, I suppose. But what about me? I was faithful to that boring man for twenty-six years, and then I fell in love too. Was that so terrible? Was it like cannibalism or matricide or something? So why in hell doesn't he at least call me? He could call even if he's still in LA. There has to be a way. A quiet corner where he could whip out his cell and just try, leave a message or something. So what the hell's going on? I know how I feel, but I have to wonder if he feels the same. He does. He doesn't. He does. He doesn't. Like picking the petals off a daisy. And now, whatever, he feels, I can't even tell him about what's happened with Harris. I'm tired of lying awake trying to figure it out. Tired of walking up and down, looking for something to kill time. Down on my knees planting the iris that Astrid gave me. Scrubbing the shower as if it wasn't clean already. But I shouldn't think of it as my shower anymore. Because it's not my house? Where will I go? I should have...but what sort of career? They're right that no woman should ever depend on a man financially. Fay doesn't. Good for her. Am I jealous? You bet. Not because of Harris. She can have him. But she doesn't have to have him. Dammit! That's the regret.

When I called his office, got his damn voice mail. What's that supposed to mean? In town or out of town? Left a message for him to call "at your convenience." Apparently not convenient. Or he's still away. Or is he? We're having an affair, and affairs are awkward. That I know. Even if I never had one before. I read books. I see movies. I know about affairs. A Touch of Class and all that. I thought we were friends—at the very least. And you should be able to trust a friend. Is this some kind of test? It's like being in jail without knowing the term, without even knowing the charge, without knowing anything.. It's like Kafka. Or Guantanamo. So what am I suspected of? Hell isn't hellfire. It's hellfire without hope. So do I have hope? Of course. Today he'll call me. He will.

I was stupid to fall in love. I should never have let it happen. But now, how not?

⸺◈⸺

Lauren turned her head to look at the clock radio. Ten after five. Still completely dark. She moved slowly to the edge of the bed so as not to open the covers, not to wake up Harris. And only then did she realize that she wasn't sleeping with Harris anymore, that she had moved to the bed in the guest room, which was now special to her in the best of ways. At last, after so many years of a dead marriage! Why had they slept together for so long? Habit? Or a form of denial? A reality forged by mere routine. She usually got up before Harris, went to make coffee, pick up the paper from the drive. While she started breakfast, she'd hear the shower running. He'd come in presently, dressed for work, looking scholarly and debonair. Despite receding hair, he was still handsome. So why didn't he attract her?

Why didn't she attract him? Not even a passing touch of the hand. They'd sit down and read the paper together, like roommates or siblings, exchanging a few comments about the news, discussing the daily schedule. Would it be so different with Fay? She'd never know.

Still dark out. Dark, dark. Won't be light till after six now. Fall's coming. Thanksgiving. Winter. Christmas. The whole rigmarole one more time. Pretenses of the season. Then sell the house. And what? I can't leave Marin. Or Matt. Can't afford to stay either. Unless I get work, but doing what? I'm useful in a way, but not economically. Good at cleaning showers and making beds, volunteering for good causes, that sort of thing. My curse is never having been sure what the next move should be. Never decisive.

Lauren usually brewed coffee, but having no energy now, she took down her mug and heated a cup of instant in the microwave. No light yet. Leaving her coffee on the counter, she turned on the porch light and went out to the curb to see if the morning paper was there. At least a distraction. But it was not. Was that a hint of light in the east or just the reflection of the East Bay cities? Hard to tell.

The moon's late. Waning now. I miss the moon when it's waning. But would I want it to be always full? I guess not. Change almost defines it. But you know it's coming back. Predictability makes it okay. God, the star jasmine needs trimming! I should do that. But is it my garden anymore? When's it ever going to get light?

When she got back to the kitchen, she found Creamy placidly awaiting her breakfast. Nice to have someone around so focused on the essentials, not prey to sexual desire—spayed of course—or work or shopping or bills or any of those things. A sort of pure being. Dependent, yes, but still her own person. How do you achieve that without being a cat?

Daylight came finally. Traffic noise from Sir Francis Drake Boulevard and the other arterials rose just before daylight like the murmur of a distant ocean, with occasional nearer sweeps of surf on their own residential street. Another cup of coffee, properly brewed this time. The morning paper had finally arrived with its usual headlines of crime and catastrophe. Foreign wars now relegated to page three.

Harris was in and out of the shower. Toasted English muffins with jam. A bowl of sliced peaches from the farmers' market. Harris observed that he missed fresh strawberries. Well, so did she, but so what? Seasons are seasons. The paper was on the kitchen table, shuffled and reshuffled to kick out the ad inserts. More road accidents, more official lies from Sacramento and Washington, the market up a little, the Red Socks going to the play-offs. David would be pleased. Lauren didn't really need to read the paper. She could write it.

Local news was a little less predictable. Sometimes. She scanned the obits for names she recognized, but there were none. Astrid was dying slowly, but who knew how long it would take? Those whom the gods love may not die young, but they should die quickly, not eaten away piece by piece like something rotten, sloughing off your body as you go.

Today nothing of interest. She closed and folded the paper brusquely and turned to stack the dishes. Later she would package *Nostromo* and take it to the post office.

Harris was getting ready to leave. God, but he did look important with his brief case in hand! By the door that led to the garage he paused and looked back at her, she thought rather a long look and thought *I look terrible. Does he notice?* But he only said, "I'll be late tonight but I'll be back early tomorrow. If you want, we can start to talk about… plans." Lauren looked at him without answering and gave only a faint nod. "Late" meant not to hold dinner, but to leave some snacks or leftovers in the fridge. A sort of code.

Plans? The only plan she had for herself was to find Matt somehow. To talk to him somehow. Even while she was nodding to Harris, she was thinking that, oddly, she didn't know where Matt lived, not in the sense of having his address. Only an approximation. East side of the freeway, he mentioned one time. Wasn't it Point San Pedro Road? A nice area, but maybe not quite so expensive twenty-five or thirty years ago. Anyway, if she knew the house, she could hardly go there. She only got voice mail from his cellphone number. Telepathy clearly wasn't working. While she pondered her options, Harris drove away, unnoticed and unmissed.

After putting the breakfast dishes in the dishwasher, she made her bed, the beloved bed that now seemed so barren, brushed her teeth, got dressed, packaged the novel for David in a padded envelope, looked over the paper again. Anything to kill time. At nine o'clock she picked up the landline phone in the kitchen and dialed his number again. "You have reached the voicemail of Matt Ramirez. Please leave your name and number and brief message." This time Lauren didn't leave message. Instead she went to her computer and got the number of the main office. Again she picked up the phone, put it down, then picked it up again.

A cheerful voice answered after two rings. "Marin Morning Journal. How may I direct your call?"

"I… I'm…This is Lauren Hamilton. I've been trying to reach Mr. Ramirez, but he doesn't seem to be in. Is he…out of town?"

"I can give you his voice mail."

"No, please… I've tried that. I just didn't know if I should be expecting a return call sometime today."

A moment of hesitation. "Maybe you should try again. I think he's in today, but probably in a meeting. Or he could be out on an assignment," she added, covering any possible dereliction.

"Thank you. That's what I needed to know. Thank you."

"Do you want me to try his voice mail for you?"

"No, no. That's okay. I'll try again later. Thanks." And she hung up. What now? She looked at her appointment calendar one more time, but she knew already there was nothing else on for that day, other than a modest grocery list and the post office. Should she start scanning classified for a job? Yes, of course, but, oh gawd, not now!

Okay. So I'm obsessed. I can't help it, so I won't really try. My luck that if I go to the office, he'll have gone out, and anyway, what am I supposed to say if he's there?

'Why the hell didn't you call me?' That sounds whiny. The one thing a person should never do is whine. Children can get away with whining. An adult? No, never. If he'd wanted to call he would have. So be casual. I was just passing by your office and… I almost never pass by the newspaper office. Not on my way to anywhere, not even the post office. So… maybe some god will get friendly and give me a thought.

After mailing the book, Lauren drove to the newspaper office and actually found parking on the street. It was metered, but she had the change for an hour. A bloody waste of coins. Finding out what was going on, if possible, wasn't going to take an hour, but she was conservative about meters.

She was about to go in the front entrance when she had a thought. Instead, she walked around the building so she could see if Matt's car was in the employees' lot. It was. The silver-gray Honda. Next to a blue SUV. She was turning to go back around the corner of the building when she noticed the back door opening, and Matt himself coming out, the camera case over his shoulder. On his way to some appointment likely. On a schedule. Not a good time to interrupt. She stood rooted in perfect indecision. Would he see her there, hovering at the edge of the lot? Yes. He stopped. Their eyes met. Then he continued to his car, opened the passenger side and put in his equipment.

"Matt," she said. No need to shout. He was only some twenty feet away.

"Lauren," he replied without any particular affect except perhaps mild surprise, staring at her over the roof of his car. Then he closed the door of the car and walked around to the driver's side, which put him a few feet closer. "I'm… I'm sorry," he fumbled. "I'm just on my way to an interview."

"That's fine. I won't keep you," she answered stiffly as she walked towards him. "But where have you been? I know, LA. But I was worried. I left a message yesterday." She came within easy conversation distance and stopped, hating the complaining tone of her voice.

"Yes, I got your message. I just didn't know… what to say. It's been too complicated. We came back from LA on Sunday evening. I was trying to catch up yesterday and this morning. My daughter, she had a baby. We just found out. We had to go. We hadn't even seen her for almost five years, didn't even know where she was. I'm sure I left you a message before I went." From the hurriedness of his delivery, she couldn't tell if she was getting an explanation, an apology, or merely a dismissal.

They stood close to each other now, but didn't touch. At least their mutual complaints seemed to be about equal. Now it was a question of who would pursue what grievance.

"Yes, you did call before you left," she conceded. "But I just wondered…" She didn't know how to say what she wondered. Or was afraid. He did look her in the eyes, but yet there was a heavy reserve that surrounded him. "So should I be happy about the baby?" she asked him. "I don't know if I'm supposed to congratulate you or console you. Did you want to be a grandfather? Is your daughter okay? You could have at least let me know you were back." Again that awful accusatory tone intruded.

"Yes, you're right. I should have. The thing is, we have the baby with us. Didi and I. We brought her back from LA. Our daughter, she was ready to give her up for adoption. We couldn't let that happen, so we brought her back with us. We're a little old to be parents again, but we couldn't leave her with strangers." He sounded like an angry person trying very hard not to be angry. "Don't you see?"

"Of course I see," she offered in a gentle voice that tried to conceal dismay.

"I hafta go," Matt said. "I'm sorry. Really. We can talk later. I admit I should've called. I do want to explain." He sounded at once miserable and sincere. His hand was on the door handle.

"Yes, I understand. But Matt, before you go, there's something I have to tell you—now. Something's changed for me, too." She hesitated and her mouth moved in an uncharacteristic tremor that might have presaged crying. Did she know herself? "Harris wants a divorce. He has a girlfriend."

"A girlfriend? As in a mistress?"

"Yes. He's having an affair." And suddenly she started to laugh.

Matt stared for a moment, and then he started to laugh, too. All at once it was the best joke in the world, and they went into each other's arms, shaking with laughter.

Coming out the back of the building, Mary McCorkle, a senior editor, saw them and paused on her way to her car. But Matt noticed her and waved her away, not wanting her to think it was a joke that could be shared, pulled himself together and let go of Lauren, still chuckling, flushed from laughter. Mary waved back and went on to her car.

"I really gotta go," he said again, but now with real regret. "Meet me somewhere—if you can—at noon tomorrow. I don't have anything on in the early afternoon. I can't... not explain." He sounded determined and confused at the same time.

Lauren stepped back, but stayed near the car. "When you're done with this appointment, call me, and we'll work it out. Maybe we could meet in Sausalito? I haven't been there in a long time. Just call. You look tired," she dared to add.

"Yeah, I guess I am," he conceded "I'll call you."

He got into the car, rolled down the window, and looked up at her. "I don't have an appointment for the paper," he said. "I'm going to our attorney to talk about revising my will. I need to put everything into a trust for my wife and Iris."

"Iris?"

"The baby."

"A lovely name!"

"My suggestion."

"Well done. I love iris." She managed not to add, "I love you too," as it seemed unbecoming there in a dreary parking lot. And it startled her to realize that love didn't necessarily make her happy, but it did make her care about being alive.

"I'm sorry about not answering your message."

"Never mind 'sorry.' Just call."

He nodded, started the car, and then he was gone.

A WALK ON THE BRIDGE

Lauren and Matt met in front of the No Name bar in Sausalito at 12:30, both on time, but the bar was so crowded that they decided, after barely a glance through the door, to walk on down the street and buy a sandwich at the deli across from Scoma's. Lauren ordered a bagel with dried tomato cream cheese and Matt, after a considerable pause and a sideways glance at his companion, ordered a roast beef sandwich with everything on it. She didn't flinch. It was crowded there too. Too crowded to talk, so they simply awaited their orders in the midst of the jostle around them. They discussed a beverage and settled on a cup of water, to share.

"What now?" she asked him, as they gained the sidewalk.

"Simple. My car's at a meter, so let's eat our stuff over by the bay, and then we can drive up to the bridge."

"The bridge?"

"Sure. Why not? I have an urge. I've had it for a while. To walk on the bridge just one more time. The water. East Bay. The city. A 'View From the Bridge,' like the play. Do you mind?"

"Of course not. I'd love it."

"Good."

He seemed different from yesterday. More than cheerful. Almost giddy. As they sat on a bench, eating their lunches, he talked about Iris, showed her some pictures on the screen of his camera. Mostly sleeping. A couple awake, lying against an adult shoulder. Didi's presumably. Funny. Lauren had no idea what Didi looked like, but so what? Had Matt ever seen Harris? But here was Iris with a mass of dark hair like a cap on her very small head, making Lauren wish again, just a little, that David had been a girl.

They folded their sandwich wrappings and dropped them in the sidewalk trashcan, along with the mostly empty plastic cup. How simply pleasant it had been to pass that plastic cup of water back and forth. Gulls watched them dispose of their trash, but made no advances, having learned the art of the possible. It was the middle Wednesday of September. Clear, warm. Made for human beings and gulls to live their separate lives companionably linked together. Tourists were abundant, but as children were in school, these people were older, more composed, enjoying *la dolce vita.*

Matt drove to the car park on the west side of the bridge, and they took the pedestrian underpass to the bay side. A strolling security guard paid them no attention, nor they him. They were entirely together, hand in hand. Even the constant traffic behind them went unnoticed. They walked in silence, but at the middle of the bridge, more or less, due west of Alcatraz, they stopped by the railing to consider the view, only a little obscured by the netted suicide barrier. "I haven't been here for a long time," he observed. "I mean on foot." "I've only been here once," she said, "and that was, I dunno, a couple or three years ago, and then I was too engaged to really experience all this."

"What do you mean?"

"A peace rally. Sound quaint? Everyone was carrying signs about stopping the war. So pointless, but fun. 'Power to the peaceful' and all that. Before we understood that the war would be perpetual. There must be a god of lost causes."

"There is," he assured her. "I think it's Saint Jude."

Matt smiled a little, and without looking at her, he put his arm around her shoulder. She felt it warm there and put her arm around his waist.

"God, but I love you," he said, still looking out to the bay.

"And God knows I love you too," she answered, also looking straight ahead, but feeling the epiphany that they had finally said it.

The early afternoon light made the East Bay hills distinct and yet soft, a painting only lightly textured. Around and beyond Alcatraz was a sprinkling of bird-perch islands. To the left the headlands of Belvedere and Tiburon, where people were either very wealthy or struggling to seem so, but at this distance gracefully unpopulated, lighted only by the sun. On the right was the city of San Francisco, calm and majestic from this famous point of view, the buildings seeming to await a camera like a group of people at an elegant class reunion, serious and jovial at the same time.

"I wanted to see this one more time," Matt said, then paused. "I mean to create it. After all, does beauty exist when there's no one there to see it?"

Lauren pondered that, even if the question was only rhetorical. She finally commented that it made more sense than asking whether the fall of a tree made noise if there was no one to hear it. Noise was sound waves, she reasoned, but beauty can only be formed by the intersection of some existing thing with a perceiving mind. Not right to say that beauty is in the eye of the beholder. It's was a connection, a kind of union.

"Yes, that's so," he agreed. "So what hole in beauty does the perceiver leave when he goes away?" Another dense question, but he didn't wait for any response.

"So this is about the last thing I wanted to have to say, but I've got to tell you. It's only right."

"What?" she asked with the reluctance of apprehension.

"I have to go away. I mean I have to leave Marin." All this he said, still without looking at her, but looking straight on across the bay to the green and building-dotted hills. His voice was steady and poignantly clear.

Lauren was too stunned to form a question, to know what question to ask.

She tightened her arm at his waist.

"It's not just on account of Stephanie's baby. Our baby now. I've had to think about what to do for the last couple of years. Never came up with anything concrete, so I just went on pretending that god—any god at all—would come up with some inspiration or *deus ex machina* or whatever. Pretense is a pretty accurate word. Not faith. People have always been good at pretending. The offspring of imagination."

Lauren said nothing. She was waiting for the rescue of an explanation, holding on for dear life, while the tide was washing her away.

"You know I don't have any money. I never denied that. But it's worse than that. I'm terribly, impossibly in debt. Which was never my way, I assure you. I never went out and bought things I couldn't afford. Not even camera equipment. Yes, sure, I've borrowed for a car a couple of times, and we had a mortgage on our house, like most people. But I knew I could make the payments, and I paid off the car loans early, every time. When times were slow, we cut back. When they were better, then we spent the money on stuff for the kids or for improvements on the house. And I borrowed to build my studio at the back, but that was paid off ten years ago. The upshot was that I never saved much, but I never owed much either.

"I always loved photography. You know that. I liked the Journal. My first and only salaried job in Marin. And then my private business. Mostly portraits. Families. Weddings. It was all satisfying. Every bit of it." He finally glanced at her. "The pictures I took of you were stunning," he added, then quickly looked away, down at the ruffled waters of the bay. And he fell deeply silent.

Lauren tried to feel pleased about the pictures, but she was still waiting for some kind of redeeming good news. To fill the void, she remarked on the number of sailboats, though it wasn't even the weekend. It was, of course, perfect sailing weather, smooth, with only enough breeze to make the tacks interesting.

Blessed are the rich, for they inherit everything," Matt finally resumed in a flat tone. "What I need to tell you," he went on conversationally, "is why I have to leave Marin, not, god knows, because I want to. It's a perfect place. But beauty costs. Like happiness. Whoever said money can't buy happiness was only partially right. Ironically, it does buy the foundation, because without it…" He trailed off.

Then he told her the whole story of Dan's documentary and failed investment, the one he had told Richard only the day before. "In a way I can't blame Dan," he concluded. "What can you say when you see some poor deluded soul staggering after the American dream, when they're sick with an illness they don't even recognize and no remedy outside of maybe a Buddhist monastery? Isn't an opulent lifestyle something you're supposed to have in this goddam country? After all, he wasn't doing anything illegal. There's no debtor's prison anymore. Just bankruptcy," he added with a harder edge.

She nodded, suddenly grateful that David was reasonably frugal. And glad and a little guilty that for her money had—heretofore, anyway—never been a problem.

All at once Matt said, "Let's walk a little more."

Linking arms loosely around each other, they strolled on toward the city. A small group of Japanese tourists coming towards them caused them to break and walk single file a short distance and then rejoin.

"I really love you." Matt said, as their arms linked again. He paused to kiss her temple.

"And I love you. Down to my bones. Down to the marrow."

They walked on. Near the southern end, they stopped again, looked back, and contemplated the Marin shore with its fingered outreach into the bay. There was still a little breeze, and the sun was warm on their backs.

"Dare I ask?" Lauren ventured. "Did your son even try to pay you back?"

Matt laughed a laugh that carried no humor. "I think he tried, yes, but his business and lifestyle, as they call it, soaked up everything that came in. They're right when they advise you never to loan money to a relative."

"God of lost causes," she observed dourly.

"You…" he said, looking at her directly. "I know damn well I shouldn't have fallen in love with you. It was like reaching for something on the riverbank and then falling in and getting taken by the current. And I'm sorry. For you. Not for me. I seem to have stabbed myself, so I deserve to feel it."

"It didn't just happen to you, you know." She returned his look in a futile effort to console. "And I'm not sorry at all."

He gave her waist a slight squeeze and looked out to the bay again.

"So…" She slipped into her question reluctantly. "You're going away. How does that fix anything?"

"I told you that one thing I maybe did right, after all, was just before Marilu was born, I took out a life insurance policy, a big one for those times. I've thought about cashing in that policy from time to time, but I never did. Now I have to. Not that it's worth a lot of cash, but it's something, and we've gotta move somewhere cheaper to live. Maybe back to LA, we can buy a cheaper house there, and maybe I can open a new studio."

"But Matt…"

"I'm sorry. You know damn well I don't want to go. I can't talk about it anymore. I can't." His tone of final punctuation was genuine. "Let's start back."

They turned back toward the Marin end of the bridge, still walking with their arms around each other's waist. The traffic beside them was heavy and constant, but not especially loud, except for an occasional massive truck that created, not only sound, but a small rolling earthquake of vibration under their feet.

"Did it ever occur to you," Matt said, sketching the image as it came to him, "that people are like drivers rushing to their destination with a broken gas gauge? They don't know how much gas is left in the tank, so they really have no idea how much further they'll get before they run out. But they drive on—most of them—as if they'd only just tanked up, as if there was an endless supply. Only a few ever have any idea when it will run out." He fell silent then.

"You're right, of course," Lauren assured him. "Just now you made me think of a woman I once drove to San Quentin to visit her son. One of things I did for the Council on Aging. Well, you know about that. Anyway, he was doing 25 years-to-life. She'd been visiting him for a long time, but she couldn't drive anymore, so I took her over there and just waited in the visitors' lot with a book. She was chatty enough before she went in, but when she came out, she didn't talk, not a word all the way back to town. Two weeks later she was gone. Dead. When I found out, I wondered if anybody would ever visit that guy again. I call that worse than empty. I mean, isn't it as bad as death to be abandoned?" She stopped walking for a moment, holding him beside her, as she considered the ramifications of her own question.

Matt was silent, regarding her profile against the backdrop of the city. Not answering.

"Matt, wait," she said abruptly, though he was waiting already. "What are we thinking? I'm finished here, too. By the end of the year I probably won't have a house either. I'll have to move somewhere. Doesn't really matter where. When you've figured out where you're going to settle, I'll come. So we can be…close."

"No! Absolutely not! You can't. You don't understand!" His outburst made her rigid. She dropped her arm from his waist, moved back a step, just out of reach of touching, staring at him. She looked at once amazed and betrayed.

"God, I'm sorry, darling, sorry, sorry." He also stood rigid, shaking his head. "I didn't mean… It's not your fault." A young couple, speaking Spanish, came along and passed beside them without seeming to notice anything was the matter.

"Then why are you doing this?" she floundered. "I really believed that you'd want to find a way."

"We can't quarrel. That's all." He cut her off. "We can't wreck this day. I wanted to come here with you for the pure beauty of it."

"Me too. But you said you were moving. I only want to be near you, somehow. Not in the same house. I understand that can't be!" She wasn't able to keep anger from forcing its way up through her bewilderment. "I just want to know—"

"Maybe you're right. But I can only make one plan at a time. It's just that I'm… overwhelmed. Okay?" He sounded gentler, but his tone still said, "Leave it alone."

"Then let's go back," was all she could think to say. "I'm a little… dizzy."

In fact, she did feel like someone just getting off a carnival ride, unsteady, churning with inertia's conflicting forces. Holding hands again, but lightly, they walked back to the parking area in silence. It was still a blue afternoon and beautiful.

White sails and cruising white gulls punctuated the blue-green of the water behind them. The crisscross of life on a planet that had life as its premier product. They paused by the car, feeling a soft whisk of wind, but had nothing to say.

Matt drove back down the curving road to Sausalito, still in silence. At the parking lot there were no open spaces, so he stopped in the lane behind her car, miserable that this clear afternoon had become so blotted. But she reached over and took his hand from the wheel in a conciliatory gesture and held it against her thigh.

"Wherever you are, I'll never be very far," she said in a low voice.

Just then a brisk middle-aged man, wearing a white shirt and tie and carrying a briefcase, came down through the lot and opened the door of a car a little behind them. When Matt saw him coming, he knew what it portended.

"Look," he said. "I love you to the edge of pain. You know that. So forgive me. What I have to do makes me feel sick, but I can't help it. We'll plan later."

"I'll find a way to be near you. There's nothing to forgive."

He lifted his hand from her thigh, pouring coolness on it as it came away.

"Darling, I'm sorry. I've gotta move the car. There's a guy coming."

"It's okay. We'll find a way." She leaned towards him and kissed him a brushing kiss that fell just to the side of his mouth, got out quickly. Going to her own car, she hit the unlock button, got in, then glanced to the left to see that his car was already gone.

LYDIA VISITS HER MOTHER

Since Lydia had a key to her mother's house, it wasn't necessary for her to knock, so she didn't. Rather she unlocked the front door, opened it a little more than the width of her head, and peered inside.

"Mama?" she said tentatively, but without an answer.

Then, having closed the door behind her, she walked into the living room and dropped the key back into her purse. There was no one in the room. Only the lighted table lamp by her mother's favorite chair was a sign of habitation.

Lydia was a little taller than her mother, or probably stood straighter, and was still pretty, with short dark hair and hazel eyes. The picture that Astrid had showed to Thorny and Richard was correct in every detail, except that the Lydia in the photo was fifteen years younger and looked more composed and confident. An able university student, ready to stride up the hillside of life. Now, well upon that hill, but with no sense of progress, this Lydia wore a slightly stretched look of practiced frustration, as if the hill itself were an unanswerable question.

"Mama?" she asked again, louder.

"Lydia?" Her mother answered from her bedroom, where she was laying out clothes on the bed, trying to decide what she should wear on her flight. She jerked a little at her daughter's voice, like a child caught picking her nose, though there was nothing reprehensible about what she was doing. "I'm coming!" she called and hurried into the hallway.

"Hi, Mama. How are you?" Lydia went to meet her mother in the middle of the room and gave her a glancing kiss on the cheek.

"I'm fine, darling. I like your haircut." That was always a safe thing to say, even though the cut had not varied in years.

"I like yours, too," Lydia replied with the same formula and stepped back.

"So what's this about a trip? What's so important that you needed me to come down?" Lydia asked the first question amiably enough and then tacked on the second without pausing for an answer to the first.

"No, please, don't rush me. Just give me a minute to think. Will you sit down? Do you want some tea or something? Joyce isn't here yet. You remember Joyce?"

"Yes, of course, Mama. And no, I don't need any tea." Lydia sat down on the sofa where Joyce would sit when she wasn't busy, when she was looking at the paper or just scratching Creamy behind the ears. Lydia put her purse beside her and waited, necessarily patient, like someone waiting at a stoplight.

Astrid sat in her chair and picked up her notebook from its place by the telephone.

"Well, you see, dear, I needed you to come because I had a couple of things I wanted to give you."

"Couldn't it have waited? Until Christmas or something?" Lydia's voice was neutral, but an underlying irritation gave it a challenge.

"No, no. You see, I want to get some things settled, you know, before my trip. I thought that it might be important to… tidy up." She seemed wandery for a moment and then went on, businesslike, focusing on her notes. "I went to see Ed Duncan a few days ago, and we talked about the trust and how to make it so there won't be any, um, what's the word?"

"You mean probate?"

"Yes, probate. Well, it was like that already, but I told him to make a separate trust for the children's education. I talked to Laura about it while she was driving me over there. To Ed's office. Joyce doesn't have a license or she'd take me places. I don't know if I told you that—"

"Yes, you did." Her voice was level, but thin.

"All right, well, I have a copy of the trust. You can look at it." Astrid looked at the end table, empty of everything but her telephone and reading lamp. "It was just here." She sounded aggrieved at no one in particular. "I don't understand." Agitated, she got up and began to shuffle through the current paper on the coffee table in front of the sofa. "I just had it. I did!" she defended herself.

"Calm down, Mama." Though Lydia leaned forward in an attitude of concern, she made no move to help look. "Everybody loses things. Calm down and think where you last saw it. Where were you when you were looking at it? When was it? This morning? Yesterday?"

Lydia got up. She had just remembered her mother's habit of reading the paper while she ate breakfast. Both her parents used to do that, exchanging sections as they finished them. She went into the kitchen and came back a moment later with a legal-sized document in her hand.

"Oh…" Astrid exhaled, relieved and chagrined.

"It was on the kitchen table. You want me to look at it?"

"Well, yes, of course. That's partly why I asked you to come here."

They both sat down again. Lydia turned on the lamp by the end of the sofa and scanned the document. "A bunch of legalese," she observed after turning over a few pages, "but it sounds okay. If the market doesn't collapse. It looks like you're setting aside the mutual funds for the kids. The house and contents go to me. But we talked about that before, you know. And the money in the bank…well, my name's already on your account, so that wouldn't be a problem. And five thousand from the estate for Joyce Cooper. How come?" She looked up from the paper.

"Because Joyce has been so good to me, and she needs work on her teeth. And she wants to find her son. The one she gave up when he was born. Maybe I told you."

"Yes, you did."

"Joyce has had to struggle."

"Yes, I know. But what about Ed? Does he go along with this?" Her tone possibly a little suspicious.

"Oh yes. He said that was perfectly fine." Without further defense of her decision, she went on. "He said that this house is worth so much money these days. It wasn't expensive when we bought it, you know. It seemed expensive to us, of course. Then…I don't remember what we paid. But Ed said he'd make sure it's in your name so that Al doesn't get part of it. Whether you kept it or if you sold it. This house—if you ever wanted to come back to Marin and live here—it would be big enough. The children could have rooms upstairs. Plenty of space, you know. I almost never need to go up there anymore. My things are all here, downstairs, everything I need. There's still some furniture and books up there, but I don't exactly remember."

"So should 1 keep this or leave it?" Lydia set the document down on the coffee table.

"Oh, you can keep that. What's his name, Ed, he has a copy. So do I."

"Okay." Lydia picked up the papers again, refolded them, and slid them under her purse. "By the way, I've got a question. When I was in the kitchen, I saw all those labels around on the cabinets and drawers. What are they for?"

"Labels?"

"Yes, those labels printed on masking tape. For the contents on the drawers and cupboards. Like 'spices' and 'flour' and 'cereal'. That sort of thing."

"Oh, those. Joyce asked if it was okay to put them on so she could find things better. She uses the kitchen to make us lunch. Then she washes up, so she needs to know where things belong."

"I see. Is she a little, I don't know, retarded? When I met her, she seemed perfectly normal."

"Oh, she's smart enough. She's just had bad luck. That's all. That's why I wanted to do something for her. In my will."

"Yes, of course. That's very nice of you. But, you know…" Lydia looked around the room, seeming suddenly to speculate. "Will or no will, just look at this house. It's too big for you now. You don't go upstairs. Maybe that's a sign you don't need an upstairs. What I'm saying," she pressed on, "is that… have you ever considered moving to a retirement community, a place where you can have your own apartment with meals provided and all that sort of thing? Some of them are really nice. So much less responsibility. You could read and chat with other people and maybe take day trips or go to concerts. Not a bad life, really. But of course you've got Creamy." She looked around. "I haven't seen Creamy since I got here. Where's the kitty?"

Astrid looked startled for a moment and then a little puzzled. "Creamy? She was here a little while ago. I saw her." She remembered. "Oh Lydia. I'm so sorry! I forgot. I don't have Creamy anymore." She leaned forward slightly in the chair, her face regretful.

"She died? Creamy died?" Lydia seemed incredulous. "She was only, what, five years old? What happened?"

"No, no. I gave her away. To Laura. On account of it was getting hard for me to take care of her. That's all. She's fine. Laura's nice. She likes cats. It's all right." She defended her decision before it was questioned.

"Oh." Lydia sounded relieved. "Why didn't you tell me?"

"I forgot is all. I couldn't help it," Astrid pleaded.

"Well, that's okay. But you really had me worried there." Lydia looked around the room then, appraisingly. "This is still a nice house," she observed, "but it needs redecorating in the worst way. Should get a high rent, once it's fixed up."

"Yes, well…" All at once Astrid was change-resistant. "What would you do to it?" Her hands tightened on the arms of her chair.

Lydia hesitated, giving the question due consideration. "The whole downstairs… It's so dark, like a catacomb. I'd cover the paneling and paint it a nice light color. Put in better lighting. That sort of thing. If I lived here myself, I'd get new furniture. Something current with a nice fabric, something with gold or maroon in it. Bright." Seeing her mother's desperate expression, she retreated a little. "Of course, I'd keep most of the bookcases. But books darken a room too, you know."

"Yes, I suppose they do, but they're so…" She lost her train of thought. "When you…when I… I hope you won't just sell it." It was her house. Was it about to be abandoned? For money?

"No, I didn't mean that. Like I said, it would fetch a good rent, or I could even live here myself. As you said, there's room for the kids upstairs, and I could have an office downstairs, where Daddy used to have his study. This neighborhood is zoned for light commercial now, so I could set up a business like graphic design or interior decorating. I mean now that the kids are in school, I could start my own business," she added brightening. She didn't mention Al.

When Astrid realized that Lydia hadn't referred to her husband, her mind cleared a little. She wanted to keep Lydia planning ahead. On her own.

"There's a school in walking distance," she observed.

"Yes, I remember. Perkins Elementary."

"I think they tore down the old one and built another. Something about…what do they call it? you know, for earthquakes."

"Retrofitting," Lydia supplied.

"Of course." Being reminded of schooling, Astrid pursued her reminiscence. "We didn't think the public school was quite good enough, so we sent you to that other school. What was the name of it?"

"Montessori," Lydia supplied again. "Well, maybe that was a good choice then, but my kids are in a public school, and they're doing just fine."

"Of course." Astrid was quick to agree.

Lydia got up then and walked over to the bookcases that covered the further wall. She began to scan the titles.

"Are there any books you'd like to take along with you?" Astrid asked her.

"No, I don't think so," Lydia answered vaguely as she regarded the collection, pausing to gaze now and again. "No, I won't take any books now. Not today, but maybe sometime." Still hovering by the bookshelves, only partly turned towards her mother, she asked a question. "Why are you going on this flight? Just sightseeing?"

"I have…well, a friend invited me. And I thought it would be so pretty to fly over the mountains. I never had the chance before. What do they say? Something about 'diem'?"

"*Carpe diem.* Yes, I understand. I used to love travel."

"Well, maybe with the children in school…"

Lydia shook her head. "Too complicated for now, but someday maybe. I'd like to take them, of course. Anyway, I'd love to show Wendy around Europe. All the great museums. She's artistic. Her class projects look professional, and she enjoys it. Joy is the main thing, isn't it?" She paused behind her own poignant question. "Look, here's your old copy of *The Secret Garden.* Can I take it along?"

"I…of course. I thought you had it." Actually, Astrid hadn't thought of it in years. "I think some of your books are still upstairs in your old room."

"Yes, I know. I think I'll go up and take a look."

Astrid suddenly felt that she had to urinate. When that pressure came on, she had to deal with it. The old muscles didn't hold anymore. "You go on up," she said, standing.

Lydia was already going up the stairs by the time Astrid got to the bathroom door, and the urine was beginning to trickle down her legs. She tried to hold it, but with no success. With a little whimper of despair, she let go, let it flow, down her legs into her shoes, onto the floor. Not a big puddle, but enough. She still went to the toilet, though she had little urine left. She dried her wet thighs as well as she could with toilet paper. Then, still sitting on the toilet seat, she worked off her sopping underpants, picked them up, and dropped them over on the edge of the bathtub. At least she was wearing a housedress, so she didn't have long pants to deal with. Then she got up from the toilet and, pulling a bath towel off the towel bar, she dropped it on the puddle that she had left just inside the door and pushed it around with one foot while she steadied herself with her right hand against the door frame. Since it was so hard to get down on her hands and knees, she didn't undertake a proper cleanup. So she pushed the towel partly behind the toilet, where maybe it wouldn't be noticed by Lydia in case she decided to use the bathroom. Leaving a mess behind had never been Astrid's way, but making a mess was never her way either.

She went to the basin and began to wash her hands, and then she had a thought. While her hands were soapy, she tried to work off her wedding ring, which hadn't been off in years. She couldn't think when, but it must have been for cleaning or resizing or something long ago. It fit well enough, but the knuckle held it like a handcuff. She added more soap, worked it against the joint back and forth, hoping it might suddenly break free. The final pull hurt, but the ring came, escaped her soapy grasp and fell into the basin, luckily not into the drain, but its sudden fall gave her heart a catch of panic. She picked it up with her right hand holding on tightly, transferred it to her left hand so she could stopper the drain and turn on the water. Then she washed it carefully. It was two rings actually, bonded together, a diamond engagement ring and a plain, thin, platinum wedding band. A somewhat conventional set, but elegant. Commitment joined to love, they used to say. She dried her hands and the ring on a hand towel and left the bathroom, having put the ring in her dress pocket. She realized then how odd it was not to be wearing underpants, but no problem. She could put on a fresh pair later, and Joyce would clean up the bathroom. Her shoes were damp, but that was endurable.

When Astrid got back to her chair, she heard Lydia coming down the stairs into the hallway behind her and turned before she sat down. Lydia made her entrance with some thin books in the crook of her arm and wearing an outrageously broad sun hat. With the knit shirt and jeans she was wearing, the effect was ludicrous.

Astrid stared for a moment in confusion, almost not knowing her daughter, and then she laughed.

"You found the hats! I'd forgotten all about them."

"They were in a box in my old room, in the closet." Without removing the hat, Lydia went back to the sofa and sat down, put the books on the coffee table. "I thought I'd like to take these for the kids. *Sleeping Ugly* and some *Frances* books. I'd forgotten about them. Wendy's too old for *Frances*, but the younger kids will like them. I want the kids to read. I brought down *Jacob I Have Loved* for Wendy. For later. That's all right, isn't it?"

"Of course." Astrid also sat down then, but a tremor touched her mind. "You won't sell my books, will you?"

"What do you mean? I just told you. I got these for the children to read."

"No, no. I mean all my books. Your father's books…"

"Well, I suppose that someday some of them will have to go. Not all. Look, Mama, don't worry. You know I care about the books. I want to look at every one, if I ever have time. You know how I love the poetry anthologies. And your set of Shakespeare, the one with the great critical notes. Don't worry, okay? So how do you like the hat?" she asked, fending off further discussion.

"It suits you, darling. So… garden party." Astrid paused, then reached deep into her memory for the old game they used to play.

Some grace allowed Astrid to remember the impromptu role-playing that taxed their imaginations, but gave so much fun. She had read somewhere that the more you play roles and make up stories with your children, the more creative they're likely to be. It seemed to work. When Lydia was older, they used to read plays together as a family, and they would prepare by putting on some item of clothing or jewelry to represent the character. Astrid remembered no details now, but she remembered that they had done this. Mostly comedies. *The Importance of Being Earnest* She remembered suddenly. She asked Lydia the name of the character she used to read.

"Wendolin, I think," she supplied. "I don't remember all their names either. And no, Wendy was not named for her. We just liked it." Then Lydia took off the hat, set it down on the coffee table, and turned into herself again. "What I was wondering was, would you care if I took the whole box home with me."

"What box?"

"I mean the hats."

"Of course not."

"I'd almost forgotten all the fun we used to have. I'd like to do more of that with my kids. I think it does them good to play roles. Not that good versus evil and all that rot in video games. Everybody needs to learn empathy. You can pretend to understand other people, but it's not good enough. That's just a form of manipulation, like advertising. You have to get inside, like you do with good literature or drama. You know?" Lydia sounded deeply earnest. It was the very Lydia who had lived in that same house before she went to the city and fell in love with a salesman. And married him.

The thought stirred a recollection. "Listen," Astrid said suddenly, "I was wondering if you'd take my wedding ring with you." She fished in her dress pocket and held it up.

"Why, in heaven's name?"

"Well, you see, it doesn't fit me anymore, and I worry about that." She had almost said that she worried about losing it, but a ring that fit that tightly could hardly be lost.

"But Mama, I could lose it. You don't know what my household is like." She suddenly sounded put upon by one more responsibility.

"No, no. I understand, but don't you have a, what do you call them, in the bank?"

"A safe deposit box?"

"Yes, exactly."

"Well, sure, but…"

"So maybe the next time you go to the bank, you could drop it in. Here, does it fit you?" She motioned for Lydia to come and try it on. "Maybe you could just wear it until you got to the bank."

Lydia went over to her mother and took the bonded rings, slipped them on her right hand. Yes, they were a good fit. She held her hand under the lamplight admiringly.

"All right," she said finally. "If you're sure."

"Of course I'm sure. It becomes you. You could take the diamond," she added, hesitantly, "and have it reset. Someday." What, after all, would Lydia do with another wedding band? And besides, being artistic, Lydia had always been very particular about design. She'd want her own style. It hurt Astrid a little to think about it, but it was all right.

"Sure, Mama, maybe eventually. Resetting is expensive, though."

"Maybe I could pay for it."

"Well, only if you wanted…" Lydia held the ring to the light again, seeming to ponder what she might have done with it.

"It's a fine stone," Astrid encouraged her. "You know your father."

"Of course. Listen, Mama…" Lydia straightened up. "I've gotta watch the time a little. I'm gonna go back upstairs and get the hats. Okay?"

"Of course, darling. Go ahead."

When Lydia had gone upstairs, Astrid looked at her empty ring finger with its worn groove in the flesh and found she could not remember quite how long the rings had been a part of her. She tried to calculate the years since Charles had asked her to marry him. It wasn't fifty. She knew that because they had never celebrated their gold wedding anniversary, but she was pretty sure it was over forty. She thought that Lydia was thirty-one. Or was it thirty-three? She didn't dare to ask. Ah well… The past is past. Period.

Was there something else that Astrid was going to take up with Lydia while she was there? She picked up her notepad and started reading from the top. She regretted to see that there was no longer any reason to detain her daughter.

Lydia came down the stairs slowly and appeared in the hall doorway with a large cardboard box held awkwardly in front of herself, crossed the room, and set it on the floor beside the coffee table.

"Oh my dear…!" Astrid exclaimed.

"No, it's not heavy, Mama, just unwieldy." She unfolded the flaps and took out the first sample. A sort of maroon cloche. "Very twenties," she observed as she put it on. "Now this is Daisy Buchanan," she announced, tilting her head a little in a saucy gesture. "Why, Jay, of course Ah remembah. You sweet thing! The jonquils you brought me…" She mimicked a vague Southern accent, then laughed at herself.

Astrid struggled to remember their old games. "Do another one," she said.

Lydia took off the cloche and put on a gray felt hat with a medium brim, bound with a red velvet ribbon around the crown. "How do like this?"

"Charming. On you. But I can't think… Some war movie?"

"Not sure, but we can call it Ingrid Bergman. I'm sure she wore a hat like this sometime. So maybe…'It's not over, Rick. It'll never be over because we'll always have Paris…' What a thought," she added with a smothered sigh.

Then, despite her eagerness to get home, Lydia took out the hats one by one until there were seven on the coffee table, and for each one she produced some kind of brief scenario. Astrid listened to her daughter, entranced and admiring. It was like the taste of a certain once-beloved food that one hadn't eaten in years, had almost forgotten about, like the tapioca pudding Joyce had lately made for her. So forgotten, then suddenly so remembered.

All at once Lydia declared that she had to go to the bathroom and then get ready to leave. While she was in the bathroom, Astrid got up and put the hats back in the box, each one like a treasure. She put on a broad-brimmed garden party hat, but as there was no mirror in the room, she took it off again and set it carefully on top of the others, rearranged them a little for a better fit and closed he flaps. Only they didn't stay closed. There was a way you interlock the flaps of a box so they stay down, but for her it didn't seem to work.

Just then she heard the sound of flushing and Lydia came out.

"There was a towel on the floor in there," she observed. "By the toilet."

"Oh?"

"It was wet, well damp anyway."

"Oh." Astrid began to remember and felt a tremor of panic. "I'll tell Joyce to pick it up," she declared sharply, as if it might have been Joyce's fault.

"I already did that."

"You shouldn't have. Anyway, Joyce can put it in the laundry hamper."

"I did that, too. I'm used to messes. I've got kids." She came over, looked at the box, and quickly folded in the flaps. "I gotta go."

"Listen, darling. Wait." A memory had emerged. "I want to write you a check."

"What for?"

"For—what do you call it? About fixing the ring."

"Oh that. Resetting. There's no hurry."

"But I want to do it now. While I think of it. How much do you think?"

"Oh, Mama, how would I know? All I know is everything takes more than you think it's going to. Maybe, uh, two hundred?" It was a wild guess and minimal.

"All right, but you have to promise you'll do it. Not spend it on…" Astrid fumbled for an alternative. "…furniture," she finally concluded.

"No, of course not. Listen, Mama, I'm missing my lunch. Have you got anything in the fridge I could just snack on in the car? Some carrots maybe? Something like that?"

"I'm not sure, darling. Go look while I get my checkbook. Joyce likes, what do you call it?, some kind of pudding. Maybe there's some pudding in there."

Astrid got up and went to the bedroom to find her purse. All at once she realized that she had on no underpants. Now where… oh yes, the top drawer. She took out a pair and sitting on the edge of the bed, pulled them on. There, that was better. Then she went back to the living room, checkbook in hand, sat down again, and wrote laboriously on the end table. Lydia came in from the kitchen a short time later, eating a celery stick with peanut butter in it.

"Maybe you can look at this to be sure I have it right." Astrid held the check out to her. Lydia took it in her free hand and scanned it.

"Okay. Just write 'and zero 100ths' at the end of the line." She pointed to the line with her bitten celery stick. "That's really nice of you, Mama." She put the rest of the celery stick in her mouth and muttered something around her chewing about taking the box of hats out to the car.

When she came back from her car, she took the check and looked at it.

"Thanks, Mama. You're so sweet!" Impatient now, "I really gotta go. Gotta go pick up the twins from daycare."

"Of course."

Lydia put the check in her wallet, slung her purse strap over her shoulder, and looked around. "Oh yes, the books. Thanks a mil…" She picked them up from the coffee table and tucked them into the crook of her arm.

The front door opened a crack just then, and a head appeared.

"Oh, sorry! The door was ajar, and I… I didn't know." It was Joyce, who came in and stood there, just inside the door, uncertain and apologetic.

"Joyce!" Astrid seemed remarkably glad to see her. "This is my daughter, Lydia. I don't know if you…"

"Sure. We met before. How're the kids?"

"Fine. Listen, I really gotta run. Bye, Mama. Thanks for everything. Have a nice trip. Bye, Joyce. Nice to see you." All this she uttered almost in a single phrase, passing Joyce in the doorway, so close that Joyce had to move aside a little to let her by and the door closed.

MATT DESTROYS IMAGES

Although the early evening was warm, Matt opened the flue and laid a small fire in the fireplace, using the classified section of yesterday's paper, a few sticks from the wood box, and the note Dolores had left him on the kitchen table. They rarely used the fireplace anymore because wood was expensive, paper was recyclable, and there was no family left to gather around it anyway. So much for Hestia. He struck a match, and when he saw that the fire was established, he went back to the kitchen and poured himself a glass of cheap burgundy. Then leaving it on the table, he went out to his studio in back of the house and took a manila folder from the locked file drawer. He didn't bother to relock it, since there was nothing else there he cared to keep secret. And there was no point in making things harder for Dolores when it came time to go through his papers.

In the same drawer were the life insurance policy, auto insurance, home owners, health insurance, and the infamous mortgage agreement. Thinking of that dark burden, he realized that he should make the payment for October ahead of time. The keys to their safe deposit box were in a separate envelope, also labeled.

Not much in that box but a deed and the pink slips for their cars, which were duly noted on a slip of paper along with the keys. Nothing about this careful organization would seem odd, as he was, by nature, orderly.

As he turned from the file drawer, he gave a cursory glance at the walls of his studio, covered, quite naturally, with examples of his own work. A few portraits of individuals and groups, a few studies of his own children when they were little, his favorite still being the shot of a serious nine-year-old Dan holding a smiling baby Stephanie on his lap. There were no pictures of Marilu, though he had taken many.

Other than the portraits, his favorite pictures were some local landscapes, especially the bay or the coast in their various permutations of light and season. Water also seemed to be part of many photographs. The one that took an award showed a ketch, sitting on its reflection just off a dock in Sausalito. The water was almost without ripples, only enough to make a perfect impressionist painting of the reflection. The pure accuracy of the colors, floating just below the transparency of the surface. A shot like that was partly luck—the subject, the film, the camera, the light, the place, the weather, the composition, the agent— all coming together for one sacred instant. He could tell how he had done it technically, and yet the miracle of it still amazed him.

An idea came. Going to his desk drawer, he took out a pad of Stickie Notes, and on the top one he wrote in a small hand, "Give to Lauren Hamilton." He paused and added underneath, "art collector" and under that, her cell phone number. Then he tore off the note and stuck it to the bottom, right-hand corner of the picture. She might or might not ever get it, but he had tried. It was all he could think of to do.

He didn't need to look in the folder he had taken from the drawer. He'd looked in it too many times already, pondered it like an addiction he didn't want to break and yet almost wished it hadn't taken hold. *Damn this feeling! Dammit! How did this happen? How the hell…* From the first time he saw her…something catching hold inside the mind or the senses, or who could say? Maybe it was something like visiting an opening at a gallery, strolling around the room, stopping in front of a particular painting and just looking at it for a long time, then leaving, walking down the street, pausing, going back, looking at it again, enthralled by something about the style, the composition, thinking *if it's still there on Friday…* going back, finding that it was. What if you had found it was gone? Did you need to have it? Of course not. But still, if you left without it, wouldn't you feel… incomplete? Wouldn't you grieve? It was too costly. But it was so perfect. Until finally, you think *yes!* Something like that.

Matt went back to the house with the folder, picked up his glass in the kitchen, and returned to the miserly fire he had built, knelt on the hearth, and set down the glass and folder on the bricks. The room was quiet except for the small chatter of crackling sticks. Since Dolores had gone out with Iris, there was no one around to distract him from the task at hand. Although it was Dolores who was getting up with the baby at night, he felt suddenly exhausted, almost unable to reach out his hand to the file beside him.

He opened the folder. Without counting he knew there were nine prints, along with their negatives, and wondered briefly why he hadn't taken more pictures of Lauren, not just in bed, but at every small encounter. Her head at a particular angle, her face in a certain light, her quick smile, just lifting a cup to her lips. But he had been too busy being entranced, hadn't thought of spending his time with Lauren taking pictures. Until that wonderful, unique Friday two weeks ago. Was it that long ago? That recent? Memory distorts time, like a reflection on water.

He looked at the pictures, one by one, setting each aside slowly. The one with the sheet drawn up just to her breasts was conventional, but nice. He started to touch the image with his index finger, and then, recollecting what he was doing there by the fireplace, he laid two of the pictures on the fire. The edges began to blacken as the fire took them to itself. He looked away, not able to watch the disintegration, and noticed the glass of wine. He drank two long swallows and set it down, nearly empty. Then quickly, he added the next five prints in a stack. These hesitated, clinging to each other as if resisting destruction, then suddenly took fire.

While these pictures curled and crackled in the grate, he turned his attention to the last two, lying on the hearth, illuminated by the fire that was destroying the other images. They were the studies of Lauren's beautiful curved back. The Velasquez studies. The natural light through the bedroom window created, as he had hoped, the perfect softening of a shadow where her body met the sheets, in the line of her upper arm against her side, the curve of her neck. There was no mirror in this one, but a slightly averted profile. Really good. It wasn't only Lauren; it was some of his best work. Taken at half a second with a steady hand. He took another swallow of wine. It was so hard to turn these mere images to ash that he knew there was no way he could take leave of Lauren again, that their inadequate final goodbye, in a parking lot of all places, had been said. Choosing not to think of that, he deliberately thought of uncompleted little Iris, taking form like an image out of fog or smoke. He thought how love and beauty lead into each other. How beauty was, at bottom, the same thing as love. Love too was essential to survival. *We must love one another or die.* Willing or not.

As he looked at the two remaining pictures again, he found the same living quality he had seen through the lens that day, and he shivered with a sense of the numinous that he couldn't account for. Even without god, there was something holy there, in a place where thought was happy to drown in complete sensation.

The fire had nearly died out. Even the sticks were consumed. The pictures and negatives would have to go in now or else the fire would have to be relit. Dolores could be back at any time. First he tossed the negatives into the fire where they curled and vanished in a spurt of flame, like lit matches. But the prints, when he handed them into the flames afterward, hesitated as though they might put out the fire rather than be consumed, and there was a brief respite from destruction while the uncertain smoke gathered under the paper and flowed out around the edges. Then black spots began to appear on the uppermost image. Matt turned his face away but could hear the crackle and feel the flare of heat. It was almost as if she herself were burning, innocent of witchcraft, but condemned all the same. He picked up his glass and finished the wine in one swallow.

When he dared to look into the fireplace again, the images were gone. The only evidence he knew of that he and Lauren had been lovers was ash. A few wisps afloat on the warm air of its own destruction, most of it cooling in the grate. Matt let out his breath slowly as he stared at the wispy remains. The fireplace, which he hadn't cleaned out since late last spring, now contained a layered mass of charred kindling and incinerated art.

Though he had been expecting it, the sound of the garage door opening startled him. Dolores was back. Then he heard the same door closing with a kind of whir and thunk. Then a car door closing, a pause, and then another door. She had taken Iris out of the car. After those, the kitchen door, with each thunk coming nearer, and Matt shrank inwardly from the immense pressure of her approach. With a small motion that took an extraordinary effort, he blasted the last scraps of paper with the poker, stood up, and closed the fire screen. He had replaced the poker and was just tucking in his loosened shirttail when Dolores spoke to him from the kitchen.

"It smells like something's burning," her voice came through the open door.

"Yeah. I was cleaning out some old stuff from my files and decided I might as well burn it instead of putting it in the garbage. Just some old photos. Nothing I could recycle."

Dolores made no comment on his explanation, but came to the doorway and simply looked at him. Matt stooped to pick up the empty wine glass from the hearth, thinking he might pour himself another, but at the moment Dolores innocently blocked the way to the bottle on the kitchen table.

"I just got back from the drugstore," she told him. "Did you see my note?"

"Yeah. Thanks. How was Iris?"

"Fine. Wonderful. She's such a good baby! Dr. Ferguson said to try her on this formula and see how it goes. She fell asleep in the car, both times I had her out today. Remember how we used to quiet Stephanie by driving around, and she'd drop right off?"

"Maybe if we'd kept her awake more when she was little, she would've slept through adolescence," he answered, then stopped ashamed of his sarcasm. "I'm sorry. I'm just tired. I bet you are too," he gave added conciliation.

Dolores had already turned back towards the kitchen, so that he spoke his apology to her back, but her hesitation implied a kind of acceptance. "I gotta put away the formula," she said over her shoulder.

Matt followed her into the kitchen, went straight to the wine bottle and poured himself another glass. Only then did he stop to look down at the infant seat by the door to the garage, the one he and Dolores had acquired at the thrift shop yesterday along with a crib. Mutely he contemplated the bundle of Iris that it contained. Her head, so nicely capped with fine, dark hair, was tipped to one side, her mouth slack. He sat down at the end of the table so that he could continue to look at her. He felt so drained at the moment that he saw himself as a rock, deeply covered by water at high tide, beset by currents, yet blind and unresisting. And very cold.

"You know that I saw the attorney yesterday, about setting up a family trust. Also about the adoption papers. We're supposed to sign everything tomorrow morning. Then he'll send a copy to Stephanie. I'm not worried about that. I mean that she won't sign. Do you think…?" he asked as Dolores turned from the refrigerator.

"No. Poor thing," she added. Which poor thing she meant was not articulated nor did he ask her, but kept looking at Iris, loadstone of his determination.

Then he saw Iris's feet kick at the blanket like something independently alive, for her face still slept. That small thump of life, like a fetus in the womb, like Dan and Stephanie, and yes, Marilu. A butterfly about to break the chrysalis, an emerging wonder, but to what? To death finally. In due time, baby Iris, thou too shalt die. So what's it for? What the hell is it all for? Why do we try? Why do we care about anything?

At the sink Dolores was putting formula into a nursing bottle. Womanwise she didn't seem to ponder the unanswerable question of purpose, but mothered on.

Was it the case that some people are always asking "Why?" while others only ask, "How?" Dolores was a good mother always. A much better mother than he was a father. Fathers were supposed to protect and manage their families. It was the male role, but he had never been "*grande, grande, grande*" like the song. Sometimes strong, yes, sometimes bullying, but more often standing to one side like a spectator, leaving the domestic struggle to her. He had claimed the pain of losing Stephanie for his own and worn it like a crown of thorns. How much worse it must have been for Dolores, and how little he had really consoled her while he wrapped himself in his own guilt and frustration. He looked at Iris and wondered if Dolores was destined to lose her, too. The courage it took to love was bewildering, but mostly based on ignorance, like stepping onto a bridge you don't know is about to collapse. Of course you trust that it won't, but there's always that possibility.

It was then that he noticed the little bend in the eyebrows that meant the baby was going to cry. The sudden familiarity of it struck across the years, another focus that brought the distant painfully near. He hadn't seen that expression since…

"Didi?"

"Yes?"

"…the baby…" But before he had formed any more words, Iris began to whimper. Her head came upright. Her whole face wrinkled and she began to cry.

To have "no language but a cry" was too poignant to contemplate. Dolores went over, bent, and picked her up from the seat, up on her shoulder where human infants fit, patted her back, jiggled her lightly up and down.

"There, there *mi' hita,*" she crooned. She picked up the bottle from the counter, and sat down with Iris at the table. Then she settled the baby in the crook of her left arm and began to feed her. That ample bosom. A pity it was devoid of milk, but nursing aside, Dolores's motion was as natural as though it hadn't been over twenty years between infants. The crying died, of course, as Iris began to suck, and there was only a faint sound as gently contented as purring.

Matt tried to feel the old anger at is daughter, augmented by her new sin of thoughtless procreation. But it wasn't anger that smashed his long resistance. It was guilt for failures he still didn't understand. And the pain of a father's unrequited love. Tears began to gather unexpectedly and roll down his cheeks. He put his head down on the kitchen table, which had seemed so stylish to them when they bought it from Sears twenty-five years ago and which now seemed both worn and tacky, and he sobbed.

Propping the bottle in a fold of the blanket, Dolores reached out one hand across the corner of the table and laid it on his arm, a touch he did not welcome, but did not resist.

"Maybe I'm a little drunk," he muttered, lifting his head like a ponderous weight. "I'm sorry. I can't help it." In fact he had drunk only a sip from his second glass, but it was on an empty stomach, and it was the old excuse of men for any behavior they want to deny. Uncommon, however, for him. He didn't think Dolores had seen him cry since the day they came home from the hospital without Marilu.

"I know it's gonna be hard," Dolores soothed him, "but we'll work it out somehow." Which sounded consoling except for that tinge of martyrdom she managed to get into her tone. "I really believe God means us to raise this baby. It's like a new life for us and a loving home for Iris. You know?" she sought his agreement.

"Yes, sure. I know."" He answered her raggedly, wishing she hadn't dragged God into the whole thing one more time, but so what? If it was a comfort…

She patted his arm again.

Although he rejected her touch, he still didn't move to push her hand away. She was trying. She had always tried. And she was right to blame him for losing Stephanie, for all his mistakes, whatever they were. Love is not sufficient, he concluded. Love, which is supposed to make a joy of duty, fails you when you need it most. As soon as it brings out your best, it cuts off that goodness with cleavers of disappointment and leaves you maimed and angry, dragging yourself through life, weighted with chains of regret or obligation, wanting to love again, but afraid now.

And if you do love again, then it all happens again. All at once it felt good to hate love.

The alternative to love was a great freedom. No citadels to defend, hence none to lose. It also meant living in a land without mountains or gorges. It meant having no place where you could lose your footing or achieve a view. It meant no destination, no welcome lights of your village at evening. It meant no Lauren, no Dan or Stephanie. No tiny Iris twitching her feet under the blanket. Not even Didi whom he had unquestionably loved once. It meant a freedom that was worse than any hell.

Dolores looked at Matt in silence for a while, as though considering if she dared to offer any further signs of consolation. Then with a sigh that she uttered purposefully like end punctuation, she took her hand from his arm and gave her full attention to Iris. Matt closed his eyes for a time and sat immobile, his right hand lightly around the forgotten glass of wine. Not long now. He'd told Dolores about the flight on Saturday. Going along to take pictures, an unusual opportunity. Would she be okay with the baby? Of course. *When Dan gets the news, he'll have to come home. And you have friends, from the church and all that. So you won't be alone. Then there's your mother and siblings and so on. You have people I never quite made part of my life, though I tried off and on. Yes, I actually did. And I don't dislike any of them. They'll give you support. I can't do it anymore.*

Can't do anything really. I can't only not *marry you, my precious, beautiful Lauren. I can't even be near you, stand by you if you need me. Not right, but true. Damn blasted true…*

"Matt?" Dolores's voice intruded on his solitary pain. He looked over at her.

"What?' he asked neutrally, focusing on her face.

"Could you maybe clean the ashes out of the fireplace tomorrow? Before you go on that trip? It's kind of a mess."

"Yeah, sure. On second thought I'll clean them out now. No time like the present, eh?"

He took one last swallow of wine, then got up, dragging himself, leaving the glass nearly full on the table. He wanted to call Thorny and ask him to beg Richard for the impossible. "For godssake, let's go now. Tonight! Let's get it over with." Because now at last he realized with complete certainty that he was about to die.

JOYCE HELPS ASTRID TO PREPARE

On Friday morning Astrid Williamson sat down at the desk in the front bedroom that had served as her husband's home office and wrote her note. Four times. Every time she read it over, there was some mistake, like a word left out, or something she wanted to change so that she could say goodbye without exactly giving away the secret. The wastebasket began to fill with drafts of her note torn into fine pieces. As the note evolved and her hand began to tire, it became shorter and simpler and more scrawly. Finally it stood:

> *Dear Lydia,*
>
> *My will and all legal papers are in the top drawr of this desk.*
> *My mind is a mess and I am sacred to leave my home.*
> *I miss your father a lot. It's time. Please don't be mad.*
>
>
>
> *Love,*
> *Mama*
>
>

When Joyce knocked on Astrid's door in the early afternoon, there was no answer. Since patience was something she knew about, she waited almost two minutes before she knocked again, a little louder. Still no sound of steps or voice. Odd. Mrs. W was usually waiting for her. She tried the doorknob tentatively, but it did not yield. She gave another knock, but this time while she waited, she fumbled in her deep baggy purse for her key ring, reaching into the bottom past her wallet and comb, a small packet of tissues, a bank book with a rubber band around it, lipstick that she didn't use, her cell phone, a small case with an emery board and nail scissors, a note pad for lists, a pocket calendar that she found abandoned last January in the laundromat, and finally she felt the key ring, which like any weighty thing, had sunk to the very bottom. There were only three keys on it, the middle of which belonged to this door. Astrid had asked Lauren to make two copies of her front door key some months ago in a sign of both trust and apprehension.

Joyce unlocked and opened the door cautiously, as if to a room where a baby is sleeping. She put in her head, then removed the key from the lock, entered, and closed the door behind her with a soft click. The living room was quiet and empty, but then she heard a kind of moan from the bathroom. Dropping her purse on one end of the sofa, she hurried to investigate.

She found Astrid at the bathroom basin, pulling a comb repeatedly through her hair, which clung to her head almost as if it had lard on it. Since her hair was cut short and permed, even wet, it should be a little frizzy. Astrid turned towards Joyce, who stood in the doorway, and gave her a broken look of dismay.

"I just washed my hair but it's all wrong. Something's wrong." She held up her comb as if that might be the object to blame or simply as an exclamation point. The comb looked both gummy and shiny.

"That's okay, Mrs. W. Don't worry." She went in and touched one finger to the side of her head and found the hair oddly slick. Something the matter with the water? Couldn't be. "Where did you wash it?"

"At the sink. I…for my little trip tomorrow. To look nice. But look!"

"You mean the kitchen sink, right?"

"Yes, of course, the way I usually do."

"You wait here. I'll be right back." Acting on inspiration, Joyce hurried into the kitchen and found on the counter a bottle of hand lotion.

"It's okay," she consoled Astrid as she walked back into he bathroom. "You just misread the label on the bottle. Let's get out your regular shampoo, and I'll help you do it over. Your hair's gonna look real nice. It'll be nice an' soft." Joyce repressed a giggle when she thought about it.

Accordingly, she got the usual shampoo from the cabinet under the bathroom basin, led Astrid back to the kitchen, where she carefully washed her hair again, lathering it three times for good measure, commenting again on how easy it is to make that kind of mistake and that it did no harm whatsoever.

While she was shampooing Astrid's hair for the third time, she suddenly noticed the missing wedding ring and gasped. She remembered it was a real ring with a big real diamond on it.

"Mrs. W! Your ring! It must've come off when you put that lotion on your hair. It couldn't of gone down the drain, could it? Omygawd!" Immediately, she bent to examine the sink.

"No, no, Joyce! No. Stop that!" Astrid protested. "I took it off. Awhile ago."

"You took it off? But where is it?"

"It's…all right. I, actually, I gave it away."

"What d'you mean? It was your wedding ring!"

"Well, of course. But I gave it to…" Astrid fumbled for a name. "My daughter."

"You mean Lydia?"

"Of course. I wanted her to have it."

"Oh, well, in that case…" Funny, but maybe understandable.

It came to Joyce that Lydia was lucky in so many ways. For example, she had Mrs. W for her mom and of course Mr. W for a dad. And she had a husband and four kids. Joyce wouldn't have minded having four—in a real family, of course. And Lydia was smart and pretty. In fact, she was beautiful. And so slender. Luck was what did it. Nobody had good luck every minute, but some people seemed to have it most of the time. How come? An old question, she thought. *I never had much luck, but it wasn't bad every minute either. There were a few times... even Pete was good to me for a while. And Coop. And for a few minutes I held Patrick. It was so perfect. Enough...*

Joyce ran warm rinse water over Astrid's head again, noticing that her hair was not only unnaturally soft, but although quite gray, it was still thick.

"How does that feel, Mrs. W?" she asked.

"Oh nice, nice. Thank you, Joyce. Thank you so much!"

And at that moment Joyce conceded that she was lucky.

Taking Astrid back to her bedroom, Joyce turned and asked, "Now, what would you like to put on?"

"Put on?"

"Yes, dear. You're still in your bathrobe."

"Oh..." as if she had just realized it by glancing down. "I couldn't decide, you see, and then I started thinking about my trip. I used to be so good at packing years ago. Charles and I, we used to go to Europe. We were planning a trip when he died. Did you know that?"

"I'll put your clothes for tomorrow in a pile on this chair, and then they'll be ready and you won't have to think about it anymore. You know, like we talked about. The pants and shirt and the blue cardigan. How's that?" It was a decision they'd already been over more than once.

Astrid nodded, and while Joyce laid out the chosen items, she picked out of the closet a bright dress whose print consisted mostly of daisies.

"So do you want to put on this one?" Joyce asked her, handing it to her.

Astrid shook her head. "I don't like it. It's… what did they call it in the old days? Never mind. I never did like it. Do you want it?"

"You know I can't wear your clothes, Mrs. W. I'm too big."

"Well, give it away then." She dropped it, hanger and all, on the bed. "Give them all away! But this one." She returned to the closet and selected a pale green housedress with faint stripes of darker green and tan. It looked very dated, like something chanced on in a thrift shop. "This one."

"Okay. I like that one too." It was true that she did. Nice colors.

Joyce returned the daisy print to the closet, then turned back to help Astrid dress.

"No, no, I can dress," she answered testily. "You just…" She unknotted her bathrobe tie awkwardly, digging at it until it came loose. "…do something else."

"Sure." Joyce hesitated in the doorway. "Did you have breakfast?"

Astrid pulled off her bathrobe, dropped it on the bed, and looked at Joyce with a certain perplexity. "I think so. I always have breakfast."

"I'll go see about something for lunch. I think we had some vegetable soup left. How's that?"

"That's fine. Now go away. I have to get dressed."

When Astrid came into the kitchen, Joyce noticed that her dress was misbuttoned, but she tactfully took care of that and then turned back to stirring the soup. She served it with crackers at the kitchen table, and they ate in relative silence with only comments about the pleasant fall weather.

"Where's Creamy?" Astrid asked abruptly. "I don't think I've seen her today. Did you feed her?"

Joyce put down her spoon. "No, Mrs. W. You gave Creamy away. Remember? You gave her to Lauren. Last week sometime."

"Oh." She pondered the news for a moment. "Oh yes. I hope she's happy. I miss her. But I had to…"

"I'm sure Creamy's fine. But Lauren would bring her back if you asked. I can always feed her for you and all that." Joyce was trying to carry on the conversation while the face across from her gathered lines of irritation between her eyebrows.

"You don't understand! I just want this trip to be over. That's all!"

"If you feel that way, maybe you shouldn't go. I mean, a trip is supposed to be fun—"

"No, it's not for fun. I'm not thinking of coming back. It's all arranged." Astrid looked more lucid than she had so far that day, which confused Joyce so much that she couldn't think what to say. Was Mrs. W worried about an accident? No, it sounded more like she was planning not to come back to her house. To move? But where? She must have made a plan with her attorney and forgot to tell about it.

"You're such a help," Astrid observed suddenly. "I don't think I could get ready without you."

"No problem. Which reminds me, we need to set your alarm. You said Thorny's coming around seven, didn't you? That's what you wrote down. But you'll want some breakfast. Like I said, I traded my shift with Nancy, so I can come over and help you get ready. But you should allow an hour anyway. It's never good to feel rushed. So let's say six o'clock?"

"Yes, that's fine."

"But first let's get this stuff cleared away." She stood up from the table and gathered their bowls.

"Do you have my daughter's phone number?" Astrid asked to Joyce's back as she put the bowls in the sink.

"Yes. I mean it's programmed on your phone."

"Of course. You can explain about my clothes. Just get rid of them. But some of the books might be worth money. There are a few first editions, you know. I already gave one to Laura. But my daughter… my daughter…" She faltered. "She can use the money. Four children and a worthless husband. Do you know my daughter?"

"I've met her, if that's what you mean." All at once Lydia sounded less lucky.

"I'm leaving her this house," Astrid added, practical. "Maybe she'll want to live here someday. She grew up here, you know, I mean in this house." She paused, concentrating on the blank place on the table where her soup bowl had been. "I guess everything's ready. I can't think of anything… except… did you set the alarm?"

"No, not yet. I'll do it as soon as I wash up."

"I worry about oversleeping."

"You won't oversleep." Joyce reassured her and began running water in the sink. She never used the dishwasher for so few dishes, which meant she hardly ever used it at all.

THORNY GOES TO A BAR

Thorny sat on the sofa in his mostly empty living room and looked at a wall bare of shelving, bare of pictures. Just a wall. Oddly, it didn't seem that he had anything else to do. He had prepared his departure so thoroughly, made his legal arrangements, paid his bills, given his share for the flight to Richard at their meeting last Wednesday, and called Astrid this afternoon to see if there was anything she needed. Joyce had answered and assured him that Astrid was ready, though "kind of confused." Well, that didn't surprise him. Anyway, she could still decide not to go, even at the airport. He refused to concern himself with any decision except his and Richard's. Their time was firm.

So what to do, except see an invisible clock on the goddam wall? It came to him, odd as it seemed, that he could go down to the local bar where he was pretty sure to run into Rudy Stanopolos getting his pre-dinner refreshment. Thorny had never been one to patronize the bar, except sometimes with Rudy, especially in the summer and early fall when they might be between jobs and a cold beer was nectar. But he went more often lately, since he didn't have Clare to go home to. He'd known Rudy since they were buddies in grade school. You couldn't say that about many people in a society that saw constant movement upstream or downstream according to the currents of money that flow through suburban communities.

Driving down to Fourth Street, Thorny focused his thought on Rudy. He was living with a woman who worked for a wealthy family in Fairfax and often stayed late in the evening to serve dinner when they were having guests. She'd been with them for about ten years, "like family" now, but of course not like family, still an employee. But Adela had no real complaints. It seemed that this family had always been rich, so they weren't arrogant, just entitled. Adela passed on the stories of the usual family problems, their fights, their flights, their kids going wild, or wildly successful. Sometimes only a raft of money kept them afloat. "So if the rich aren't happy, who is?" Rudy would ask rhetorically. But both he and Thorny knew the answer: it lay in wanting what you have. Knowing when you're happy. Just that.

Pondering that great truth, Thorny nearly walked past the entrance to the bar, but was signaled by the sound of voices when the door opened to let someone out. While the door was still ajar, he went in. There he stood for a moment, adjusting his eyes to the lower light.

"Hey Thorny! Over here!"

So Rudy was there, down near the far end of the bar. Thorny walked over and planted himself on the next stool. Rudy was a big, bearded man of splendid strength who had gotten himself quite a beer belly since he retired from full time sheetrock and carpentry. Now he did odd jobs for people, but didn't put in enough work to stay entirely fit. "Drywall, lumber, and beer keep a guy in shape," he used to say, but now it was mostly beer. Nevertheless, he defended himself by adding that at some time in your life you should relax and humor your belly. Rudy was both widowed and divorced and had lived with a couple of different women in between his changes in marital status, but now he'd been with Adela for about six years, so maybe he was actually settling down.

"So Thorny, how goes it?"

"Okay. Yourself?"

"About usual. I'm still doin' that little remodel job over in San Anselmo. I got the sheetrock up yesterday and taped it today, so I'm ready to start painting on Monday. Painting's a drag, but it's part of the deal. I hope she's not one of those who wants to change color about the time you're half done. Or decides she wants to know if you do wallpaper. 'No, Ma'am, I don't,' and then they get mad. Y'know? Well, hey, I haven't seen you in a while. I started thinkin' maybe you died or somethin'. Whatcha been up to?"

"Nothin' much. Just sort of wrappin' up my business. I'm retired, y' know."

"You mean, like totally? I don' believe it."

"Yeah, totally. Just finished my last job. Like I told you, I got arthritis. Can't work anymore, man. The doc says to take aspirin or something. Doesn't help much, and I don't believe in those expensive drugs. Side effects an' all that. Know what I mean?"

"Yeah, I know. Shit, man, drug dealers come in all varieties."

Thorny nodded. Then he looked at the bartender, Howard, who was waiting across the bar expectantly, though he already knew the probable order.

"A dark draft."

"You got it."

He drew the beer and set it down in front of Thorny with a napkin. The head teetered on the edge of the glass and then gently subsided.

"So how's Adela these days?" Thorny asked Rudy as soon as he'd taken the first sip and licked a wisp of foam off his upper lip.

"Just great. Y'know, that woman's the best cook I've ever met. I mean it. She can cook anything and never opens a cookbook. Hell, she can't even read English, but she sure can cook!"

"Yeah, it shows all right."

Rudy laughed. "Sure. The belly's a sign of a satisfied man just like with a satisfied woman." He laughed again. "Shit man, you know what the trouble is with you? Trouble is you haven't got any woman to cook for you—or nothin' else either. Now don't get me wrong. I mean I know Clare was the greatest, and you gotta grieve, sure, but you gotta go on too. Life isn't just a slog, it's an adventure. Something always around the corner, maybe not perfect, but you know… You can go fishing and not catch anything and still have a great time. You take me an' Adela. Maybe she's not perfect, but who wants perfection anyhow? Perfection just makes a guy feel…inadequate. Know what I mean?"

"Yeah, sure." But Thorny didn't want to discuss women or even life, past or future. Rudy was great, but his greatness wasn't consoling now, it was exhausting. His attention strayed to the beer ads behind the bar, those decorated mirrors that announced Coors or Budweiser and all the rest of them and actually managed to be kind of pretty. There was movement in the mirrors as another patron came in and settled himself down toward the other end of the bar. It wasn't anybody Thorny knew, but he was known to Howard, who greeted him affably and fell to pouring a whiskey and soda.

It came to Thorny all of a sudden that he'd never be here again, that this time next week, this time tomorrow actually, he'd be dead. But he didn't find the thought either frightening or depressing. It was a kind of relief—like a man who'd suffered so much pain in one of his legs that he willingly consents to have it taken off. Thorny finished his beer and set the glass down with a slight thunk, wondering if he wanted another one, not sure if he was still thirsty.

"I swear to god, Thorny, you just need to get out more. Come on over sometime and have dinner with me an' Adela. Maybe she can invite a friend, one of her nice Latina girlfriends…"

"No, none of that," Thorny cut him off, "but thanks anyway. Appreciate it. I'll let you know."

"Okay, sure. I worry about you. That's all."

"Nah. I'm okay…"

With that assurance, they turned their attention to the baseball game that was in progress on the TV at the corner of the room. The Giants and the Astros, the Giants leading one-zip at the bottom of the second. Maybe worth their attention. "That was good about Eckersley," Rudy observed at the end of the inning. "Now they should put in Gossage and Sutter, like they say."

"You mean in the Hall of Fame?"

"Sure. I mean it's the end of the game that counts, isn't it?"

Thorny nodded. "Can't deny that. 'It ain't over till it's over', huh?"

A roar from the TV set told them that the third inning was not only under way, but that a hit that looked like homer had just gone foul.

Impulsively, Thorny ordered another beer, which he sipped slowly as they watched the game, made idle comments, and assessed the possibilities for the World Series. The shiny bar in front of Thorny took on a graceful pattern of overlapping wet circles of condensation from his glass as he alternately sipped and set it down. All at once Thorny got to thinking about the World Series. Although he hadn't followed baseball much since Greg died, he always watched the play-offs and the Series. He and Clare. They made little parties, ate hot dogs in front of the TV set, cheered their preferred team (not always the same one), and behaved like kids. When it struck him that he'd never know who won the pennant, at that moment he came as close to regretting his decision as he had come, thinking it could wait until after the season was over, only another couple months planted in front of the TV set, beer in hand, cheering the Giants, who didn't really deserve it, not this season anyway…and breaking his promise to Richard, who was counting on him. The others could still turn back, but he couldn't. And no, he didn't want to. To hell with games! No game makes you happy for very long, even if your team wins. Anyhow, when somebody wins, somebody else loses, which Clare always said was a shame.

All of a sudden Thorny didn't want to be with Rudy anymore, didn't feel like being entangled in a world he was about to leave. It made him feel like the only kid at a skating party who didn't know how to skate, who just tagged along and watched. It was about like hearing a jack hammer in the street to hear Rudy rattle on about the current ranking of the Red Socks and the Cards and the latest case of over-management when the Giants lost to the Dodgers in the tenth. This sort of thing had been interesting to Thorny once, but now it was just noise, and he wanted quiet. He finished his second beer without really attending to either the conversation or the beer, and when he had sucked the final drop out of the glass, he pushed it unceremoniously away and stood.

"You leavin', Thorny?" Rudy demanded. "You only just got here. Like you said, it ain't over till it's over," he added, grinning.

"Yeah, I'm sorry, but I got stuff to do at home. Guess I better go to the head first. Like they say about beer…"

"Yeah, right."

Thorny paid Howard for the beers and then went back to the restroom. When he came out he saw that Rudy was talking to Howard and a couple other guys who had just come in. He caught a phrase that told him that the subject had turned to the upcoming football season, but he didn't pause to participate. Just as he was at the door, Rudy's voice snagged him from behind.

"Hey, Thorny!" he hollered, over the noise of the television.

"Yeah what?" he answered, turning.

"Remember to give me a call. Remember what I said about comin' for dinner."

"I'll do that. Thanks. Say hi to Adela."

"Will do. Take care, man."

"Right. You too."

Thorny went out onto the sidewalk to find that, although the sun had dropped behind the mountain, it was still perfectly light out. There was a softness in the blue-pink halo along the outline of Mount Tam, enhanced by the slightest wisp of breeze.

Thorny blinked for a moment to adjust his eyes. The street was clogged with the tail of rush hour traffic, and he stood back against the building to let a clatter of pedestrians go by. Mainly young women off work from local offices or stores, trailing chitchat behind them. Thorny followed them into their future with his eyes. Just for a minute. Then he set off down the street to the carpark. All he wanted was to go home.

RICHARD TAKES LEAVE

Richard Young stood on the back deck of their house, leaning slightly forward with both elbows resting on the railing, the very place he had stood when he began to formulate his pact with John Thornton three weeks ago. Since the house was set on a hill that sloped downward from the street, the sense of solidity it gave on entering at the front turned to an impression of aerial suspension at the back, where the deck with its stout redwood railing might have been the deck of a sailing ship, high above the water. Below it were other houses, of course, but straight ahead at eye level was the bay and beyond the bay was San Francisco, a city that managed to be noisily, messily real and fantastic at the same time. Pale now in the day's afterglow. Sprinkles of light would soon begin to show. Sailboats were mostly gone from the bay, a few remaining like bits of white lint on a blue-green spread. Richard had looked at this scene thousands of times since they bought the house and always found it freshly beautiful. In sun or fog or starlight. They used to joke that, yes, money *can* buy happiness, but only if happiness is what you spend it on. The money that bought this house had worked.

Since the sun was just down behind the Marin hills, he could look directly to the west without the pain of brightness. The air was calm and still warm. There was no hint of fog. Off to the left, the hills of the East Bay were pink with the sun's final illumination. The venerable East Bay hills with their spreading mold of human habitation that became so dazzlingly beautiful by night. No ship's prow could offer a better prospect of port as it glided home.

Perspective is everything, he was thinking. When seeing the earth from twenty thousand feet, dotted and wrinkled and furrowed below him, he had sometimes thought, "This is the way God sees the world, not in bits and pieces, but as a totality, like the picture of Earth from space, gem-like and glowing."

But one day Susie came running to him with an oak leaf, on the underside of which was a golden spot, a little larger than the head of a pin and slightly slimy to the touch. He looked at it, but couldn't tell her what it was, then looked again with a magnifying glass and discovered that the golden patch consisted of dozens of insect eggs, and it came to him then that this was also the way God saw the world, in its infinite detail, every cell of it, every atom. In fact, in the divine mind—if there was one—there was no near or far, no inside or outside, because these were all just artifacts of human perception, and God would surely perceive everything equally, from every point of view at once, everything in constant motion, yet always fitting together. Individuals will die, but the pattern goes on season after season. The golden insect eggs hatch, creep, grow wings, fly, sink, decay, but the whole remains. Ripples rising and falling. The universe moves in waves. Maybe death is really an illusion, as some say. A mere transformation.

This beauty, this heart-wrenching beauty of earth and sky, he could never imagine leaving it, if he hadn't been leaving it already, but as he had no choice, he responded to the force of the horizon line as the best and only proper place for his transformation. To shatter like a phoenix at the point of union. For other people there might be other, better places, but for him…

Just then Karen came out and stood beside him on his right, also leaning her arms on the deck railing, looking out at the same scene, companionable.

"Hi there," she said finally.

"Hi, yourself."

"Beautiful evening."

"Yeah, almost too much."

"I trust the girls will be grateful."

"What do you mean?" he asked, not meaning to sound startled.

"This property. Like we just said. It's worth a bundle. Our children and grandchildren will cash in."

He didn't comment on luck then, but thought about it. The nature of real estate. Location, timing, having the cash to invest. In a constricting middle class, their mobility had been gracefully upward. Unless they blew it, his daughters would be able to stay afloat, no matter what the passing economic storm.

Yes, they'd been lucky. No explaining it. When he thought of what had happened to Thorny, he realized how really lucky he had been. Uncanny in a way, except for the prolonged and pathetic illness of his grandfather, how his family had never been touched with a serious tragedy. It was true that Karen's father had died quite suddenly in his fifties, but her mother had remarried, happily. His own parents lived the complacent life of the comfortably retired near his sister in Tucson. Of course he didn't want to grieve them, but he knew them. They had their church, their hobbies, their friends. They'd be all right.

"You okay?" Karen asked him suddenly.

"How's that?" Startled again.

"You seem a little tired. Are you sure you want to take this flight tomorrow? You could just call Thorny, couldn't you? Tell him you'd like to put it off."

"No, I'm fine," he countered quickly. "I think the flight'll be relaxing. It'll be beautiful. You know how spectacular the country is between here and Reno. And Thorny's counting on going, like I said. I only charged him expenses because he's a good guy."

"I like Thorny too. And I like you." She smiled at him then, and he returned her smile. He would have hugged her, but he was afraid he would cry. "Look," she said mercifully, "I gotta check on something in the oven. Can I bring you a drink?"

"Mineral water, if you don't mind."

"You got it."

Karen disappeared off the deck. Richard could hear her talking to their cat, Mandy, in the kitchen. That chipper voice people use with animals.

Richard ached for some way to comfort her against his death, the way he comforted her when she lost her father. Just to hold her, to let her cry. He felt sick. His own pain suddenly wrapped itself around his side and ran up into his armpit, harsh and unexpected. *Christ, just let me get through this!*

It was his first deliberate prayer in years, beyond the formalities of their Episcopal religion. He had prayed, despite himself, when he was suiting up for his first solo flight, and when each of the children was born. *"Dear God, let Karen and the baby be okay."* That sort of prayer. A wish really. It now gave him no particular comfort to remember that these prayers, or wishes, had been benevolently answered.

He thought his hand shook a little when he took the glass from Karen, but hoped she didn't notice. He covered his distress with an idle question about dinner. He wasn't hungry, hadn't been hungry in days, but pretended. It was the pretending that made him weariest. He wasn't a natural actor.

Karen answered something about a casserole and went back to the kitchen.

Christ, just get me through.

Contrary to his expectations, Richard actually slept for a couple of hours, but he woke up quite suddenly, feeling how his pajamas stuck to his body and realizing that he was covered with sweat. Again he felt a pain, though dull, that found its way into his armpit. The pain was a relatively recent experience that he could no longer smother with standard pain relievers. It was rather like the shape of someone closing in on him, as a man who knows he's being followed feels the stalking presence in a crowd. So he lay perfectly still for a time, trying not to move or shiver, half hoping that by being completely motionless, he could convince the pain that he wasn't to be found there after all, and if he only waited, it would turn away like a bill collector from the door, frustrated.

He no longer worried about the decisions of his passengers. At first he couldn't believe he'd be willing to take anyone with him, but he knew he had to take someone, and he never really doubted Thorny's resolve. Then he gave in to Astrid, then Matt. Was it only three days ago? But they didn't have to go. They could turn back at the airport. You can't take total responsibility for the decisions of others. Once people were aboard, then their lives were in his hands, but he would never make anyone go on board. That wasn't his business. He tried to take that attitude now. Anyway, he had no energy to argue anymore, not even with himself, especially not with himself.

Like any pilot, he'd had a few close calls in his career, unforeseen down drafts, a collapsed landing gear once at Kansas City. He'd never liked KSO anyway. It only confirmed his prejudice. A near collision with a light plant at Albuquerque. At least he could pretty much count the near-mishaps on the fingers of one hand, and none had been through negligence of his. He examined the flight path again in his mind's eye. He knew the place where Thorny wanted to scatter the ashes, some fifty nautical miles southwest of Reno. No problem there.

After a period of mental review that seemed long, but probably wasn't, he turned his head slightly and looked at the glow of the clock radio. A quarter to five. He might as well get up and prepare to meet the morning that would be the end of his enemy. He needed a certain anger now, against the monster he intended to destroy.

Putting his feet over the side of the bed, he stood up cautiously, both to avoid attracting the further notice of the pain that searched his side for better purchase and to keep from waking Karen. He stood by the bedside for a moment, cold with sweat. Then he turned to the chair and drew on his bathrobe, paused, listened for the quiet breathing that indicated no disturbance of her sleep. Many times over the years he'd gotten up in the dark to go to the airport, and most times he'd gone without waking her. He kidded her sometimes about being "sleeping beauty," and said he'd have to cut through a hundred years of thorns to get back in. But it'd be worth it.

Only this time, he couldn't see her because of the dark. Nevertheless he looked towards the place where he knew she was, warm in the covers and couldn't help thinking to her, *Wake up once more, my darling, just once before I go. Reach out and draw me in. It would surround my going like a halo to merge our bodies one more time. Only we can't because it would break my heart and because in the middle of love-making I'd feel the cancer's claws and wouldn't be able to go on. Damn it to hell! Our marriage has more strings than a harp, and I can't strike any of them now.* He thought his longing to her so vividly that suddenly he was almost afraid she would hear his thinking, and he turned away.

Quietly he went to the bathroom where a nightlight shed a dull glow, urinated, and then took two ibuprofens, for what it was worth. Next he went to the kitchen and made a cup of instant coffee. With his cup in hand, he sat at the kitchen table, reviewing the flight chart in mind yet again, almost bored by it now, like an actor who has rehearsed too many times and longs for the performance to begin.

He was finding it almost funny that Richard Ryan Young, known for his safety record, could have an accident. People who knew him would shake their heads and finally fall back on the law of averages, for which there was no law. But they wouldn't think of suicide. He remembered the case of Harry Rice who flew his plane to Napa, had breakfast at the airport and crashed in a field on the way back to Marin. But his case was different. There wasn't a note, but everyone knew. The difference was that Richard wasn't depressed. Had never been. He was always a cheerful guy. He knew that most people liked him, like the Richard in the poem. How did it go? *"And Richard Cory, one calm summer night, went home and put a bullet through his head."* Mysterious, granted, but the bullet had not been an accident. His bullet was a steep granite wall, a twin that he hadn't flown very much, and weather. He would report lightning. He would make it explicable.

By the time he finished his coffee, he felt warmer and more relaxed. At the moment there was no pain. Getting up, he put his cup in the sink, crossed the living room and opened the sliding door onto the deck, where he had taken leave of the bay on the evening before. Although the cold of morning slapped his body, it was a welcome stimulant.

There was always the sound of traffic nowadays, no matter what the time, but the sound was whispery and distant, laboring up the Waldo Grade. It was Saturday after all, not a big commute day. A waning half-moon in the middle of the sky was looking backward at the pursuing sun that even now rushed over Nevada towards the craggy landscape of the Sierras.

He watched the horizon for the path of light that opens at the feet of the sun and imagined rushing out to meet it, like a child to his homecoming father. He expected no immortality, but maybe at the last moment of life a conscious feeling of escape, of flight without instruments or wings or the roaring chrysalis of metal.

However it happens, death is a lonely thing because it's yours, like your dreams, your thoughts, your life, only more so. A thing unsharable, even if someone who loves you is close by, doing everything possible to soften it. But the only way to console the dying is to let them go. He had watched his grandmother, bent like a melting candle by the bed of his grandfather, who was dying of the same disease. But his grandfather smoked. Was there a genetic weakness? It wasn't fair. Shut up about fair! Where did the idea of "fair" come from anyway? Only last night he'd been thinking of his remarkable good luck. Keep that thought. Only this time your good luck will be your bad luck. Or vice versa.

Finally, as he stood there, he saw the margin of his last day begin as a pale gray line between the denser stars of human electricity below and the more scattered stars of the universe, a gentle dimming as though the higher stars were receding into the sun, and the human stars fell away before its golden wheel. Soon color would begin in the sky, on the hills, the bay, emerging as though from within, like the beating heart of an embryo.

Turning away from the railing, Richard went back into the house. It was time to go. Although he'd be driving against the traffic, there'd be enough between himself and Gnoss Field. So he went back to the bedroom, picked up the pile of clothes he had left stacked on the chair, ready, and took them into the bathroom, where he dressed by the pale circlet of the night light.

As a reflex, when he had finished dressing, he reached for his toothbrush, paused to wonder with a kind of ironic humor whether there was really much point in brushing his teeth, but then did so anyway. As he was putting his brush back in its holder, his hand just touched Karen's brush, barely green in the dull light. Taking it out, he held it in his hand, held it like a delicate piece of glass, wished he could take it with him like a totem or an amulet, abruptly put the handle to his lips and kissed it, then put it back. Everything he did, except for running water in the sink, was silent. Still, as he was about to pass through the bedroom, shoes in hand, he heard the covers move. He paused by the door.

"Rich?"

"Yes. I'm just getting ready to leave. Go back to sleep."

"What time is it?" she asked with a voice half-buried in a pillow.

"A quarter to six, give or take."

"Do you want me to see you off?" Not enthusiastic.

"Certainly not. I'm just on my way. No point in you getting up."

"Okay. Well, have a good flight."

He was grateful she wasn't inclined to get up, but he had counted on that. "Thanks." He wavered sickly then, almost went back to the bed to kiss her goodbye, but mastered himself. "G'bye, sweetie," he said from the doorway.

Then he left the room, closing the door behind him. When he took his hand away, the knob was damp with sweat.

He left her a note on the kitchen table, according to custom, confirming his schedule. "K. See you this evening. Don't wait supper. R." and followed the initial with an X, the usual one, that had a long crossing tail that streamed off the edge of the paper.

JOYCE MAKES A DISCOVERY

When Joyce pushed the doorbell button, a few minutes after seven, there was no reply. Ironically, it was Joyce who overslept that morning. Of course, she had intended to be there much earlier to give Mrs. W her breakfast and make sure she was ready when Thorny showed up. But it happened that after waking up automatically at her usual time at four, she fell asleep again. Which was okay. But it seemed she'd forgotten to pull out the little lever on her bedside clock when she reset it for 5:30 the night before. Really stupid. She'd jumped out of bed at ten to seven, realizing that Thorny was due at any time. It was fully light out.

Joyce put on her underwear, pulled on her jeans and shirt, then over it, her favorite blue sweatshirt, grabbed her purse, and hurried out into the cool morning without really waking up. So what? She could always get coffee at Mrs. W's. See her off. Then get another cup.

Walking along the street at her most brisk pace, panting a little, she was reviewing the wonderful idea that came to her just before she fell asleep the night before. It came like an inspiration out of somewhere else, like a voice that spoke only inside her head, a thought that was like a nudge when someone next to you wants to draw your attention to something special without making any noise. Is that the way God talks to people? Not in actual words, but in ideas? Anyway, it was a proposal she wanted to make to Mrs. W, and she kept thinking how best to make it. *How about if I, because I know you worry about having to leave your house... I mean I understand that, so what if I could just sort of move in here, upstairs, which you don't use anyway, and take care of you. I' d still work at the coffee shop, but I' d be with you most of the time, just in case you need help or if something you want gets lost."* Something like that, but not so raggedy.

Joyce hadn't told Astrid about finding a pair of socks carefully tucked away in a drawer with dishtowels in the kitchen, or any other of the oddly misplaced items that turned up from time to time. But all this now fell in with her new idea. As she walked, she kept on rehearsing how best to put her case for moving in.

"Gee, Mrs. W," she murmured to herself, *"maybe you could even get Creamy back. I don't think Lauren would mind, and I' d take care of her. I could do everything you need. Cooking, cleaning, laundry, all that stuff. Sort of like I do anyway, only more. Maybe I could even get a driver's license. Like I said, I pretty much know how to drive and all the rules. I just never got around to taking the test. Maybe Lauren would let me use her car for the test. She's nice about things. And if I could get together a little money because, see, if you would let me live in your house, I wouldn't need to pay rent, so I could save a little. And then I could even buy a car, just an old one. Then I could drive you places. We could even go to the beach sometime. If you wanted. The front room upstairs overlooking the street is really nice. I' d fix it up. Make new curtains and all that stuff. I wouldn't be any trouble, but I' d be close if you needed me. I think it' d work out great. Like they say 'win/ win.'"* But her internal monologue came to an end at the top of the porch, which she reached sooner than she expected because her mind was so occupied.

Routinely she rang the doorbell, but since no one came to the door, Joyce fished in her purse, brought out the key, and opened it.

Mrs. W was probably in the bathroom, having a pee before she left. Or still brushing her teeth. She always seemed to take a long time at that. It was lucky that at her age she still had pretty good teeth to brush. But it turned out that Mrs. W wasn't in the bathroom, or the bedroom, or the kitchen. Joyce was about to go upstairs, even though, as far as she knew, Mrs. W never went up there anymore, when she thought of the study at the front of the house. And there on the desk she found the note, right in the middle. The hand was somewhat shaky, but quite legible and definitely that of Mrs. W. The way teachers write.

> *Dear Lydia,*
>
> *My will and all legal papers are in the top drawr of this desk. My mind is a mess and I am sacred to leave my home. I miss your father a lot. It's time. Please don't be mad.*
>
> *Love,*
> *Mama*

Joyce stood by the desk with the note in her hand. A funny thing to say, but then she remembered that she used to write "sacred" for "scared" herself sometimes when she was in school. Like she wrote "dinning room" for "dining room." But it came to her then that it wasn't the spelling that seemed to odd. It was the message. The whole thing.

All at once the restraint of conventional thinking let go like an old window shade that flies up with an unexpected, frightening snap. Just how they planned to do it she had no idea, but when Mrs. W had said she wasn't coming back, it wasn't about moving. She meant it. And it had something to do with an airplane and Thorny and that other man who had visited lately. It was crazy but not crazy at the same time. She began remembering other funny things Mrs. W had said lately, like about getting rid of her clothes. Giving Creamy away. Having to clean up this and that "before I go." *Dumb me! All that stuff I planned to tell her when I got here…I should've told her days ago. Weeks ago. How I could live with her and take care of her. Why didn't I? Only I didn't think of it. Now it's too late! I'm too late! She's already gone. Maybe she planned to leave early on purpose. Could she plan that? Or maybe that guy Thorny… Shit! I was gonna give her some breakfast an' tell her my idea. She doesn't have to go and do something stupid because she's scared. Poor thing! Of course I don't blame her, but this is so stupid! Only maybe she just left, like two minutes before I got here. It's only just a quarter after now. I probably just missed her, so maybe it's not too late after all.*

Joyce took Astrid's note to the living room and turned on the light by the telephone. She was rushing in mind, but getting nowhere. She knew from some comment that it was not the San Francisco airport, but the local one. She could look it up in the phone book and call, and say… what? "Stop Mrs. Williamson and Thorny from getting on a plane"? That made no sense. If she called the police or the sheriff and said there was going to be a suicide, they'd ask her how she knew, and even if someone believed her and went out to the airport, Mrs. W would probably say no, it wasn't true, that they were just going up to look at the scenery. If Joyce showed someone the note, Mrs. W would say it was for her daughter. Private. Like she left it in case of an accident. Like insurance, sort of.

As she pondered, she actually opened the drawer in the end table with the telephone, since that was where Mrs. W kept her phone directory. It wasn't there, probably misplaced, but there were five ten-dollar bills, joined with a paper clip. No, Joyce did not have a theory for that.

Then an inspiration. She could call Lauren. Lauren would probably know what to do. Have some idea, anyway. Joyce remembered that Lauren's number was on button 3 of the cordless phone. A good thing she remembered. So she hit the third button and waited. It was no longer early, not for Lauren anyway, who said she always got up early.

Well, not as early as Joyce. No one got up that early unless they had to. But the ringing seemed to go on for a while.

When Lauren said "Hello?" she sounded sort of tentative, like hopeful it would be somebody else, but not sure.

"Hey, Lauren. It's me. Joyce. I gotta…something really bad is happening, and I really, really need some help." With that almost hysterical opening, she went on to tell her about the note for Lydia, about finally getting the meaning of it all. Although she was blathering as she talked, she gathered her wits into the proposal that had come to her as she was waiting for the phone to be answered. "Could you possibly go up to the county airport? Would you just go up there and find her and stop her from going and tell her that she doesn't need to do anything stupid because I plan to come and stay with her and look out for her so she won't have to leave her home. I can take care of her for a long time, maybe even until she dies. I mean dies naturally. I mean you can tell her for me. If you would, please. Can't you?"

Lauren's voice in answer sounded as if the request was more peculiar than urgent. "Yes, I suppose I could do that," she answered hesitantly. "I suppose I should—if you're that worried. The traffic. It's Saturday, isn't it? If she just left, I'd be there almost as soon as…" Her voice trailed off, like someone considering other possibilities, but not coming up with anything. "Yes, I suppose I can do that," she repeated. "Okay. Do you want me to come down and pick you up? Then you can talk to her yourself."

"No, no, I don't think so! That'd waste time, because, see, I don't know how long she's been gone. I'm just guessing not very long. I just want you to tell her what I said. Get her to come home. Make her come home if you have to. Just… please… I'm not all that religious, but I'm sure God doesn't mean for her to do this. He means for me to take care of her." All of a sudden, it did seem that there really was a divine plan. Not just her plan. It wasn't that Joyce knew the Bible. She'd only been to vacation Bible school a few times when her foster mother sent her, but she knew that one way or another God often worked through people to get things to happen. You had to do something, but God would help out. Like that.

"Yes, all right. Don't worry," Lauren sounded vaguely reassuring. "I'll give you a call from the airport. Get some coffee. I'll see what's going on. It'll be all right. Calm down, okay?"

No, not okay, not really, but Joyce agreed gratefully and hung up the phone, trying to trust that if God had a plan for her to save Mrs. W, then it couldn't fail.

AT THE AIRPORT

Harris was right about one thing: the commute wasn't worth the effort. Even on a Saturday and even driving against the main flow of traffic, getting onto 101 was a pig, then advancing warily, watching out for the mergers and the weavers. Like that blue van sweeping in off the overpass lane as if there was no one else on the road. Lauren pretended to herself that there was no urgency anyway, that Joyce was overreacting, but even if she wasn't, even if she was right about this stupefying plan, was it really her business to intervene? Lauren recalled the case of an old woman—Marilyn was her name—someone she had visited for a short time when she had first volunteered with the Council. Marilyn had a clear directive that called for "no resuscitation." And yet they had brought her back from a stroke that she shouldn't have survived. For the year of life that remained, she was helpless and morose and, of course, incapable of suicide. So... But first she had to get there and at least deliver Joyce's message. If Astrid was even there. Lauren felt more curiosity than anxiety. All some sort of mistake on Joyce's part.

She got to thinking again how Harris did this on week days. Poor guy. Today he said he'd gone in early to give some kind of adult class, or did he just go to have a tryst with Fay? Well, if he was right about the commute, he was probably right about the rest of it.

Time to get on with his life. It took courage for him to admit it. *That much I have to admire. Good ole Harris. He is, in fact, starting to bald a little. Yes, it is time. For me too. Scary. But good. I'll gather all the money I can from the divorce and move wherever Matt moves. Even LA Palm trees are fine if he's under them. I can review my Spanish. I'll look for some kind of job. Clerking. Anything. I'm not too proud. Why have I been such a wimp? Like an adult child who refuses to leave home. Had to be kicked out. Embarrassing. I should've left him, but I've been so secure all these years. So I'm scared. Why not admit it? But then too, why not admit I never liked LA? Every time I was there, even at Disneyland or the Getty Museum, still, all that traffic and heat. Of course Harris was driving, Harris was always driving... But I could adjust if I could be near Matt, but if only there was a way to keep him here, anyway in the Bay Area. My comfort zone. Only I've had too much comfort zone, haven't I?*

She passed Highway 37, which bled off quite a lot of traffic to the east. After that it was easier to maneuver. Get in the right lane after you pass South Novato. *I haven't been to the county airport in years. When? It had something to do with David going up in a light plane with one of his buddies. Can't remember, but his father was a pilot. All the same, I shivered when they took off, but luckily David didn't catch the flying bug. Harris would've paid for lessons. Thank gawd that didn't happen. Driving is bad enough. They say flying is safer, but can you really believe it? Can't be far to the Atherton exit. Yes, there's the wetlands. So-called.*

It was only as she took the off-ramp that she forced herself to think again of her mission. *What the hell am I doing here anyway? What am I supposed to say to Astrid, even if she's there? What if she really is part of some kind of suicide pact? It's like a damn soap opera. Let's just say she's there. And then I'm supposed to tell her to come home with me because Joyce wants to live with her, and if she says, "I don't want to go home," then what?*

I'll stand there like a ninny with my mouth open. I should've told Joyce to leave it alone. As if she could. Little bulldog Joyce.

The dry grasses and reeds along the narrow entry road brushed her vision. Cooler days didn't mean the end of the seasonal drought, but a nice period of not much fog, an indrawn breath before the rains began. If and when they did. There were always water wars in California, but climate change... Wildfires reported in the LA area, but then there were fires everywhere. The road curved into the airport entrance with its spread of ugly, massive, square, steel buildings. So functional.

Lauren drove past the first building that carried the logo of a private aviation company and pulled up in a parking area behind the next one, happy to find a space in its morning shade. Few other drivers had arrived. There was an older model blue pickup two spaces away and beyond that a couple of SUVs, then a Volvo sedan, and next to it, a silver Honda sedan that reminded her of Matt's. A painted sign on a low building to her right read AIRPORT OFFICES, which looked like a place to start. She got out, pressed the lock button, not hurrying, neither knowing where to look nor what to say if she found Astrid inside. Or was she already aboard a plane? That would simplify things. She would simply tell Joyce that she had arrived too late. Then whatever happens, happens.

As she was about to enter the building, she noted that on her left two lanes of light planes were tied down, mostly single engine, a couple of twins, and what looked like a private jet. The field area was separated from the buildings by a chain link fence, with an opening near the office. She squinted into the new sun, then away again to her left. On the farthest row away from the fence a lone man seemed to be doing a walk-around, but hard to see against the light. Then in the nearest row, but close to the end of it, she saw a man releasing a tie-down cable on a blue and white twin. Just on the other side of the plane was another man, or rather a pair of trouser legs and a small, dark lump on the ground, no doubt a piece of luggage. No one who looked remotely like Astrid Williamson. Lauren was momentarily distracted by the approach of a light plane doing touch and goes. She watched it land and take off with vague interest. The procrastination of uncertainty.

Then with an effort that came only from the resolution of her commitment to Joyce, she turned and went into the office building, still not sure what she was going to say or do. No sooner was she in the hall than she saw a man maybe in his sixties hovering outside the door of the women's restroom. Waiting for his wife? A sign and arrow on the wall pointed to the main lobby.

"Excuse me…" he spoke to Lauren diffidently as she was about to pass him.

"Yes?"

"I… could I ask you a favor?"

"Sure."

"There's a lady inside, and it's been several minutes. I'm starting to get concerned about her. But I didn't want to go into the 'ladies,' you know… If you wouldn't mind just stepping in to check on her. Be sure she's okay. She's elderly. Gets kind of confused."

"Sure. Of course. I'll be right back."

But when she went into the restroom, there was no one there, at least not visible. Two toilet stall doors were partly open, a third closed.

"Hello?" She paused outside the closed door. "Is someone in there?"

"Oh, thank God!" answered a familiar voice. "Please! Can you help me? This door is stuck!" An urgent request that was near a cry.

Astrid!

"Astrid, it's me. Lauren. Don't worry. Don't be upset. I'll get you out. Maybe it's just the latch. Don't worry. Astrid, listen to me. Let's try the latch again. Do you see it? There's a little knob on it."

"Yes, yes, I know," Astrid answered sharply from the other side. "I pulled and pulled it, but it doesn't come." She was pleading now like a child on the point of crying.

"No, dear, don't pull. Just try to slide it to one side. Just take ahold and slide to your…away from the crack where the door opens. Away from the crack," Lauren repeated, hoping that it made sense, but not at all optimistic.

There was a fumbling sound inside the door and a sudden opening inward, revealing Astrid, dressed in beige pants, a print blouse, and a familiar light blue sweater. Her purse strap was over her shoulder. Very travel-ready. She smiled at Lauren without seeming surprised to see her, a quick social smile.

"Oh Sarah—I mean Laura—thank you! I was getting a little scared and I didn't know how to get ahold of Thorny. I tried calling, but no one came. Where is he? Is he still waiting? I don't want him to go without me!" Her words came in little clumps like someone breathless from running.

"No, he's there. Right outside. It's okay." Lauren put one arm protectively around Astrid's shoulders. "Do you want to wash up?" she asked, guiding her to the sink. "Did you say 'Thorny'?"

"Yes. He brought me. In his truck. We're going together. He promised to wait by the door. Is he still there?"

"Yes, right outside the door. He was worried, but he didn't want to come into the ladies' room. You know how it is."

Lauren turned on the faucet for Astrid, watched while she routinely washed her hands. As there was only a blow dryer in the room, Lauren fished in her pants pocket and handed Astrid a clean handkerchief. Astrid dried her hands in a partial way and handed it back. Though it was now damp, Lauren folded it in half, then in half again, and returned it to her pocket.

"Okay, so let's go tell him you're okay," she said, pulling the door open for Astrid to go first. Thorny was there, leaning on the wall, not ten feet from the door.

So that was him. The guy in the paper, the one who donated his house. Even though his picture hadn't appeared with the article, when she looked at him more closely, it fit. His age, his compact frame, his roughened hands with a slight knobbiness in his finger joints. Quickly Lauren introduced herself and told him she knew about his generous donation, at which he nodded, but didn't comment. In fact, he barely looked at her.

"Astrid," he said simply. "Richard's out at the plane, looking it over. So are you set? If you want to change your mind and go home, well, here's your friend. I guess she'd take you," he added with a slight nod towards Lauren.

"Astrid, listen," Lauren said as her original mission came to mind. "I came here because Joyce asked me to. She was so worried. She wanted you to know that she'd like to come and live with you and look out for you. She really wants to take care of you. For the rest of your life, and she wants me to bring you back home." Lauren knew better than to issue a rush of words to Astrid, but she had to get it said. "That's why I came. Maybe we should call her, so you can talk to her about it. I've got my cell right here." She glanced down at her shoulder bag, but hesitated, then looked at Astrid helplessly, silently begging a response.

"No! Tell Laura, no, I mean tell Joyce, that the house belongs to my daughter now. It's in my will. I have everything ready." Astrid looked at Thorny. "I want to go now," she said simply. "I'm ready. I want to go with you."

"Okay then." Thorny guided her to the outside door with a light touch on her back and pulled the door open. He was behaving as though she had not just said something very odd and as though Lauren had not been standing there, hearing the whole thing.

Lauren followed them out and jogged a step to catch up, so that Astrid was between them. "What's going on?" she asked Thorny, talking across Astrid. "Don't tell me this is really some kind of... plot." She came to a full stop. "Is Joyce right? Is this really a plan for... suicide?"

Thorny made no answer, as if not hearing the question, while Astrid walked a little bent forward, like someone leaning into a wind or just hurrying to be on time for a lecture or concert.

"Is that why Joyce is so upset?" Lauren persisted. "Because she found the note Astrid left for her daughter."

"For god's sake, I hope not!" Thorny burst out, pausing to face her. "What the hell did she say?" Astrid stopped beside him, as he faced Lauren, appalled. "A note, for chrissake…" but then he drew Astrid's arm through his elbow and patted her hand to reassure her that he wasn't angry with her, though he must have been. "What did she say?" he demanded again.

"Nothing explicit, but enough to make Joyce suspicious about the plan. Because of other things Astrid had been saying, I think. That's all it was." She tried to reassure him. "And don't worry about me saying anything. Really." She instantly understood something. Somehow or other, if there was a plot, maybe it was best for Astrid to be part of it. How could she say? As for Thorny, she had no right to an opinion, only to think it was somehow a shame. Such a decent person.

Thorny shrugged then, but looked unhappy. He patted Astrid's hand again, lying lightly on his arm. "It's fine, Astrid," he reassured her. "It's going to be all right." And they moved on, with Lauren still trailing slightly on Astrid's right side. So they passed through the opening in the fence that separated the parking area from the field.

Then Lauren noticed that someone was walking briskly towards them, a tallish man in a green polo shirt and light tan pants.

"Hey Thorny," he said loudly, but not shouting. "Richard wants to know what's the delay. He's ready…"

Their eyes met at the same time. Both froze for an instant, and then Matt came up to them. He looked tired and was unshaved. He spoke first.

"What are you doing here?" he demanded of Lauren. Amazed?

Annoyed?

"What are you…? I came on account of Astrid. But you…?"

"Take Astrid," he said to Thorny, without answering her question. "Tell Richard I'll be right along. You guys can be getting Astrid on board."

Again Thorny patted the vein-ridged hand that he held lightly in the crook of his elbow. "Come along, Astrid. We're going to get into the plane." And he began to lead her away toward the line of tie-downs. She went with him, not looking back.

"Matt, what are you doing here?" Lauren repeated. "These people, I think they're in some kind of plot. Do you know anything?" She could not even find a coherent sequence of questions. "Do you know what they're planning? Or else why are you here?"

"It's okay." He found his voice, though it seemed roughened. "I'm here for Thorny. He's a friend. In case he wants something—for me to do."

"What in god's name do you mean?"

"I mean, yes, he's confided in me, and I'm confiding in you. I shouldn't but I have to. Have to trust you…There's a man who's dying of cancer, who's planned the whole thing, but it's the right thing. I'm sure of it. So for chrissake, don't wreck it. Let them go. Do you understand?" He held her with a hard look until she nodded, and then he turned back towards the twin-engine plane where Thorny and Astrid were stopping. Lauren fell in beside him, but he stopped then and turned on her sternly.

"You can't know any part of this! You have to go home. Just go!"

"But Matt…"

"No! Just go." He paused. "I'll call you," he added a reassurance.

So Matt wanted from her a difficult, yet small thing—to ignore a terrible event. Lauren wavered, half waiting for a small smile, even a quick kiss, but there was none. He turned away abruptly and walked ahead of her then. She watched him with a mixture of fascination and dismay. While she stood uncertain, he reached the plane, just after Thorny and Astrid had disappeared around the wing tip.

She went on towards the plane a little, then stopped. As she was still standing, looking, she suddenly heard a shout behind her. More like a cry, like a warning of danger. She whirled around. Some two hundred feet behind her was a heavyset woman trotting awkwardly along the walkway, dressed in jeans and a faded blue sweatshirt. A large shoulder bag bounced against her hip.

Joyce!

"Joyce!" Lauren called and waited till the woman was closer. "What in god's name are you doing here?" she demanded as Joyce came bouncing towards her. Lauren had forgotten about Joyce. All that she had come for had been erased by a new revelation. "You were supposed to wait…"

"I couldn't." Joyce came to a stop next to her, breathing hard. "I found some money in a drawer, so I got a taxi. I couldn't just sit there. Where's Mrs. W? Did you stop her? Where is she?"

"I think she's on the plane by now. She doesn't want to go home." It took a great effort for Lauren to shift her mind to this, to try to sound reasonable, definite. "She understands that there's going to be an accident…it's what she wants…"

"Didn't you explain to her? Didn't you tell her what I said? About taking care of her?" The bulk of Joyce and the weight of her accusation were daunting. "Look, here's the note she left." Joyce fished a crumpled paper out of her shoulder bag and shoved it at Lauren. "The one I told you about. She's scared and lonesome. That's all. I can help her with that. Didn't you tell her?" Joyce spoke as if Lauren were to blame if her offer wasn't accepted or maybe for not delivering the message at all.

Lauren quickly smoothed out the note and read it, as though she hadn't already been told what was in it. She played for time to think, but nothing came. She folded the note twice, and although Joyce reached out to take it back, she shoved it into her pants pocket.

"Of course I told her! It didn't work. I'm sure she cares about you, but she doesn't want to go back. She's made up her mind." Lauren found herself to be firm against any private doubt.

"But you don't understand! It's like God sent me to take care of her. It's like something I'm supposed to do. It's something I want to do, because I love her. You don't understand." Joyce seemed less angry now, but still accusatory. "Let's go and tell her that. Get her out of there! Out of the plane!"

It was clear by then that Joyce had no intention of retreating. Rather she pushed past Lauren and hurried towards the plane where there appeared to be two men standing just in back of the right wing. Lauren tagged after her, wretched with the turmoil of this tragedy within a tragedy. What to do? What not to do?

The door to the plane was open. It looked like the pilot and Astrid were already on board.

The man Thorny had not yet gone in. He was talking to Matt.

They both turned abruptly when Joyce bustled up to them. Stunned. Staring. Lauren hurried to catch up.

"Who are these women?" the pilot called out through the open door.

"I told you to go home," Matt said to Lauren with unexpected harshness.

"I don't know one of them," he called back to the pilot, "but it's okay. They're leaving." In a tone of heavy certainty.

"No, I'm not!" Joyce retorted. "I'm here to take Astrid home. She doesn't understand how I'm going help her. If you don't get her out of the plane, I'll…I'll stop this thing. I'll go to the office and tell them what you're planning to do. I'll call the sheriff if I have to. Maybe they won't believe me at first, but if you do this…this accident, whatever, then they'll have to wonder, so it won't be an accident, after all, so you see you can't do it," she concluded, triumphant. For a moment Lauren was impressed with Joyce's threat, even hopeful she would bring it off. A thought that hadn't occurred to her.

As he leaned toward the open door, there was a look of amazement on Richard's face that gathered into something like anguish. "You can't stop this flight! You women will have to get off the tarmac, both of you!" His voice was thickened with the effort that conceals a plea.

But it was Matt's voice from beside the mounting step that Lauren heard, hard as the scream of brakes before an inevitable collision. His own anguish suddenly replaced Richard's.

"Lauren, for chrissake, get this crazy woman away from here! Do it for all of them. We…they need you to do this!" His eyes were directly on hers, a command. "Get her away from here and keep her quiet. For chrissake!" He ended raggedly, like someone near gagging, struggling to speak.

Lauren shivered, looked around at Joyce's equally wretched expression. All at once she knew what she had to do, but uncertain how, afraid of using the wrong tactic, agonized for the lack of time to devise a plan. She passed through that long moment like falling before crashing against the rocks, even as she reached out and put her hand on Joyce's shoulder, and kept it there, though Joyce made a motion to step back. But Lauren grasped the fabric of her sweatshirt.

"You don't understand, but then you couldn't. Look Joyce, you couldn't have known, but you can't take care of Astrid."

"But I could!"

"No, dear. You didn't know. She has a brain tumor." Lauren urged her point, not sure if it was connecting. "She's dying anyway. Soon. Maybe a month or two."

"No! She's got Alzheimer's! She can still live a long time," Joyce said fiercely, into Lauren's face. "I don't believe you!"

"No, please, Joyce. I wouldn't lie about something this important. I mean, we all thought so, and maybe she really has Alzheimer's, but Lydia found out from her doctor, and she told me. She phoned me about it. Wanted my advice about hospice. I probably should've told you, but Lydia said it was confidential. But really, I think Lydia would have told you, soon, so you could be prepared. She knows how much you think of her mother. I know it, too. But it's too late! They can't operate. No one can help her." Lauren felt she was blathering, but she also saw that at least she had Joyce's full attention.

"Does Mrs. W know?" So she seemed to believe what Lauren was telling her.

"No, but she knows she's getting worse. She revised her will, with you in it, so you could hire someone to help find your son. She told me that she knew how important it was for you. I think that's part of God's plan, too…" By now, she could see the usefulness of an argument from God. "For you to use the money the way she wanted. And I can help you too."

Joyce was looking at her directly then, her expression puzzled and pinched, her eyes gathering tears. "I can't just go away. Not without a goodbye. I love Mrs. W. I really do love her. Like if she was my gramma. Yeah, even a lot more."

"I know, I know. But believe me, she'd only get more upset if you told her goodbye. Honest. Listen…" Lauren loosened her grip on Joyce's shoulder, but only to give her an encouraging pat. "Sometimes you just have to let go, even if it's the hardest thing you can imagine. Even when it tears your heart out. You know that. If we tell the authorities anything about the plan and make them stop, then they'll probably put Astrid straight into a hospital. It'll be awful for her, and you wouldn't be with her anyway. So you can't help her now, except by letting her help you. I mean with the money. She loves you too. You know that."

Cautiously Lauren began leading Joyce away from the plane, back to the walkway, one arm around her shoulder, a painful step by step. "It'll be all right. In time. You'll see how God's plan will work out, after all. You'll feel so much better when you find your boy and know he's all right. You'll find him, I promise you. Come off the field. We'll go somewhere together. I'll…I'll take you to my house. We'll talk about it, make plans. You couldn't have known about the tumor, but I'm glad I told you. You needed to know."

As she talked encouragingly, constantly, and they made their way along the chain link fence and through the opening, Lauren's earnest assurances were suddenly lost in a blast of noise that made both of them jerk involuntarily. The light jet was starting its engines in front of a hanger just to the left of them, a storm of noise that made Lauren shudder and tighten her hold around Joyce's shoulder, as if to keep them from being blown away.

"Let's get out of here!" she shouted, not sure if Joyce heard her. But they quickened their pace, Lauren having released Joyce now and hurrying ahead, not talking anymore because their words would have been drowned out by the engine roar. Lauren led Joyce past the massive yellow steel building to her parked car in the back, still in shadow, though the mounting sun was rolling up the shade behind it. The building blocked the jet shriek a little. Then she couldn't avoid seeing that the car she had noticed earlier *was* Matt's car. She fumbled in her purse for her car key, pressed the unlock button with a shaky hand. Her head had begun to throb.

She leaned against the car. "I can't drive."

"What's wrong?" Joyce asked her, standing just behind her.

"It's…it's because loud noises do this to me. I can't function. I have go take an aspirin." There was truth in that. She turned away from the car, brushing past Joyce's body. "Get in the car. Wait for me." A clear command.

Joyce paused, her hand on the door handle. "Where are you going?"

"The restroom. I need water. Just get in the car. Wait for me. I'll be right back. Wait!" As though commanding a dog to stay.

Lauren turned away and began running towards the office building, pulled the door open and went inside, gasping for breath. In the hallway a man who was passing in the direction of the lounge gave her an odd look, but she brushed by him and went into the restroom, where she had found Astrid not fifteen minutes earlier. No one else there, thank God. She was panting now, like an exhausted runner. She bent over the washbasin, pressed on the cold water control, and splashed her face with both hands until the automatic flow stopped. She breathed deeply, realized she didn't actually have aspirin. Didn't matter. The water helped.

That's a little better. Gotta get ahold of myself. Take a breath. No towels. Wait, I have the handkerchief that…Astrid…still damp.

But as she pulled out the handkerchief Astrid had used just minutes before, she felt more than the handkerchief in her pocket. Something crinkly. Paper… She pulled it out and looked. Of course. It was the note that Astrid had left for Lydia. If there was an investigation… *Must get rid of this.* Even if Joyce remembered what was in it, there'd be no evidence. She shoved the handkerchief back in her other pocket, then tore the note into small pieces, dropped them into the nearest toilet and flushed them down, then flushed again to end a few floating scraps. *Pray God Joyce stays in the car. Shouldn't have left her there.*

Lauren wiped her damp hands on her pant legs and hurried out. The jet noise was still rattling the air, but less as the plane moved onto the head of the runway. She didn't look toward the field at all, didn't try to see what was going on. She made for the car at a trot and saw Joyce, bent over, with her face in her hands. Lauren scurried around to the driver's side and got in.

At the sound of the car door closing, Joyce turned her face towards Lauren. It was wet with tears. Lauren had read or heard of people who had cried so much that their face looked like it had been in a basin of water, but she had always thought that was probably an exaggeration. No, it was not. "Oh Joyce…Joyce. I don't blame you. I don't blame you in the least," she said as soothingly as she was able. "You're all heart. You're wonderful!"

With a kind of gasp Joyce answered her.

"Life sucks!" she said simply. "I wish I was dead!"

"Oh no, not that…"

"Yes, I wish I'd been smart enough to kill myself when I tried once before." She gasped again. "I was just too dumb. I didn't know how." She paused with a sudden new idea. "I should've gone with Mrs. W. I should've made them take me!"

"They wouldn't. You know that. And anyway, look Joyce, you have something to do." Lauren begged her, gathering her thoughts. "You've gotta find your son…"

"Patrick."

"Yes, Patrick."

"It won't work. I won't find him. Ever."

"No, I think you're wrong. Come home with me, and we'll start searching right away. On my computer. I mean for ways that you can track people. If that doesn't go anywhere, we'll go to a lawyer. Someone with experience. These things happen quite a lot. You know that. It's going to work out this time. We'll make it happen," she added, taking a kind of responsibility she hadn't intended. "Look, Joyce, I have a son. I know how important it is."

Joyce sniffed, turned her attention to the hefty purse on her lap and drew out a tissue. Blotted her face. Blew her nose. Suddenly she looked at Lauren keenly.

"Would you die for him?"

"Well, yes, of course." Lauren responded to a question she had barely ever thought of. David had never seemed like a person who would need dying for.

"I'd die for Patrick," she repeated.

"Yes, I believe you would," Lauren answered automatically.

"Have they gone? Could you see?" Joyce asked her all at once.

"I didn't look, but we've got to get out of here. Go to my house, like I said." Lauren turned the key, her hand shaking, but able to get into reverse and back out of the space. No cars coming in. Good. She paused to fasten her seat belt, reminded Joyce of hers. *You can want to die, but still why not be careful?* she thought wryly.

Anyway, it's the law. She shifted to low and started down the entry road. *Don't look towards the field. Just the road,* she thought. *It's working…at least Joyce has stopped crying. Matt must be pleased that I got her to leave, and yes I'll try to help her out. I will do that.*

"Do you really believe that God…?" Joyce turned to Lauren with the eternal question.

"Yes, absolutely." Lauren reassured her as she steered the car onto the freeway on-ramp, looking for a way to merge into the muddle of southbound traffic.

On their left now was the wall of ugly steel buildings and, disappearing behind them as they headed south, the landing field with its rows of small aircraft, lined up like toys on a shelf. The jet had taken off and disappeared to the north. Then a blue and white twin was in motion. Gradually it passed behind a hanger. But Lauren only watched the gray asphalt ahead of her, leading her onto the freeway.

Now the Cessna pauses at the head of the runway, ready for take-off. Now it begins to move forward, gathering speed, rushing down the runway, lifting, climbing steeply, heading due north up the valley, the gear retracting, and then, just on the edge of sight, turning east into the sun.

ACKNOWLEDGMENTS

To Johnnie Mazzocco
for myriad corrections and astute suggestions

To Barbara Zeiger
for attentive reading and essential encouragement

To Eva Long
for an amazing combination of commentary,
esthetic judgment and technical skills

To Jenny Gusset
for her friendship, and for being an Argus-eyed reader

To the Reading Glass Books production Team
for their assistance and expertise